PULSE

Ed Adams

First published in Great Britain in 2020 by firstelement
Copyright © 2020 Ed Adams
Directed by thesixtwenty

10 9 8 7 6 5 4 3 2

A CIP catalogue record for this book is available from the British Library.

ISBN 13 : 978-1-9163383-4-0

Ebook ISBN : 978-1-9163383-5-7

Printed and bound in Great Britain by Ingram Spark

rashbre
an imprint of firstelement.co.uk
rashbre@mac.com

ed-adams.net

To Elizabeth
and
The Kendricks

THANKS

A big thank you for the tolerance and bemused support from all of those around me. To those who know when it is time to say, "step away from the keyboard!" and to those who don't.

To thesixtwenty.co.uk for direction.

To Topsham, for being lovely.

To the NaNoWriMo gang for the continued inspiration and encouragement.

To the edge-walkers. They know who they are.

And, of course, thanks to the extensive support via the random scribbles of rashbre via http://rashbre2.blogspot.com and its cast of amazing and varied readers whether human, twittery, smoky, cool kats, photographic, dramatic, musical, anagrammed, globalized or simply maxed-out.

Not forgetting the cast of characters involved in producing this; they all have virtual lives of their own.

And of course, to you, dear reader, for at least 'giving it a go'.

Books by Ed Adams include:

Triangle Trilogy		About
1	The Triangle	Dirty money? Here's how to clean it
2	The Square	Weapons of Mass Destruction – don't let them get on your nerves
3	The Circle	The desert is no place to get lost
4	The Ox Stunner	The Triangle Trilogy – thick enough to stun an ox
		(all feature Jake, Bigsy, Clare, Chuck Manners)
Archangel Collection		
1	Archangel	Sometimes I am necessary
2	Raven	An eye that sees all between darkness and light
3	Card Game	Throwing oil on a troubled market
4	Magazine Clip	the above three in one heavy book.
5	Play On, Christina Nott	Christina Nott, on Tour for the FSB
		(all feature Jake, Bigsy, Clare, Chuck Manners)
Stand-Alone Novels		
1	Coin	Get rich quick with Cybercash – just don't tell GCHQ
2	Pulse	Want more? Just stay away from the edge
3	Edge	Power can't be left to trust
4	Now the Science	the above three in one heavy book.
Edge of Forever - Edge Trilogy		
1	Edge	World end climate collapse and sham discovered during magnetite mining from Jupiter's moon Ganymede.
2	Edge Blue	A human outcome, after a doomsday reckoning, unless…
3	Edge Red	An artificially intelligent outcome, unless…
4	Edge of Forever	Edge Trilogy

Triangle Trilogy		About
1	Triangle	Money laundering within an international setting.
2	Square	A viral nerve agent being shipped by terrorists and WMDs
3	Circle	In the Arizona deserts, with the Navajo; about missiles stolen from storage.
4	Ox Stunner	the above three in one heavy book.
		(all feature Jake, Bigsy, Clare, Chuck Manners)
Archangel Collection		
1	Archangel	Biographical adventures of Russian trained Archangel, who, as Christina Nott, threads her way through other Triangle novels.
2	Raven	Big business gone bad and being a freemason won't absolve you
3	Card Game	Raven Pt 2 – Russian oligarchs attempt to take control
4	Magazine Clip	the above three in one heavy book.
5	Play On, Christina Nott	Christina Nott, on Tour for the FSB
		(all feature Jake, Bigsy, Clare, Chuck Manners)
Now the Science Collection		
1	Coin	cyber cash manipulation by the Russian state.
2	Pulse	Sci-Fi dystopian blood management with nano-bots
3	Edge	World end climate collapse and sham discovered during magnetite mining from Jupiter's moon Ganymede
4	Now the Science	the above three in one heavy book.
Edge of Forever - Edge Trilogy		
1	Edge	World end climate collapse and sham discovered during magnetite mining from Jupiter's moon Ganymede.
2	Edge Blue	Endgame, for Earth – unless?
3	Edge Red	Museum Earth – unless?
4	Edge of Forever	Edge Trilogy

Author's Note

Pulse was written ahead of the series of novels Edge; Edge, Blue and Edge, Red. Collectively they discuss Earth after a major series of dystopian catastrophes.

Pulse features as a pre-history of the series, set some 300 years earlier than Edge. To a reader of Edge and particularly Edge, Red, it will become increasingly apparent that Pulse set in motion events with a very long arc.

I hope you enjoy!

Ed Adams

TABLE OF CONTENTS

PART ONE

1

Where all were minds in uni-thought
Power is weird by mystics taught
No pain, no joy, no power too great
Colossal strength to grasp a fate

David Bowie – The Supermen

Scrive

Scrive clicked the new cartridge into place in his forearm and felt the cold rush snake from his arm to burst somewhere inside his head.

Next, he checked the small plexi-inspection window briefly and could see his blood already changing from a bright red back to orange, and he knew that within another twenty minutes it would again be the safe yellow colour.

Like everyone, he knew that red blood spelled danger and he had been particularly careless to let his system deplete its supply of the tropus for so long.

He felt the pulse bubbling on the left side of his head above the eye-line. He knew this was his body regaining its equilibrium. He squeezed both his hands into a fist shape the way they were taught and used his two middle fingers to massage the fleshy areas below his thumbs while his system adjusted.

Another five minutes and he was walking across Chelsea Bridge to the Tube station. He lived less than ten minutes on foot from the nearest stop, and his ride to today's meeting was around fifteen minutes. He could feel the cartridge working, and his relaxed acceptance of the day's tasks was already returning.

He looked briefly toward the sky. A jagged spark had flicked across. Now gentle vapour trails were crawling behind what had been a brief tear shooting along the path of the River Thames.

Others walked at a similar pace towards the station, although he ducked to the right into a quieter street that also cut a corner and missed some traffic crossings.

He glanced as he prepared to cross the diagonal into the station and glimpsed someone he recognised.

She had a petite almost boyish build, dressed in black, dark hair in a black band. Scrive had noticed her for three days now, at the same spot, the same pace and the same appearance. He knew she would look up and he'd see the small tattoo by her left eye. At least he assumed it was a tattoo and not consistently applied daily make-up. As she passed, he thought he could hear her gently humming a tune. Maybe from a streamer, but he couldn't see any signs of her wearing one.

He descended into the TfL transit. His new cartridge meant he had a good range on his transceiver again and could access the transport system without overtly waving his arm over the sensor.

Most travellers referred to the sensors as 'oysters' although this was a reference to a long-defunct technology, much as the Tube itself was merely a reference to the shape of the original tunnels that formed the original wheel-based transport system.

He used the moving floor system to get to the high-speed transit level and stood for a moment waiting for the next transit pod. He clipped himself into a free TPOD seat and punched in his destination. The system was pretty fool proof. His cartridge provided the principal co-ordinates for his routine travel, and a short, personalised menu of options had appeared on the screen. He'd just tapped his planned destination.

Of course, he could go to other points within his regular routes or pre-authorise other destinations in advance, from the HomeLink system. Today was ordinary, though, or at least that was what he needed to suggest, despite what had happened yesterday.

Janie

Janie was exhausted. Not from the morning jog, which had been one hour at a fast pace. It was because of the idiotic requests that she was subjected to in the workplace. If anything, the morning run had boosted her mood, but it was from a pretty low starting point.

"Hi," she said to Karin, as they sat together for a morning coffee, "How's today?" Karin threw a knowing glance toward Janie.

"Not great, we are still going downhill, I think. But the coffee is good."

Janie's work colleague was Karin, and they'd been friends since just after Janie had started. Karin had been in the company slightly longer - just enough time to mean she could show Janie around and warn her of any subtle office hazards. The machine coffee, the inefficient procurement process and ways to circumvent it and the slightly sleazy Leonard who worked in accounts.

Karin seemed to be able to operate around most of the recent chaos of the changes without being as perturbed as Janie. Even her functional move just after the new management arrived didn't seem to have affected her spirit. But Janie also noticed that Karin could be somewhat different if they went out together for an after-work drink or occasional cup of coffee.

"I don't know how you do it," Janie exhaled, intensely watching Karin scraping some of the foam from the coffee.

"I asked for a flat, and they've given me a latte," Karin replied,

"Considering I'm in here most days I'd expect them to get it right by now."

"No - I mean about the firm," continued Janie, "It's beginning to drive me nuts. They are constantly changing things at the moment, and each time they do so, a few more people seem to disappear."

It was over the last two months that things had changed. There had first been rumours that the company was in some financial trouble. Then a set of new people had arrived, superficially polite but rapidly asking for increasingly ludicrous changes to the way that they were supposed to operate.

It was supposed to be about boosting profitability, but Janie had seen several of her colleagues summarily dispatched, some to overseas and a few to leave the company.

The ones remaining had been instructed in no uncertain terms to refrain from contact with those that had moved away. It was officially because of privileged information, which was supposed to remain secure, but Janie was far from convinced that this was the real reason.

Janie's unit had remained mainly unscathed except when Mayer and Nikolai, who were two of Janie's bosses, moved to the USA. Replacements were new people from an external consultancy firm, and Janie understood that they would be temporary so-called 'interim' management while the operation was revised.

"I tried to contact Nikolai, after the swap around," said Janie.

"It was a personal matter - I'd forgotten to return a couple of items before the move. I sent an email to check whether a small package I'd sent through the internal post arrived. I was surprised when the mail returned with a non-contactable message."

"Not just an out of office then?" asked Karin.

"No, I don't think so. It landed me in trouble with the new management, who explained that the 'no contact' protocol was rigorous. I was told not try to reach anyone that moved, and if anything were to be forwarded, then the managers would handle it. "

"It doesn't surprise me," said Karin, "So much is changing. Even the email system itself. My workstation was upgraded to a new model and now needs a biometric scan of fingerprint and retina before I can use it.

Several of them had made macabre jokes about this because the technology was in some ways more traditionalist than merely using the proximity detector built into their tropus arm cartridges. It was slightly irritating that they could use the cartridges to access phone systems, the transport system and most types of door access but now had to revert to bio scans for something as simple as browsing the infranet.

Biotree

The Biotree company they worked for was a producer of biotech equipment. It had developed several of the nanotechnology-based products which had created a renaissance for British industry. The most famous was the Aport, which could be used within a bloodstream to manage the walls of veins and arteries. It had revolutionised healthcare since its originally controversial introduction and development into a range of products which could manage blood flow, cholesterol build-up and some aspects of the cleansing of contaminated organs. The Aport ran as a series of nanobots, which inserted into a person's bloodstream via the same type of cartridges used to manage general health.

The company made its fortune from the devices and the sophisticated software that was required to make them run successfully and without error.

London was still the global headquarters for the company, with other administrative locations in most major countries. The tentacles from the company spread wide, and the product base was routinely customised to markets.

The huge secretive manufacturing plants for Biotree's core nanotechnology resided in several locations around the world. Nevada, US; Toulouse, France and Shandong, Eastern China.

Research and Development had been moved to Bodø in Norway as a strategically safe location. Just within the Arctic Circle, it still had good infrastructural connections including fast land transit, extensive seaborne links and the small matter of a major NATO airbase nestled within the town. The origins as a strategic base went back to annual shows of strength known as the Cold Response, which still occurred under the less obvious title of CORE.

It had other advantages. A local population with their own language, while also possessing excellent English language skills for handling the incoming scientists. A university base developed extensively as part of the run-up to the creation of the research faculty.

The location also had appeal for the people stationed there, who were attracted by world-class research, the best facilities, no practical budgetary limitations and a premier lifestyle during their term.

Many tried six months and then remained for much longer.

Additionally, the Norwegian government had been particularly understanding since the changes in global energy policy because they had needed to re-provision from the decline in North Sea oil and natural gas. They had granted the area a special status as a world economic development zone, and it had boosted the relative ranking of the still sparsely populated Norway to a top fifteen economy in terms of its economic freedom.

The subtext was the immense security that surrounded the environment and the commitment of those employed to maintain the secure nature of their work. Bodø was also small enough to mean that unusual activity would be quickly spotted and with the added incentives of the Norwegian kriminalitetsforebygging (KRÅD) – the criminal intelligence organisation providing added rewards for useful intelligence.

In its heyday, Biotree was simply a money machine as the demand was pretty much world-wide, and the patents and manufacturing processes locked down during the prototyping cycle.

Therefore, the employees of the company were routinely subjected to heavy screening before they joined, were provided with extensive benefits and the equivalent of 'golden handcuffs' making it exceptionally undesirable to want to leave.

That had been the case until when a Chinese manufacturer had started to produce the first clones. Strictly, they were not clones at all. They were a different way to provide the same outcome. It was evident that some brilliant people had somehow reversed engineered the 'bots and also the operating systems and now created something remarkably similar in its function, but at what worked out to be one-tenth of the price.

That had tipped the market and the little nest egg of un-vested shares that Janie and Karin had received when they joined the company was now worth less than one-tenth of their original value. These changes had heralded the management changes and the new people that walked the corridors.

It was understandable that the company was now jittery and that many of the longer serving associates were beginning to look at the job sites again for new roles.

Janie and Karin continued their coffee.

"I think we are still at the very beginning of something," replied Karin, "I won't be surprised if the new management also gets replaced within a month or two."

"What, just a revolving doors management style?" smiled Janie.

"No, more a double-blind protocol," responded Karin, "Remove the people who know what is happening, replace them with new ones and break the chain. I've seen it elsewhere; it severs the Corporate knowledge before another move is played."

"How come you know so much about this?" asked Janie.

"I'm letting you into one of my secrets when I tell you this." said Karin, "This process is the reason I joined Biotree".

She looked long at Janie. "We're all smart people in this organisation, but some of us have roles that are far enough down the organisational tree not to be a threat. We won't get replaced like Mayer and Nikolai. And that's important because I've been sent here to find out what is happening."

"Why are you telling me this?" asked Janie, "It all sounds a bit far-fetched."

"Tonight," said Karin. "meet me - this coffee bar at six o'clock - and I'll show you something."

Tube

Scrive was travelling across London. He looked around the TPOD compartment. It was a recent model and had the evaluative advertising module that had been creating a commotion in the media. Linked to the occupants, it would select advertising materials with apparent associations with the people in the compartment.

Despite the trials, it had proved something of a disaster. People wanted to see aspirational products like expensive holidays but instead were presented with perspirational products like deodorants. When the adverts were non-selective, it really didn't matter, but when the demographics of who was in the vicinity chose the banners, then it became a question of 'who triggered that one?'. The marketeers had an answer for it all based upon product weighting. Still, most people assumed it was either them or their neighbouring travellers that had created the demand for unpleasant cereal selections or dating agencies for the lonely.

The countdown began, and ten seconds later, they were moving towards their next destination. They accelerated to a couple of metres from the next pod and hurtled through tunnels at blurry speeds towards East London. The scheduling was impressive, with individual pods able to manoeuvre around one another and to take the right branches, guided by a lidar and radar system that avoided collisions.

For most of the journey the windows were black, not because of the view, but to avoid inducing vertigo into the passengers. Everyone knew the buckle-up protocol on the system, and it was frowned upon if anyone fumbled too long getting into their seat.

There was a moment of phase shift which sounded like a suction motor as the pod slowed and stopped suspended on its soft magnetic levitation while a few passengers swapped for the second part of the ride.

Scrive was flicking idly through the touch screen pages, which had been interrupted by the safety announcement before the pod started again. He noticed the newsfeed was referencing the Biotree financial difficulties and the emergence of the Chinese alternative biobots.

It wasn't exactly new news, but the media liked to recycle the same few facts every way they could, and there were now plenty of cartoon simulations of how a nanobot worked and the various components used to make them.

Scrive had been through surgery after a fall which had broken a bone. The medics injected the local area with nanobots to speed the repair. He was astonished at the way they had linked into a structure which effectively fused the bone halves and then as he healed naturally, the nanobots progressively reduced their links and eventually flushed from his system.

He had no idea how it all worked but had been given a monitoring device while the 'bots were working so that he knew how many were operating. It had been several thousands 'bots but eventually dropped away to a couple of dozen.

That had bothered him at the time because he was aware that they hadn't dropped back to zero and he sometimes wondered what the remaining few were doing inside of him. He'd tried the monitor on others. Those who underwent nanosurgery seemed to have residue; everyone else didn't show any readings on the device.

A sharp ping broke his reverie as the TPOD arrived at the second stop. His destination in Canary Wharf. He'd been lucky to catch a fast transit that had only made one stop along the way. Sure enough, about two-thirds of the passengers unclipped and left the pod, back onto a platform surface and then through a series of moving floor-ways back to street level. He would use the underground retail levels to get from the Tube stop to the office.

That certain something

Janie's afternoon passed with yet more unexpected company changes. Laughably they were being sent out via email, but the new system had a fault, and so many of the recipients were getting blank messages with just a title. Janie felt this summed up the current situation, all title and no content.

Janie prepared for her evening meeting with Karin. She knew her well enough to think she was serious about something, rather than it being some form of a practical joke, and it didn't look as if it would be about boyfriends or partying. At about five minutes to six, Janie headed into the coffee bar and ordered a drink. She'd not got much of an evening ahead, so a chat with Karin would be an entertaining diversion, whatever the basis.

Another ten minutes passed, and Karin hadn't appeared. Janie sipped on her coffee and looked around. She hadn't prepared for a long wait, because usually the two of them were pretty punctual when they met.

Another five minutes and she decided it was sensible to call Karin's phone. She tapped the number and diverted straight to messaging. She decided to tap in "I'm here" instead of leaving a voicemail and was surprised when an immediate response returned saying that 'the holder of this number is no longer available'.

Janie looked down to check the code. She had used the right number; it was a click from a call that she had made to Karin earlier today. Janie decided to try again, this time by speaking. The number rang, and she heard a click. No voicemail, no messaging at all this time.

Janie pressed her recall facility and ran back to the message from a few moments ago. She saw it pop back onto the display, but then she noticed it rotate and disappear. It had been deleted, but not by Janie.

She flipped back to Karin's contact entry. It had also gone. Janie looked around the phone for the on/off switch. She cursed that she'd forgotten how to turn the whole device off, it wasn't something that one ever did after it had been powered on for the first time. Eventually, she found the switch, flipped off, counted and flipped on again.

A few seconds for the animated initialisation and this time Janie could see that the contact had been deleted. There seemed to be a few other numbers missing as well.

"Hello." said a man's voice behind her. It was quietly spoken as if to soothe. It didn't work because Janie was already turning to confront what she expected would be someone panhandling for money right there in the coffee shop.

"You must be Janie?" he asked before she had a chance to get angry. He was around the same age, clean-cut and lean but wearing a slightly crumpled looking outer sports jacket. The sort of jacket that would be seen at the top of a mountain. In snow.

"Hello...Who are you?" she responded, "I don't think we've met, at least I don't recognise you?"

He smiled as if trying to look like a friend.

"No, we haven't met, but I'm a friend of Karin's"

"Where is Karin, then?" replied Janie.

"I don't think she will be along, in fact, I don't want to alarm you, but I don't think either of us will be seeing her again," came back his response.

"Now you are worrying me," said Janie, "In a creepy kind of way. I will make a fuss if you don't explain yourself right now." The cafe was busy. They were at a table right in front of the serving area. It would be hard to imagine anywhere else more public. If Janie made a commotion now, there would be people intervening in seconds.

"Look - I'm here for a reason. Karin said she would bring something along this evening. That something was me," he began to explain.

Charlie

Charlie could hear the room. Apartment 123. It made two different sounds. One was a buzz, which seemed to be the refrigeration unit. The second was a low growl, which sounded as if someone had left a music system switched on but without anything playing. A kind of low-frequency hum.

She removed the mirror shade sunglasses that she'd worn into the building. Better to be remembered for dark glasses that are easy to exchange.

Charlie had felt that spin-down relief wash over her too. She had been busy and hyper-alert for the last two weeks. An assignment in Milan had almost driven her to distraction.

She'd been driven back to the airport in a black limousine, which seemed to have priority access everywhere. The driver only spoke Italian but had a black liveried look that said to anyone outside the ride, "Don't mess with me."

Cedar woodland streams

Scrive passed through Biotree's elegant entrance lobby through which permeated a smell which he thought of as a woodland stream. There was a greenish-blue water sculpture between the entrance desks for visitors.

The building divided into different businesses and a couple of the main ones had entrance lobbies on the ground floor. Further up the building were more entrances and some quite ornate environments designed to suggest anything except a world that was many stories from the surface.

His access was pre-defined, and he could walk through the scanners and harmless-looking glass turnstiles and towards one of the elevator banks. He knew about the glass shield that could drop silently from the ceilings and rise from the floors if someone was attempting unauthorised entry to the building.

The security style of this enterprise was muted, compared with offices having steel cages separating inside from the outside. It was as if the security was in inverse proportion to the appearance. The fanciest buildings appeared to have no protection, whereas a corner shop would have the overt grills, chains and bullet and bombproofing on display.

Scrive hadn't worked with the low-end organisations for several years. He'd made his reputation which meant his line of work was recognised with the big players and the related high fee-rates. He usually worked through other organisations but still considered himself a free agent, able to pick and choose and without the hassle of a long-term boss breathing down his neck.

Today he was deliberately operating through another company and had some special idents made so that he could tow their corporate line with his client. It was a kind of unspoken situation between him and his clients. They knew he was freelance but didn't ask. He would appear to represent the agency or company that fronted him but wouldn't confirm that he was a full employee. It worked for everyone because the clients he worked with knew he was one of the best at what he did.

The elevator pinged open on the 63rd floor. A woman's voice politely announced the level and the company departments represented.

"Company Compliance," she announced. Scrive crossed the lobby to another set of reception desks.

"Hi, my names Mallinson, Scrive Mallinson, I'm here to see Makatomi San".

He presented his ident on a handheld device, and it blinked onto the receptionist's screen. He had used the Japanese traditional method to show the ident. It seemed slightly arcane to grip the handheld between both thumbs and forefingers and to bow slightly, but this was part of a business tradition that swept back through many generations with the Japanese and was somehow updated to cope with current technology.

"Mr Mallinson, I see you already have full access authority; would you like to be escorted to the meeting room, or do you know your way? I will inform Mr Makatomi of your arrival," responded the receptionist. It was all very formal here, Scrive knew he was in one of the places where ceremony and protocol would still be necessary.

"I'd be pleased to be escorted," he replied, realising that although he knew the way, the client would feel more comfortable seeing him in their keeping rather than running loose, at least until he'd kicked off the assignment.

Another person, slender, Japanese and suited appeared from behind a partition. "Hello Mr Mallinson, let me show you to the meeting area - My name is Takuya, if you need anything while you are here, please let me know." He bowed lightly, and Scrive returned the gesture.

Scrive noted the perfect London English of the Japanese-looking person. He wondered if Takuya was his real name or was an adaptation for his role in the company. As they walked, he thought about asking, but then decided to play it low-key until at least until the assignment was underway. He was ushered into the meeting room.

"Mr Makatomi will be along in a few minutes," said Takuya, "Would you like some coffee, tea or water?"

Scrive thanked Takuya but declined any drinks. He would use the few minutes waiting to scope the working environment. Takuya quietly left the room after pressing a small button which lit an engaged signal. Scrive realised that this would probably also start a monitoring process with sound and vision, so he decided it best to play dumb and settle into one of the comfortable leather chairs.

He noted the camera spots on the walls. One large obvious video camera, facing towards the floor and switched off. Three more small pinprick-sized cameras with tracking arranged around the wall. He couldn't tell whether they were activated, so he pulled his handheld and took a silent picture of one of them. He glanced at the result, and there was a small pinprick of light from the infra sensor. Something not noticeable to the eye, but easily spotted by another camera. They were on; he was undoubtedly being watched.

He walked across to the door of the room and glanced at the panel that Takuya had pressed. It was the latest generation operating system and a specification that he had not seen before. This room and probably this entire floor were kitted out with state-of-the art technology.

There was a muffled noise from outside, and then the door clicked open. Takuya re-entered along with two other people.

"Let me introduce Mr Makatomi and Mr Arusen," said Takuya, "and this is Mr Mallinson". They all briefly bowed to each other, and Scrive extended his hand for a handshake.

"Mr Makatomi, Mr Arusen, you may call me Scrive", he smiled.

They both smiled back, shook hands and took seats around the long rectangular table.

"Mr Mallinson, ...Scrive, we have something of a problem and require some extraordinary assistance. I believe you will be able to help us." began Mr Makatomi,

"This is Mr Arusen, from our legal counsel. He is in this meeting as a matter of record. Afterwards, he will have taken notes from our conversation, and they will form a permanent record of what has been discussed today. That will be the only record, and it will be non-deniable. Do I make myself clear?"

Scrive nodded. He realised the situation. The three of them were about to talk off the record. The notes from Arusen would describe an entirely different discussion which had no bearing on the actual conversation.

"Mr Arusen, you had better provide me with a copy of this conversation", he smiled, "You may beam it to me for simplicity."

Mr Arusen nodded, "Actually, I have taken the liberty of already doing so. I noticed your use of your handheld device a few minutes before we entered the room and beamed you a copy just after I wiped out your picture of this room".

Scrive felt the hairs on the back of his neck tingle. He would need to be on top game. They'd just signalled to him that they knew what he was doing and that they could access his well-protected handheld computer. And even wipe out content.

Scrive smiled again, "My test of your systems worked then," he replied, "you detected my scan and were able to remove the content and replace it with your file. That's my point about your current technology. It looks modern, but if you can do that, then so can someone else. It's a situation where the strength becomes a weakness."

Scrive secretly thought that he was the one turning his own weakness into a strength.

"Let's get to the main business", continued Scrive, "beyond the theatrics, you seem to have a real problem. You've already checked me out, long before I appeared here so please can you explain to me the basis of your need for my assistance?"

Mr Makatomi grinned, "They said you would be direct with your discussion. Let me be as direct with you…"

Tract

Lars lived on the Tract. It was an area outside of the Ellipse where the poorer people lived and survived in the old ways. No biospheres, no transport apart from self-powered systems, because access to fuel was prohibitively expensive.

The Tract dwellers had access to fire, water and farming, but the economy was completely separated from the area inside the Ellipse.

Fundamentally it was an economic model similar to something from the Middle Ages. Protectors ruled, workers survived, and everyone paid a lien to the local Protector who would keep order and prevent incursion from neighbouring tribes.

There was no hope for a Tract dweller to legitimately enter the Ellipse. Lars sometimes wondered whether people inside the Ellipse even knew about the Tract world outside.

He and his partner Carolin knew about the outside, because they had both arrived in the Tract from Norway. They had been children when they crossed into the area, both with their families. After one of the meteor strikes they found that the land had become part of the Tract.

There was a large area separating the two environments. It comprised a white band of light and a power source activated by movement. It sparked first as anyone approached and would destroy anything that crossed into the white area. As a child, Lars played dare games and had thrown stones and even small branches into the light, to see them burst and disappear. As he'd grown older, he'd realised the danger of getting too near and nowadays, like most people, he would stay away.

There were plenty of signs of the previous habitation in the Tract areas. Whole towns were visible and many consumer goods but without power sources nor means to make more than token power from fire or through static bicycling, the energy from which was stored in old-style car batteries. There were some wind farms which still worked, but the energy was erratic, and the control systems for routing the energy was mainly destroyed.

Lars and Carolin belonged to the Dals. They mainly spoke Norwegian and English and also had another language amongst some of them from which he'd only ever managed to pick out a few words. His nearest town still had bookstores and libraries, but they had gradually been raided, and nowadays many of the books had been used as fuel. It was still possible to make a living, and the old metal coins were used as a means of exchange. The coins had a higher value than the banknotes, and only a particular type was generally exchanged.

The biggest threat to Lars and his tribe was from various biohazards which would sweep through the Tract areas. These could be simple ailments although there was still a significant number of conventional pharmaceuticals in circulation, there were also virulent bugs that would strike and wipe out a whole tribe.

Consequently, most tribes stayed apart, and a delicate balance of equilibrium was maintained based upon survival rather than territorial disputes.

Lars had no idea how large the Tract or the Ellipse were. He knew he could walk all day, but the terrain would hardly change. There were markers on the old highways which represented the ends of his domain. They were words describing what had once been county boundaries. It was usually easy to stay inside the boundaries because the main routes all had signs at their edges, which often, ironically, welcomed people into the next area. Some of the county signs picked out something famous about what the county contained.

Along the side of some of the main routes were also advertising for domestic items or even high technology equipment. He had seen one for an author, Jo Nesbo, as he approached a town. He knew Jo Nesbo had written books and had once found a couple of novels that were dismissively supposed to be used as fuel, but which he'd hidden in order to read.

Despite all of this, Lars could still sometimes feel very happy. A warm day, sunshine on his face, a run along one of the highways and he could feel a kind of exuberance. He was careful though because he knew that if he fell and injured himself, it would be another story. Many people who fell and broke bones would never recover — the same with people who suffered from deep cuts. There was something like a fifty-fifty survival chance in this case. And even with the remains of a past civilisation to use, it was like seeing an infrastructure gradually weakening.

He wondered for the next generation, and whether there would even be one beyond that.

Today was a special day. It was Protector's Day, and the Protector would be in town to collect lien via his taxmen and to provide an update on the current state of the Tract. He was heading for the town centre, not to meet the Protector, but because he had been selected for a special assignment.

He knew it was special, because he had been told he would be leaving the Tract, to visit the Ellipse.

Coffee Bar

In London, Janie looked more closely at the person who had replaced Karin for the evening coffee. The first impression of mountain climber was somehow reinforcing itself. He had a tan, but it was a kind of weathered look, more from snow and wind than direct sunshine. His face was angular and with slicked-back blonde hair. The dark jacket had a small logo with a picture of a mountain. And almost irrationally Janie was deciding he looked very athletic.

"Okay," she said," We'll stay here for a couple of minutes while you explain yourself. Then I will leave".

"Okay," he replied, "My name is Lars." Janie noticed the slight accent and then the name. Before she could ask, he continued, "I am Norwegian and had come to London to meet with Karin. I saw her yesterday for about an hour, and she has told me some things that I will share with you. I don't want to alarm you, but Karin has been in some trouble, and I think that is why she won't be along this evening."

Janie looked around. She could still make a fuss if needed and leave without difficulty. She was across the table from this guy. Outside, he could undoubtedly outrun her if anything weird was going on.

"You'll have to tell me some things that stop me thinking you are a weirdo", she clumsily replied," I've never seen you before; you tell me you've come from Norway to see my friend and then she disappears. It doesn't seem right." She could feel her pulse quickening as the gravity of the situation increased.

"I didn't expect you to embrace this situation", he continued," But frankly, I need your help. Karin was sent into Biotree to investigate some things. She has been undercover since she started. I work with her, and we are investigating a serious matter."

He looked down at his plain black coffee and stirred in a small amount of sugar. Janie noticed a small tattoo on the underside of his hand. She thought she had seen it somewhere before, like a skinny 'S' shape.

"We've been looking into the plans for Biotree," he continued, "We're from an organisation that checks civil freedoms. Like an Amnesty International crossed with a Greenpeace, but we do our work without publicity or public profile. It is better that way, or we get targeted and refused access and even work."

"You'll need to show me some proof," replied Janie, trying to think of her best exit strategy. She needed to know whether to trust this person or to find the fastest way to escape. Janie was concerned that he knew who she was, what she looked like, and where she worked.

"Okay," she added "Suppose I believe your story. I still want to know where Karin is, and then when we are both together, I may co-operate a little more."

"As I said", he responded," I don't think either of us will be seeing Karin again. I believe she has been dis-appeared like a number of your company management. Try her number, try her email, I think she will have been removed from the systems already."

Janie knew this was the case but wondered if it was some trick. An electronic erasure done like some conjuring trick to persuade her that this wasn't a hoax.

"Here's the situation", he continued. "I expect Karin has given you something to look after in the last couple of weeks. It will be something minor, a book, some papers, a loan of some kind — That's how it works. The person investigating discovers something, passes it along to someone who doesn't know anything about it and then one of us collects it. A kind of drop box but with a person rather than a location."

Janie was thinking fast. "Okay, but if Karin has disappeared, it could be because of you, in any case. How do I know you aren't trying to get something from Karin by tricking me?"

She stared at him.

"You don't", he replied. "But why would I go to such elaborate ends to talk to you like this? If I was hostile and had done something to Karin, wouldn't I do the same with you? No. I am who I say I am. Here is my ident."

He held his arm towards her, and she scanned him onto her handheld. A Norwegian passport appeared. His picture. Lars Fjelstad. Journalist. It looked authentic and had the little authenticated icon on the top corner when she played it back.

"Look. I can see you don't want to get involved with this. Think carefully about the last couple of weeks. If you can think of something like I describe, let me know and after I receive whatever it is that Karin passed you, I will be gone forever."

"Also, please don't tell anyone about this, or I will probably also disappear, and then you'll probably get another visitor with a similar request."

He looked towards her. Their eyes met. Janie thought he looked both genuine and a little bit nervous.

"Okay", said Janie," I'll think and then contact you tomorrow if I can remember anything."

"We will need a different meeting place," he replied. "You choose it now, and I will remember it. Don't write it or email it".

"Okay..." Janie felt she was getting drawn into this.

"We'll use Smollensky's by the clocks at Canary Wharf. Whichever day, it will be six o'clock in the evening".

He nodded. It was another very public place in a busy area. Easy to find but impossible to guess.

"I'll go first", he said and slipped quietly towards the door.

Janie looked around. It was six forty. Her world had changed considerably in the last thirty minutes.

Chinese theft

In Biotree's offices, Makatomi stared at Scrive,

"We know that the Chinese stole the designs for the Aport nanobots," he began.

"We also know that they didn't want them for the basic commercial cloning that they have been taking to the market. It is highly likely that they have other plans."

"Why would you need me for that?" asked Scrive. "You know what I do and what you describe is little more than the speculation that we've seen in the media. Conspiracy theories and all. China steals trade secret, makes copies, makes something else as well, makes pots of money..."

"All of that might be true," replied Makatomi, "But we need to track back to an alternative source of work that the Chinese are running."

"What is it then, some weapon?" asked Shrive, "That was the typical criticism of the nanosystems, that they could be used for good or evil purposes."

"Correct. In a way." said Makatomi, "There are certainly options that would allow an unscrupulous group to do something bad with this technology.

"The thing is, we believe the Chinese that took the original design have themselves been compromised. They are in a similar position to Biotree, except their design is weaker and their ability to trace what has happened is probably non-existent. We don't even think they know they have been compromised. That, Mr Mallinson, is where you come in."

"You want me to penetrate the Chinese system and then follow the trail to the second set of thieves? Presumably without anyone noticing?"

"You are astute, Mr Mallinson, that is what we want you to do. We will require the geo-coordinates of the second group and will take actions from there."

"We will need to discuss fees for this, Mr Makatomi"

"That can be taken care of by Mr Arusen; it should not be a problem. We will pay you some upfront expenses too; this will involve significant preparation, I am sure. Exceptionally, we will make Biotree facilities available for you as well. I suspect we have some technologies here which you will not have seen before."

Scrive looked at Makatomi San and nodded. Then he bowed. "I'll be pleased to assist with this. I will find the source of the original leak and then trace the second leak from the Chinese."

Makatomi stepped forward. They shook hands. He looked across to Arusen. "Please assist Mr Mallinson to get started. Mr Mallinson, you realize this is covert and deniable?"

"Always the way", replied Scrive.

Scrive made his way back to the Tube station. He'd return on the same system. Low profile. Traceable. His training meant he wouldn't do anything to trigger alerts from the surroundings of what was his new employer.

As he crossed the pedestrian area back to the curved dome of the station entrance, he could hear the recharge cycle of a high-powered transit. A V-Blade. Commercial version. He could tell from the engine note. Two tones were rising through octaves from a rasp to supersonic frequencies in around three seconds.

He listened for the tell-tale bass thump as the systems prepared for take-off and looked upward to the apparent source. It was from his building and almost certainly Makatomi San making his less low-key departure. The private V-Blades were still in the luxury goods category, so he knew it would be someone with corporate leverage and in a hurry. A few seconds later, he saw the flash as the 'blade departed. Makatomi could be back in Japan before Scrive reached Chelsea.

Scrive had used V-Blades plenty of times. Mainly the military versions which didn't need the dual engines. Commercial versions had to provide full system redundancy as part of safety measures. For the military, the reasoning was it was better to have two of the transports, which would anyway be moving into hazardous terrain. He'd used them since the early days when they required occupants to wear pressure suits to handle the G-forces. The later models had a new atmosphere and pressure walls which dealt with the forces as a kind of electronic cradle around the passengers. When he'd first travelled on the commercial versions, he couldn't believe it was the same craft as he'd experienced in the military field.

Scrive had never been 'in' the military but had worked with them much as he had with his commercial clients. He'd been a system engineer by background and had found a natural ability to see past numbers and sequences. They popped out to him almost as pictures, and he could manipulate huge matrices mentally to look for unusual patterns. Some would say he was gifted, but he had also experimented with some of the biometrics that he ran into in his professional life. He'd seen others running upgrades on their metabolisms and computation and decided he'd run the same tricks on himself.

There were practical limits based upon human systems, like maximum pulse rate and breathing, so the approaches used a blend of pragmatic limits and ancillary adjustments.

He knew how to run himself at 'human speed' but could over-clock his thoughts and reflexes to around ten times normal. At a burst, he could go even faster. It made other people appear to slow down when he was using these capabilities. In a stressful situation, it could make a huge difference. The physics of movement were not quite as accommodating though, and although he ran himself to a high athletic level, he couldn't outwit nature for running or strength.

He sold himself and his abilities around the pattern and analytics capabilities. It was because of this that he needed the best physique to get himself out of the occasional trouble.

Scrive learned that a low-key presence coupled with the ability to ramp up his pattern work was the best and most survivable way to earn the kind of money that would get him a V-Blade or any other flying thing one day if he wanted it.

Santa Monica

Makatomi San had further deals to conclude in the rest of the day. That was why he was using the V-Blade. He didn't like the ostentation of the craft, but it was the most convenient method to travel very long distances for face-to-face sessions. Much of what he was doing now required that type of stealth. He was next heading to Los Angeles, to meet with another figure similar to Mallinson. The task he was setting was pretty much identical because Makatomi knew that there was a better chance of success with two people involved. They wouldn't know of each other, and despite the fees, his corporation could easily afford to pay them both, ideally with both of them bringing results.

Before returning to the 'blade, Makatomi had stopped by the vendor floor in his building. He'd bought a disposable paper phone from the automat. Ten minutes of signal, enough for the calls he was to make. It was to a fixer who could provide him with support in Los Angeles. He tapped the number, and the line clicked with a kind of static that didn't happen on the newer circuits. The old 3G cellular structure was like a barely loved base utility now, and most people had moved onto wave plex. He spoke softly to the fixer about the need for support in LA, then folded the phone into his inside pocket. He'd throw it away later.

Makatomi and Arusen had settled into V-Blade seats for what would be a deceptively short journey, considering the distance covered. The craft would be entering space and then re-entering the atmosphere as part of its journey. Yet, the buffeting of 20th-century space travel was no longer a concern since new intelligent moleculars had been used in flight craft design. In effect, the V-Pulse used technology to make it super slippery, blended with its transit environment and consequently didn't suffer re-entry burn.

As they approached their destination in L.A., Arusen looked out of the windows at what was still a night sky, approaching dawn.

"We'll be at their office before they are even awake", he commented. "I doubt it", replied Makatomi, "Don't underestimate the people at Marina del Rey. I expect they are tracking us incoming".

Makatomi was right, Denny and Suze had been watching their scanner for the last couple of hours.

Not just watching the scanner, they were also working on a plan for their expected task.

"We don't know where Makatomi will arrive from, but we do know he'll be using a five-wing or a V-Blade for his incoming journey. When he departs, he will probably route scramble. but there's less need on the way in, so I doubt whether they have gone to the trouble." Suze flipped around a few radio frequency spectrums and checked some high incidence angles for unusual propulsion mechanisms.

"I've got this worked out and am picking up Andrews Airforce Base and way into the Pacific", she commented.

"It'll be a fast entry, probably, so we need to keep the monitoring so we can try to work out the reverse trajectory. I'd like to know where Makatomi is flying from."

Danny already had suspicions that Makatomi would be setting more than one team onto this case. He'd had a tip-off from the beam that this was a big situation and the implied fees supported the claim.

"Got something!", said Suze, she fidgeted in her seat and then stood to point at the screen. "Look, I've put it onto the big one", she flipped a button, and a large plasma displayed several arcs of co-ordinates, one moving noticeably faster than the rest. Almost immediately, it slowed to a similar crawl to the others, and then disappeared from the chart.

"It has to be him", said Denny, "Incoming fast, then going slow stealth for the last part. They won't have picked up our monitoring, and we've got a good arc to run back to work out their take-off spot.

"Easy," replied Suze, "It looks the most like London, with side options on Amsterdam or Paris. I doubt if they ran any evasive pattern so I think we can assume Makatomi has just flown from the company headquarters.

"Broadens the field somewhat", said Denny," If he has come from Corporate HQ, we don't really know if he's been with anyone or not."

"Let's ask him where he's been in the last 24," said Suze. "There's a higher likelihood that this is part of a setup if he was only passing through London".

"Yes. We may be working with paranoia here, but it is the best plan at this stage".

Denny and Suze's office was an apartment south of Santa Monica Boulevard. It was one of the areas that had picked up from the bad-old days and was now quite respectable while being on trend with the local fashions.

It worked well as an area to operate from, because the itinerant population and the side orders of tourists always flickering through between Melrose and Hollywood Boulevard.

They could do most things here without getting picked out as unusual, and long gaps or absences were quite commonplace among residents.

They'd arranged a completely different location for the meeting with Makatomi. An office block across town close to the Santa Monica Airport, which had the trappings of business but was clearly a front for what they were doing. It was a call centre, and Denny had called in a favour from one of his friends to borrow a supervisor's office for the meeting.

He wondered why Makatomi would make such a journey in person and decided it must be high profile. He'd seen Makatomi's picture in Fortune and on various media bulletins and was quietly impressed that he and Suze were sufficient 'players' to get a personal visit. He was also aware that there could be some danger around the situation, hence the separate precautions around the choice of location.

2

A bad day in London is still better
than a good day anywhere else.

- *Unknown*

Scrive's Apartment

Scrive walked the ten minutes or so from the Tube station back to his apartment. The Thames sparkled as he crossed the bridge, into another borough of London.

The sheet glass of the Japanese-developed shopping mall glinted as he made his way towards his building. Two sets of sensors to get inside, across a small security moat that had been constructed as part of the original building. The security was good all around this area. Suspended structures, gated parking and no direct access from roadside or pedestrian walkway. It required the two sets of secure identity to enter, a further set for the elevator and that was all before the entrance lobby for his own apartment's door.

He smiled as he approached. He could see that someone had entered. He knew it would have to be Charlie. He also remembered that he'd agreed that she could visit, but that she didn't have the requisite access.

But he also knew that Charlie could walk through walls. Not actually, but to be able to spoof past most systems.

"You could get into a lot of trouble doing that", he said as he walked into the apartment. Charlie smiled. The plasma was on, but nothing was playing.

"I decided to get a few minutes sleep while I waited for you", she said, getting up and stretching her arms for a hug. She'd changed from her travel clothes and was wearing one of Scrive's T-shirts.

"Hey", replied Scrive, "Hey Hey" responded Charlie. They kissed. "How long will you be in town?"

"It depends. Depends on whether what I've heard is true? You sound as if you might need some help with your latest big business?"

Scrive smiled. Charlie had connections and an uncanny ability to know where the big games played. Scrive would trust Charlie totally. They had a history.

Scrive had run into Charlie when he was solving a middle eastern puzzle. Things had started to cut up rough as he got closer to the truth.

He'd been told that he would be given backup and then Charlie had arrived. He had been taken aback, because he'd expected a small army, rather than a single 'girl'.

He'd soon learnt that Charlie was combat ready because within a half an hour of their meeting someone had tried to drive a truck into his apartment. They were on the third floor, and the truck had been launched from a building across the street, several stories higher, from the roof.

Charlie had shown her reflexes to be able to get them clear of the building and also to take down the skycrane jet that had dropped the truck onto the adjacent roof. It was a messy scene, but Charlie's jacked-up reflexes and remarkable use of weaponry had probably saved his life.

But Scrive had seen that Charlie's talents didn't stop there. She was fast and accurate with weapons, but also had pretty good tracking skills too. Not to his level, but easily fast enough to be a good sidekick. The difference between them was one of degree, with his world more digital and Charlie's a great deal more physical.

They were both effectively mercenaries and generally held to a code of non-involvement although sometimes drifted into a fling.

Scrive knew that Charlie had other male followers but had set some life goals around making a fortune. He knew she'd been trained by a Para-military group, but she remained silent about how this had come about. He had seen her in action with planes and 'blades too and knew that wherever she had trained and for whatever purpose, it made her one of a global elite.

Scrive realised that Charlie knew about his ultra-fast compute abilities, but Scrive also understood that Charlie was probably the only person that could almost keep up. Even when well-apart they kept an active link running, using one another as sounding boards. Scrive also realised that when Charlie had collected enough cash, there was every chance that she would simply disappear, as a way to break all connections.

"Yeah, I've just been to see Makatomi, He's asked me to find out how the Chinese have accessed the Aport, and what they are trying to do with it."

"What beyond profit-making by selling a variant at a tenth of the price?", replied Charlie. "It'll be some government deal - which superpower wants to get something over on someone else".

"Yes, my speculation also, but Makatomi seems to think its a double-cross or something".

"It's time we dug deep?" replied Charlie. "I'm on my way to a small gig on the Swiss border, but this sounds way more interesting. How come you've got the deal? I'd have thought Makatomi would shop around."

"Cheeky! I expect he did!" replied Scrive. "He seemed in a hurry to leave after our meeting. I thought he was heading back to Japan, but I suppose he could be seeding a duplicate operation somewhere else".

"Are you ready to take a look at this?" asked Charlie, waving the remote for the streamer.

"First things first", smiled Scrive.

Los Angeles

Suze and Denny packed some telemetry and other gadgets before they headed for the basement and into a hire car that Denny had randomly selected from the online Hertz desk. They wanted to run this as anonymously as possible, and the car and office they were using should help them stay unobtrusive.

Denny flipped the start button on the car. It whined into life. It was a fuel cell power plant, one of the new types that could run silently. He grimaced at the noisy engine tone that came as a default setting and selected another one, more a solid tone and less sporty sounding.

"Let's not draw attention", he said to Suze, who nodded in agreement.

They took the car up the four levels to the street and joined the slow-moving traffic as they headed towards the Freeway.

"It shouldn't take us long to get to the venue, especially at this time of morning, said Denny. "Don't jinx it", retorted Suze.

Dawn was breaking, in a half-hearted kind of way.

There were signs of the nightlife still in progress, as people had lost their sense of time altogether. Additionally, a few tired looking tourists were wandering around and there was a police situation on a nearby street corner. They moved along through the traffic, within the speed limits and as low key as possible.

Ahead, taillights from other traffic snaked out in as they took another on-ramp for their short ride.

"We'll be early, and prepared," said Denny, knowing that Makatomi was already in town and had probably landed at Santa Monica rather than LAX. Makatomi and his partners could be very close.

Makatomi and Arusen had a short meeting before they met Denny and Suze. They had arranged for some local support because their meeting with the trackers would be taking place away from Biotree company property.

Makatomi hated it that he was asked to meet like this, it was away from his systems and controls, but it seemed to be the only way that he could get to these two specialist trackers.

He's also done his homework, or rather, his fixer had done the homework and established that these people were the best. That was why he was meeting them on their turf. Being trackers, they knew how to hide. That they would break their own cover for this suggested that they were interested in the size of the reward. Makatomi didn't think there would be any more altruistic reasons for the trackers to agree to this meeting and the likely pursuit.

He asked Arusen to make the arrangements for the hired help and also requested that they lose the land cruisers and acquire some more low-key transport. A compromise was agreed, where Makatomi, Arusen and a couple of the hired team would take conventional transports, but that the rest would still provide less than discreet backup in the black-windowed cruisers.

"I hate LA," said Makatomi, "everything has to be so brash and dramatic. This is why we prefer these type of meetings to be in our own properties," said Makatomi to Arusen.

"Too true," nodded Arusen in agreement, "This type of situation can get so untidy."

They looked at one another knowing there was some risk of a trap or that the trackers would ask for some unacceptable terms. It would have to be something extreme because fundamentally Makatomi was desperate to get this resolved and needed the support from the likes of Denny, Suze and Scrive.

Of course, he wouldn't tell these trackers about Scrive. Part of the plan was to have the insurance of two separate investigations.

Janie gets help

In London, Janie was unsure about whether to meet Lars again, she'd gone home but kept looking over her shoulder to see whether she was being followed. It was partly irrational, but she wanted to be sure that neither Lars nor an accomplice would be behind her. She'd used her regular route so that she could go through the systems without having to stop, but then deliberately overshot her destination and made her way back. That way, if there were anyone following, it would be more visible. She wasn't sure what she would do if someone had followed her, in any case, but to her eyes there didn't seem to be any trail.

At home, she pondered about the meeting the following evening. She thought she should go but wanted to take some insurance. Maybe a friend to accompany her? But who? And how much should she say? She didn't think it should be anyone from Biotree, because of the nature of the conspiracy.

Janie lived in a flat with two others. They'd shared for about a year, as a way to get somewhere central in London. London gave them access to the best jobs, but at the cost that none of the three of them could afford a place to live, based upon their salary levels.

Janie decided that her flatmate Chantal would be the best option. They'd been in plenty of scrapes together, and shared thinking to the degree that they would wear each other's clothes. Or more precisely, Chantal would frequently borrow some of Janie's clothes.

Chantal's tastes were a little extreme for Janie. Although Chantal could scrub up real fine when required. Janie knew that Chantal operated with some of the more dubious parts of London and had quite a street scene going.

Janie was more the Ms Corporate and was used to wearing business attire, or when on courses or training, something they called business casual. It was even funnier watching the men. They'd all don polo shirts and beige chinos when it was an 'awayday' meeting.

The thing was, Chantal was out somewhere and had been for the last couple of days. It wasn't particularly unusual but meant that Janie would need to call to check whether she could help out. Janie clicked the number on her handheld and was immediately routed to voicemail. Instead, she opted to leave a text message.

"Need your help when I'm meeting a guy called Lars tomorrow - It's to do with Biotree, and I could do with some support. Fit guy, but this is business".

She thought the message was to the point, looked innocuous but would get Chantal's attention. She pressed send, and it flicked into the network.

Within a couple of minutes, a short reply from Chantal

"Sure ... How fit?"...Followed by an old school emoticon of a lascivious face. Janie smiled. She knew she'd got Chantal's attention and that she'd provide the backup.

Oil field digitizers

Orange LA sunrise, and Suze and Denny arrived at the offices.

"Not bad," said Suze, "Just above seedy and quite beige and sand coloured bland. We have found a great place to look anonymous."

Denny backed the car away. "We'll do better to park in that area the other side of the building", he commented, that will give us a couple of routes out. They could exit through the car park or the Mall. He nodded towards the adjacent Mall entrance which would put them into a zone filled with shoppers.

As he pulled up at what he now considered to be the optimum spot, he looked around.

"I think we should also look out for our friends," he added. They will be unlikely to visit us alone," He grabbed a bag from the back seat and looked through the content.

"Oil field digitizers", he said. "These little units allow us to build a grid to chart the area around here. We need to drop about 20 of them around and we'll have monitoring of the whole zone front and back".

Suze looked at one of the units. "Neat." she said, "self-powered, small transmitter, geo-sensitive and a motion camera included?"

"It's motion-sensing and also controllable", replied Denny. "These are quite new; I heard about them from a friend in the military. Don't worry; they are commercial grade and used by the large oil companies, so they are commonly available - if rather expensive. Let's sprinkle a few around".

They created a small coverage zone on both sides of the office with the units. The units had a grey speckled cover which helped them blend into the background, somewhat like pieces of discarded building material.

"They remind me of rodent traps", mused Suze.

"Surprisingly appropriate." replied Denny. He picked up another bag from the trunk of the car and they walked towards the offices. It was still early enough that they were not expecting it to be too busy.

However, as they entered there were sounds of activity. "It looks like a 24x7 operation?" said Suze.

"Yes", replied Denny, "But I didn't know it would be 'full on' all of the time. They made their way to the office that Denny had been loaned. His friend had provided access and covered off the paperwork, so they were expected and able to get straight to work.

They decided to treat a couple of the chairs to some transparent self-adhesive bugs. "Just don't sit down there," said Suze as she placed a few of the small bugs onto the chairs.

"I can't help thinking that Makatomi will be way above this stuff?" questioned Denny, "What with being into nanobots and all".

"Maybe", replied Suze, "But on the other hand his strength could also be his weakness."

They looked at the time. It had moved from 4 am to 8 am at lightning speed., They were both used to the early morning effect where the brain's processes change pace during sleep, giving the impact of a speeded-up return of the dawn.

"One hour and they will be here. Bang on time, I'm sure" said Denny.

"And I wonder what they have been doing for the last few hours?"

"My paranoia suggests they've been meeting some backup. I doubt whether they are used to operating this kind of thing on someone else's patch. That's why we have extra surveillance".

Denny pressed a button on his computer, and a whole bank of TV monitor screens appeared as small squares across the screen.

"We are ready to watch you, Mr Makatomi".

The Makatomi files

Scrive and Charlie were sipping wine. "Okay, so what brings you here to London?" asked Scrive, "I thought you'd pretty much settled in New York now".

"Work, in a manner of speaking", replied Charlie. She sipped the wine slowly and looked hesitant. "I'll tell you what happened, but you must promise not to say you told me so..."

"Sure thing", replied Scrive smiling and looking down into his glass.

Both Scrive and Charlie worked around the edges of the security environment. They'd known each other since before nanobots had become such big business. The so-called Great Leap, when technology had made a few giant steps forward.

They kept in contact and had paths that crossed haphazardly. Three years ago, they'd briefly been an item when they worked together on an investigation during which Scrive had found out that Charlie had other 'get rich quick schemes' that didn't seem to be working. Scrive had helped Charlie get out of a somewhat illegal situation, and despite growing apart, they'd kept their friendship and trust very tight,

"I've been working with the security agency in New York and Washington. They asked me to look at the rate of change of the nanobots that Biotree have been making – to try to find out if they were being deliberately weaponised.

We all know they went through a big series of upgrades in the first few years and then pretty much stabilised. I had been asked to take a look at whether there was anything else happening, like a secret 'Version 2'. Anyway, it meant that I had to join a team experimenting with the Nanobot operating system, to see if there were any obvious hooks for them to provide updates. We designed a few changes of our own."

Scrive smiled. He knew that Charlie had a swift and creative mind for software and a 'few changes' would be an understatement.

"They let me join their lab, and we started with just emulations of the 'bots. We knew we would need the real devices to try putting sets of them together. The way that their heuristics work meant that it is chains of nanobots that deliver an outcome rather than individual devices."

"It sounds like that old Lemmings game to me!" said Scrive, trying not to laugh.

"Well, it is, kind-of. In Lemmings you have diggers and flyers and climbers and so on. With bots it is the same except instead of each unit being self-contained, they join together to make the device that does the work. A machine might comprise 2,3,4 or even more separate nanobots.

Scrive nodded. He knew the theory of this as well, but whilst he would be good at tracking the originator of the devices and could probably, right now, find a trail in the 'net that lead back to Charlie, he wouldn't be able to do the same complex logic that Charlie was describing.

"I arranged for a selection of the nanobots to be provided, and I first ran them as intended. They were designed for cell wall repair and did join together to create chains to achieve this. It was like a ribosome conveyor belt. You know, the way that ribosome can stitch polymeric protein modules together via messenger RNA molecules?

Scrive looked blank," No, I missed that session," he quipped," But I get the idea, nanobots copying biological processes?"

"Yes, that's kinda right; they were pretty good and speedy. Some of their inbuilt logic was to slow the 'bots down, so that normal body tissue has a chance to keep up."

Scrive continued to drink the wine. "So far, so good, but what is the point of it all?" he asked.

"Exactly, our lab wondered whether the 'bots were just copying biological functions. Then we tried a few modifications. They were quite small, and we were mainly checking the ability of the Nanobots to support new command structures.

"Big Mistake. It all went horribly wrong. The 'bots have been designed to include failsafe. If you don't know the keys and secure modes, it looks impossible to reprogram them. They have their own self-checking logic and if they spot a variation, they just stop functioning. In fact, they go one further than that."

"what exactly?", asked Scrive.

"They attack each other and destroy each other. It really is a 'leave no trace'. Quiet a sophisticated design really. The manufacturers can modify them, but if anyone else tries then the whole system is rendered useless."

"Reminds me of some consumer electronics," smiled Scrive. "Take one screw out, and you might as well throw the entire device away".

"Yes - although the purpose here is a more security-minded one. To stop tampering and remove the ability to try out different processes."

"So why did that get you sent to Europe?" asked Scrive.

"Well, the thing is, I got rather bored with the programming of the 'bots each time I was testing my ideas, so I created a small handheld unit to punch in the code revisions. It is based on something that I used back in the Casino days".

Charlie's previous history had a few dubious moments when she was raiding high roller casinos by reprogramming the payout software. It had to be undetectable to the house and Charlie had created a small device to fire the software changes into the system.

Scrive knew about Charlie at Vegas. He helped her get out of trouble when she was in danger of being caught. He'd shown her how to mess up the electronic trail, which had previously led back to her.

"I took the Casino injector and produced a sub-scale version. It's a lot easier now than when I built the original because of the improved scanner resolutions available. I could use laser light to improve the sensitivity and then fire the new software into the bots, in much the same way that the old version fired software into the Casino devices."

"NSA hadn't seen anything like this before, and they've asked me to show them a breakdown of how it works. I'm heading for CERN to show them in detail. It is my comeuppance for the damage I caused when I was testing the bots I'd been building, and they kept failing and destroying one another.

She pointed to a small titanium box with an elaborate digital lock. "There," she said. "the Nano injector is in the box. It's loaded with 'nanoreductives'. They are my attempt to rebrand the dud nanobots which self-destruct one another!"

"Its' not a bug, it's a feature," smiled Scrive. He looked quizzically at the lock.

"Birthday?" he asked.

"Yes", replied Charlie, "Plus 666 - I wanted to add an edge to this devilish device."

Scrive knew that the box would destroy its contents if the wrong number was entered. But knowing Charlie there would be a twist.

"Yes - birthday will open it but destroy the loader logic. birthday plus 666 will open it and keep the device intact"

"what about anything else?"

"Three goes and thar she blows", smiled Charlie. "I thought I'd give a pirate hacker a sporting chance."

"Are you getting paid?"

"Yes and no," came the reply. "I should be, but I'm sort of paying off the cost of the destruction I created at Biotree with my hack. But now it's your turn. What are you working with at the moment? I assume it is still with Biotree?"

"Direct at the moment. And big. The biggest probably. Corny as it may sound if I tell you then you might be in some sort of danger.

"Yeah, right," responded Charlie," As if that would stop me, but first, another refill of the wine?"

Scrive reached across, picked up the wine and gently poured.

"You know what? You might want to help out with this. I can split some fees and it is worth it to me to have someone alongside who isn't known to the client. But wait until you hear before you answer."

"I'm intrigued already," said Charlie, ...and fees would be beneficial at the moment."

"Okay, so I've been asked to find out the origin of the cloned Chinese nanobots. There's a leak somewhere and the impact of the copies has collapsed the Biotree share price. I'm supposed to track the leak and pass the information back. Sounds simple, but we are talking about government level conspiracies. Hence the potential danger."

"Wow. This assignment sounds great. I assume the fees are in keeping with the magnitude of the challenge?"

"You know something; I think I could have named any price. I've gone high in any case. The thing that worries me is that they seem almost too happy to accept my terms. It makes me concerned that they won't honour the agreement."

"What can you do?"

"I already did it", said Scrive. I negotiated the money in two stages. "all of it now and all of it again when I complete. If I don't, they will come for me and take half back. I don't want that to happen."

"You've already been paid and can get the same again?" asked Charlie, somewhat incredulous.

"Plus, expenses...I said they didn't seem to care about the amount. And don't worry - it's a lot. Come in with me, and I'll split the second amount. You'll be my safeguard that we get paid based upon our successful outcome."

"How much?" asked Charlie.

Scrive told her. It was a huge sum.

Charlie nodded and started to feel like a big prize lottery winner.

Polka dot bodysuit

Chantal had arranged to meet Janie at Canada Water. It was across the River from their planned rendezvous with Lars but would give them a chance to plan how they would handle the session before they met. It was also a five-minute trip to their planned meeting place so they could be 'in position' very quickly.

Chantal arrived in a polka dot bodysuit. Three different colours; shorts, top and jacket.

"I took the ears off," she said as she hugged Janie. "And I brought a black topcoat as well in case we need to wear disguises." She pointed into a bag where a black compressed micro-fabric nestled amongst some fashion headgear.

Janie's mood briefly lifted at Chantal's appearance. They'd party together sometimes, and Chantal would usually go for something extravagant. Janie's appearance was more conservative, and today she was wearing a dark business suit.

"Thanks for agreeing to cover this", she said to Chantal. "I'm a little bit worried that this is all getting rather weird."

"I wouldn't miss this for anything. You're about to meet a dishy Swede or something," replied Chantal.

"He's Norwegian, or says he is," replied Janie. "And it is something to do with the firm and the way they are operating."

"What do you want me to do?" asked Chantal, "Hold your hand or what?"

"The main thing is to cover the situation and to follow my lead if I say anything." I may want him to think that we've spread the word about this, so there's no point in trying to keep it to just the two of us."

"Does he look as if he would be violent?" asked Chantal, making like a karate move.

"I don't think so, but put it this way, I think he could outrun us if it came to a race".

"Okay, so we'll listen to what he has to say and what he asks. I suggest we move from the first location to somewhere else to keep him on his toes, too. If we take him to the end of the walkway, we can grab a taxi and then go almost anywhere".

"Good plan. I suggest we go to Westminster, it's full of police and security so we can get out there and if needed we could easily attract attention."

Janie looked at Chantal.

"I don't think you'd have any trouble doing that, anyway".

They giggled briefly.

"Okay, that way, he can tell us his story while we are in the cab. It will only take a few minutes and put him under pressure to get to the point."

They nodded and walked the short distance to the transit point to Canary Wharf. They would be at Smollensky's on time.

Strip Mall Call Center

It was ten minutes before nine in the morning on the busy roads of California, and Makatomi was in a regular wheeled saloon car following another saloon and trailed by a land cruiser. A couple of small buzzy drones circled the land cruiser.

They arrived at the parking lot by the side of the offices where Makatomi was to meet the tracker. The parking lot was adjacent to a large shopping mall, which had car parking and a service road running alongside the offices where he was due to meet. He could see the signs for the call-center. Low rise, maybe four stories and adjacent to a few strip mall retail outlets. A pizza place, realtors, a financial institution. These were lower rent locations, and Makatomi was confident it was a short-term front used for his benefit.

Two of the heavies his company had hired approached the door of the offices first, and he could hear them asking for Mr Denny Amelung and then calling through to his car to say they were about to be accompanied to the office. He stepped out of the vehicle, along with Arusen.

"Same protocol?" asked Arusen.

"Exactly", replied Makatomi, "We need to keep this to the least people knowing. I don't want the hired help in the room with us."

They stepped into the office reception, and Arusen had a word to one of the men sent in ahead. He nodded, and the two men withdrew. Arusen led Makatomi to the office where Denny was seated.

"Mr Amelung?" said Arusen, looking at the casually dressed twentysomething sitting on a leather sofa in the room. Denny rose and moved to shake hands.

"Hi, I'm Denny, Denny Amelung." He shook Arusen's hand and turned towards Makatomi. "And Makatomi San? I am pleased to meet you." He bowed slightly towards Makatomi, who returned the gesture with a nod.

"We will be keeping this off the record," began Arusen.

"...and you'll have a record of a different meeting for your records?" continued Denny. "I know the protocol."

"We're running a surveillance sweep on this room," said Arusen. "I'm sure you know that protocol too".

"Yes, and you'll find plenty of electronics here. This is a call centre, with walk-around headsets, computers, high-speed comms, video links and satellite coverage. We are highly wired."

Arusen nodded. The small unit he was using to check for bugs was utterly useless in the current room. There was so much interference, and the EMF emissions were off the scale.

"If you prefer, we can delay for a couple of hours whilst you run an isolation sweep, or we can continue, in the knowledge that it is as much in my interest to keep this quiet as it is in yours," continued Denny.

Makatomi interrupted, "We'll keep this brief. I'll explain the situation and the terms. You'll need to make an immediate decision."

Denny was aware that Suze would typically be in the decision, but they had decided that Denny's view would prevail, and it was too much of a risk to reveal Suze's involvement.

"Please, Mr Makatomi, take a seat and do explain."

Makatomi repeated the story of the Chinese cloning and the need to track the leak. He didn't mention Scrive, but he did explain the generous terms.

The situation was pretty much as Denny and Suze had predicted. A search for a leak, an enormous reward. Almost too large, which implied extra danger.

Denny questioned the situation slightly but accepted the terms and a large down-payment from Makatomi.

As Makatomi and Arusen left the offices, they were tagged by the self-adhesives in the manner that Suze and Denny had hoped.

Denny waited for the Makatomi entourage to depart. The small telemetry units in the car park tracked the exit of two saloon cars and another two land cruisers. Denny waited for another twenty minutes before calling Suze back from the main office where she had been waiting, wearing a headset.

She behaved as if a staff member, whilst they started their conversation, aware that there was an equivalent possibility that Makatomi had dropped tags or sensors in this office. It was easier to exit, so they headed for the Mall's sports center, via a sportswear shop.

They both bought T-shirts and shorts as well as tracksuits before heading to the sports centre where they added new swimwear to their collection. Then into the respective changing rooms, change and both a swim and a sauna, followed by a change into the new clothes.

"That should have separated us from any bugs or trackers," commented Denny as they made their way to the car they had parked in the Mall.

"Let's get back to base." They gently edged the car from the Mall car park and took a long route back to the apartment.

"Let's see what we can trace of Makatomi," said Suze as she flicked on a geocentric tracking device and zoomed into the local area. They were using GeoSat to ping the small tracking bugs now on Makatomi and Arusen's clothes. These would give a short timeframe for information, useful as they tried to gather new intelligence about their new employers.

"Yes, we have them," they are heading back to Santa Monica Airport," said Suze and looked at the Map display. I'm patching to the tourist view camera to see whether we can spot their craft".

Two minutes later they had access to the airport's tourist cameras, and sure enough, they were pointed towards the more interesting craft in the airport, which included the V-Blade.

"I'll get its call-sign", said Suze and she zoomed onto an aero-map which showed planes at rest and amongst them the V-Blade which displayed the N registration of an American plane.

"Gotcha,", breathed Suze as she scanned for the registration,"...and you are from the NSA?? That's a surprise, and I thought you'd be registered to Biotree!"

Suze and Denny looked at one another. This was something very unusual — way beyond the request to drill into what the Chinese were doing.

"Are we being played?" asked Denny to Suze.

"We've been careful so far, and we've already received a down payment, so it doesn't make a lot of sense?"

Denny had flipped onto a Chinese web site. He was trying to run probes into the large corporates of China. Simple stingers designed to elicit port responses from the major sites. He wanted to find some loose links that would allow him to dig deeper into some of the principal Chinese corporates and maybe a few government departments.

"Steady," said Suze, "You'll swamp their networks, and then they'll trip intrusion and saturation detection. If that happens, we'll get tracked ourselves."

"Not behind these walls," smiled Denny. "I'm after speed but not being reckless". He made a gesture of a hand rising in front of his face.

"Shields up", he said, as he hit the Chinese and also the Biotree site with port scans and intrusion probes.

94

3

Be on the lookout for coming events;
They cast their shadows beforehand.

Fortune Cookie, King's Chinese Restaurant, Odiham

Beijing

The Chinese Ministry of State Security based in Beijing was monitoring traffic from airwaves and networks into and out of the Republic. Less well known than UK's GCHQ or USA's NSA, the Ministry of State Security (MSS) is the intelligence, security and secret police agency of the People's Republic of China, responsible for counter-intelligence, foreign intelligence and political security. MSS considered itself one of the most secretive intelligence organizations in the world.

It used the common triggers of blacklist and whitelist words and additionally looked for unusual activity. In this case, it was coming from a couple of US-based nodes that were repeatedly running interrogation probes.

The initial reports noted that the probes were quite sophisticated, but that they jittered and sparked their way around North America.

Den Xiapau noticed the signals first," It's a range of messages, but they seem to be different orientations than from the usual mischief-makers. It looks sophisticated, but a little bit rough at the same time."

Of course, that was what Denny and Suze wanted. To shake the tree, to see what fell out. In a few minutes, the Chinese would be running countermeasures, because they perceived it as a more worrisome than average attack.

That was when they would drop their catcher link into the system. It could decode the cryptologic that the Chinese were using as a countermeasure and then replicate itself into the core. Suze knew how to make the logic hopscotch over the kernel, and Denny's logic loop was so tight that he could drop this into play before a gnat had time to blink.

In Beijing, Den Xiapau had flagged the hostile to his superiors and was readying a crypto bomb which would take down the ports that were being probed and move them into a sophisticated sandbox.

The hacker would think it was still running its penetration logic, but all it would be doing was getting ever more complex prime numbers to calculate.

It would run out of computing power within ten minutes.

Den Xiapau fired the logic algorithm. The post scanner flickered for a moment and was gone.

"Wow", said Den Xaipau," That wasn't much of an attack, but it also wasn't static".

"Slam-dunk," said Denny, "We're in- they did just what we predicted". Suze and Denny did a quick high-five.

Den Xiapau wasn't satisfied to leave it at that point though. The disappearance of the trace probe had been almost too perfect.

He'd seen something like this before in the literature. It could be a decoy probe and an iceman insertion into the system. He remembered this software usually stayed dormant for extended periods. Iceman was so named because it had to thaw out but then ran everywhere.

He looked around and ran a few port scans of his own. He may not be able to find it, but he sure would escalate it. He punched the code for escalation. "There's something strange happening here - I know it is not right..." he began to explain, and a small chain reaction started.

Probed double

"Did you notice something?" asked Denny. "When we were running that decoy search, there was someone else doing something similar? It was incredibly fast but seemed to be targeting the same area? If we hadn't been running a decoy probe, I don't think we'd have seen it."

Suze punched a few keys.

"I'm going to re-run that last couple of minutes," she said, "from the log, as an e-Discovery."

She set up a couple of monitor screens, and they watched the party piece that Denny had created. Sure enough, a few other probes were running as well. They were both able to see past the usual scam artist attacks and into something more systematic. "It is coming from London", said Suze. And there seem to be two sets running, suspiciously like us.

"But way, way fast," said Denny. They were running their playback at one-twentieth of normal speed, and even then, they were missing sections.

"...it is someone in the business", said Denny, "look at that switching."

"...and look at that second probe," added Suze. "It is going into Biotree."

"I think we've found our doubles," said Denny, "And they seem to be in London. Makatomi has hired someone else to do the same job."

London

Scrive looked at Charlie," I know we are using some brute force techniques to test the Chinese systems. We need to see what kind of response they provide.

"I just want to see how they react. If it is overt, then we can assume they are treating us as normal hackers. If they do anything special, then maybe they are hiding something in the way that Makatomi suggests."

He ran the scans, initially in a quite visible way and received back the equivalent of a perfunctory 'not authorised' signal. The response was typical for the Chinese, who had managed to suppress parts of their systems from investigation for years and mainly with quite simple techniques involving feedback like 'not available' or 'busy'.

"Let's up the game!" said Scrive and he started a second script simultaneously pinging the Biotree site. It was a fairly blatant attempt to be seen 'red-handed', if there was a situation to hide. One hand in China, the other in Biotree.

"It is no different", said Charlie, "look they are still treating us as normal hackers or spammers".

"Yes - they aren't making any connections. Either they are masking their response very well, or there's nothing to hide?"

"Wait," said Scrive," did you see that?" Someone else running a perfunctory digital attack, but it just stopped suddenly. They killed that one in a heartbeat."

"Let us take a look", Charlie adjusted a couple of settings.

"A pro. that was a decoy attack. They've dropped some code into the Chinese system. It's impossible to tell where its originated though. Pretty slick work."

They looked at one another. "Someone else is playing with the Chinese," said Charlie, "Maybe a threat to us?"

"Or possibly an ally?" added Scrive.

Makatomi was back in the V-Blade. He'd had enough of today's haggling with what he considered to be hackers. At least Mallinson had been polite. Mr Amelung (if that was his real name) had been downright scruffy and rather discourteous.

But it was the price to pay for getting these people to track down the security leak. If he could get it fixed, then his company stocks would start to rise again despite the leakage of data from the hacks.

A signal bleeped. Makatomi was ready to sign off for the day and let it go to voice when he saw it was Holden. His boss. The chair of Biotree. He would have to answer it.

"There's a problem", said Holden. "One of those hackers you've been hiring has annoyed the Chinese. They are creating bad ripples. It will damage Biotree further. They say it's something from London. Fix it."

Makatomi couldn't believe it. In less than a day, the so-called professionals were rattling cages.

If the Chinese got nasty, what could happen next? They'd lower their prices further, and the faltering Biotree would go legs up.

"I'm going to have to contact London", he thought, "...and fix Mr Mallinson. A pity".

Smolly's

Chantal knew Smollensky's. It wasn't her kind of place. She knew it had its share of investment bankers engrossed in discussions about the latest fancy cars.

Chantal decided to have some fun. She would walk in first and draw the stares.

She took out her headgear and replaced it on her head. The polka dots, the colours and the fashion accessory that looked a bit like ears would do it. Minnie Mouse meets Mui Mui.

She heard the silence as conversations missed a beat. Even Lars looked. He was with someone too, as Janie moved across to meet again. A slim woman with boyish looks and a short dark haircut. A small S-shaped tattoo by her left eye.

"Thank you for coming here", said Lars. "I've brought Carolin as well this evening; it may give you some comfort that I'm doing all of this for the right reason."

"Okay and I've brought Chantal," said Janie before Chantal could introduce herself. Chantal realised that they hadn't thought about using a different name or anything clever, despite their preparation.

"You'd better explain what this about and what has happened to Karin."

Lars nodded. Both he and Carolin were drinking small glasses of wine. A waiter appeared. "We'll have the same", said Janie and nodded towards the glasses that Lars and Carolin were drinking.

"Maybe a bottle?" asked the waiter, smiling. "No just two glasses will be fine", replied Janie. Chantal knew they would be leaving any moment.

"Okay, let's introduce ourselves more accurately", continued Lars, in quiet tones "We are both originally from the Tract."

"Outside of the Ellipse", said Carolin, "So we're using quite a lot of Tract resource to come here today and to look like Ellipse people.

"We're leaving right now though", said Janie and pulled Chantal from her seat.

Janie looked across to Chantal. It wasn't a normal situation. Janie hadn't met many Tractwalkers, who mostly had reputations as thieves and roughnecks. She had hardly spoken to any of them before, now being with two of them in Smolly's was quite a revelation.

"We're catching a taxi, right now. Are you coming?" They moved outside and across the short pedestrian walkway to a line of waiting black cabs. They were parked on their landing wheels, and Janie walked to the expensive rank that didn't use the street rail.

They clambered inside and Janie asked the driver to start the run to Westminster, "But follow the rail", she added, effectively forcing the driver to take a slower route.

They sat two across from the other two. Chantal noticed that Carolin looked as if she hadn't been in a cab before.

"I hope you don't mind me asking...but how do you afford to come into a bar like Smollensky's?", she asked.

"We have been selected from the Tract dwellers to make representations because of what has been happening. I think we see things from the Tract that most Ellipse dwellers are unaware of," continued Lars.

"It links to the economy and governance of the Ellipse people by the major corporations".

"You mean since the lifestyle improvements were introduced after the Great Leap?"

"Exactly, so-called improvements since the division between wealth economies and the agrarian cultures"

The taxi was running smoothly now; it had taken one of the road tunnels from Canary Wharf's island back towards the City of London.

Chantal knew that Lars's comments were referencing the progressive split as service industry-based economies became wealthier and the land dwellers who farmed and fished became separated and eventually separated. Then barriers had been introduced that made the free passage of people from one environment to the other more difficult, unless for economic sustenance of the Ellipse.

"Carolin and I are Tractwalkers, who are part of a small group who can pass from the Tract to the Ellipse and back. For reasons we don't understand, our bodies don't trigger the 'glimmer' which enforces the boundaries.

We are considered as the servant class, but today you can see we are trying to blend with the Ellipse people."

"Are, are you really from Norway, then?", asked Janie," or was that part of your cover too?"

Lars nodded, "It's true, I am from Norway originally, although, after the introduction of the cartridges by the Nordic governments, I opted out of the healthcare program bracelets, and then found myself opting out of the economy"

Janie looked at Carolin, who was wearing a dark long-sleeved sweater which concealed her arms.

Chantal assumed that Carolin wouldn't have a cartridge and it was evident that Lars didn't. Chantal also wondered why Janie hadn't spotted this, but with cartridges being so commonplace it was like not noticing whether someone was wearing a watch.

Lars continued, "Remember, the cartridges were originally introduced as a response to the N3Ro virus. N3Ro occurred patchily around 20 years ago and very suddenly had reached an inflection point where it voraciously attacked large parts of the population.

"Some were immune, but the level of death had been on a scale greater than world wars."

Janie nodded, "Yes, some in our family were affected by this."

Lars continued, "A Biotree vaccine was already available and was progressively rolled out. As the virus became epidemic, governments shifted through single-shot vaccines and but soon had to deploy the cartridge solution."

"I remember those days of needing to get regular shots of vaccine. The cartridge was a much better solution," said Janie.

"This was because the virus was also self-modifying, and the consequent protection required regular changes. In effect, the medicinal properties of the tropus cartridges could be adapted to combat the new strains.

"That's how the cartridges became the standard form of inoculation. They were fitted to infants at birth, and to the majority of the population that lived within 'The Ellipse'.

Lars waved his arms, "There was a huge part of the planet which had the economic wherewithal to support the ongoing cartridge programme.

"The other parts of the world were referred to as 'the Tract'. There was also a variation of The Tract around the edge of significant conurbations, where more impoverished people who had the resilience to survive N3Ro had moved."

Chantel said, "I always thought of the virus as Nero." Janie nodded, "Yes, we were taught Nero in school."

Lars said, "There had also been a challenge for those with immunity. Ellipse dwellers were distrustful of Tract dwellers for a variety of emotional reasons. Mainly it was the risk of Nero morphing faster than the cartridge immunity could handle, and so the Tract people might become carriers for a new strain.

"This thinking created the disadvantaged status of Tract dwellers and the rumours that they were all roughnecks and thieves. It created a caste system at a global level. It was stronger than anything from the eras of segregation or the castes in India. All driven from fear.

Lars continued, "So you'll appreciate that we are feeling a lot more threatened here than either of you. One word and you could have us removed from the Ellipse and even with our current special status, we wouldn't be able to come back. Please listen carefully to what I'm about to tell you."

He looked across to Carolin, and she removed a small device from her bag. It was a handheld, but it looked several generations older than anything that Chantal or Janie had seen.

"Wow, vintage," said Chantal, looking with some intrigue towards the device.

"It is all we can afford," answered Carolin," And I've brought it to show you a recording." She flipped it on, and Chantal was surprised at its relatively small screen surrounded by some kind of carbon fibre surround.

It showed a few seconds of what looked like a transit station and then a blur of some feet and a three-second image of a man. He was walking on a path that cut across the field of vision. It looked like Sloane Square, thought Chantal.

Carolin paused the device and made the hand gesture to rewind it a few frames. She paused it on the face of the man.

"This is Scrive," said Lars, "He is our key to a different way of things in the future."

He pointed to the face, and Carolin also looked intently at the freeze frame picture.

"You are still talking in riddles," said Janie, "You'll need to be more explicit. I'll give you another five minutes and then we are out of this cab."

"Okay," continued Lars,

"Some big secrets are being kept by Biotree. The company has always projected itself as very kind and generous, but we are sure there is another agenda at play. Every time we have got close, our friends have disappeared, and we have not seen them again.

"They have all been from the Tract, and that has made them relatively easy to spot, even if they have cartridge implants added."

He put his hand into his pocket and pulled out a cartridge kit. Chantal recognised it as an after-market graft, the sort of thing used by people who wanted a boost beyond the level given by the health service.

"Yes, it's a booster," said Lars, "not a straight cartridge implant, but once it is in, you need to look carefully to spot the difference."

"We have information about some kind of attempt to penetrate Biotree, not by the Tract, but by a National government. Someone is hunting for power. But we think they'll get more than they bargained. The reason it is so important is that we believe Biotree is effectively the planetary power broker."

"What makes you think this is the case?" asked Janie.

"It is simple," replied Lars. "No one dies from Nero. We haven't seen a single death from it in the last 15 years."

Chantal looked at Janie, not sure whether to believe the conversation. "You'll need to prove that," replied Janie.

"It is easy to show you that," said Lars as Carolin also nodded, "...but people are still being affected. We don't know how, but people simply disappear. Much like Karin, but from the Tract it is a regular occurrence. That's where Scrive comes in.

"He's been asked to investigate something by Biotree. We want to adapt his agenda. He is one of the few people globally that can get to the bottom of what is happening. But we can't pay him, and he works strictly as a mercenary."

Carolin nodded again. Janie looked at Chantal.

"I'm ahead of you," said Janie. "You want me to help this guy named Scrive."

Lars nodded. "I do...We do. And it's because you are not from the Tract, you knew Karin, and you work at Biotree. It is the area where you work as well."

"...And in return for this, I get 'disappeared' like Karin?" asked Janie, "It doesn't sound like much of a deal."

"I agree; we have no leverage in this situation. All I can say is that our mission is trying to put things right. To rebalance the world and remove some injustice.

Janie looked at Chantal. Chantal thought that neither she nor Janie had ever stood up to anything at a political level. As far as they could tell the world was kind of 'sewn-up' about politics. People just got on with their lives.

Chantal was always slightly more edgy than Janie, but that was because she diluted her cartridges. She did something highly illegal, which was to siphon out about half of the cartridge and sold the content on the black market. The half shots were called 'boosts' and for certain parts of the population, they were a form of additional rather pleasant relaxant.

Chantal always thought she was taking risks by doing this; she saw her own blood through the plexi, and it ran close to a red colour, rather than orange or yellow. It meant she was usually on a very low dose of the tropus that everyone was supposed to take. But it made her feel more alive.

Others did this, but it was frowned upon in much the same way as 21st Century class A drugs were considered harmful. Chantal wasn't addicted to the low dose lifestyle, but it certainly gave her more freethinking and what she considered to be sharpness.

"You're a sife", said Lars, "You siphon," looking towards Chantal.

"I can see it in your eyes. Show me your wrist." Chantal extended it and Lars noticed the plexi was almost red.

"That's how we feel," he said to Chantal," No tropus and a much clearer was of thinking, acting and living."

Chantal replied, "But that's because you are immune to the Nero virus. I'm taking a risk."

"Not really," replied Carolin, "I'm not immune but have lived in the Tract all my life. My parents had the immunity, but it didn't pass on to me. The whole Nero thing is a big conspiracy now, but no-one would ever listen to the Tract on this. The conspiracy works well because everyone is frightened and therefore won't let the Tract people into Ellipse, except under stringent control."

Chantal was thinking about this. She knew that she'd been siphoning for at least a couple of years. She'd started with an eighth, but now it was half that she took out. When it dropped below a quarter, her blood started to change colour, and now it was almost the raw red colour that they had been taught was dangerous.

Janie looked at Chantal and then back towards Lars. "I'm trusting you on this far more than I should do. I need some way for you to prove you are on the level."

The taxi had just crossed Westminster Bridge and the rail it was following ended by Parliament Square.

"We're here," said Janie. "Chantal and I are leaving you now. I'll help Scrive Mallinson if he shows up at the office, but I don't know what I'm supposed to do."

"Neither do we at the moment," replied Carolin," Scrive is a tracker. He'll be looking out for signs of what has been happening. He'll need access to some things in your area, but we just don't know what."

"I'll be in contact again," said Lars. He opened the cab door on the pavement side and pushed it wide. Carolin climbed out, and he followed.

Shred

Makatomi cursed at the news that one of the trackers he'd hired was creating a problem.

He'd have to get it fixed. In a low-key way so that no-one suspected or followed any link back to Biotree. It couldn't be a disappearance, the hiring of Scrive was too recent, and the limited people who did know would think Makatomi was implicated.

He decided to call the fixer that had just helped him out to locate the heavies in Los Angeles. He needed something done quietly, and without fuss.

Makatomi reached into his pocket. The disposable cell-phone was still there. He smiled; a low-tech solution and the same phone he'd used to set up the earlier appointment. He should have already destroyed the phone. On this occasion, it worked to his benefit, because he still had the link. He hit the redial, and the phone indicated two minutes left.

"Arusen, please terminate Scrive Mallinson. I will message you his address. Use a cartridge. I want it to look clean."

In turn, Arusen sent another fixer the information about Scrive's land address as well as the IoH address of Scrive's current Plexi unit. With the Internet of Health address, the fixer could arrange for Scrive's old tropus cartridge to be decommissioned, necessitating a replacement.

4

"This isn't a ride you can take again,
but one, I'm guessing,
that is simply impossible to get off."

— *Scarlett Thomas, The End of Mr. Y*

Head-Up, Head Down.

Scrive was playing with a Head-Up Display. He wanted to try the virtual support before he took it outside. It was a new unit, and he wanted it to run very fast. He'd pressed the button-shaped device into a small carbon fibre frame attached to his left ear. It was one neat device. As he ramped up the speed, he heard a beep. It was his cartridge. It was giving out the depleted tone. He looked at it and could feel the little ripple on his wrist where it sent a small alert requesting a replacement.

Scrive thought about it. He had only put a new one in that morning. They were supposed to last for four weeks. He'd never had a defective one before. He looked for his supply. The package he'd left out this morning had been tidied away. It must have been Charlie. She'd have put it away, as part of a tidiness campaign. He flipped open the cupboard, and there was the pack. He opened it and reached for another cartridge. He was supposed to keep the old one if it was defective, but in truth, he couldn't be bothered and pinged it into the waste disposal.

He flipped the new one in and instinctively looked at his plexi. The tropus hit caught him unexpectedly, the one he'd been using before had given him a rush, but once he was back to an average tropus level, the replacements didn't usually have the same effect.

He wondered briefly whether the previous cartridge had been faulty from the start.

Then he saw the impact in the plexi. Instead of staying yellow, his blood colour was running towards red — the danger colour.

He gasped.

It was turning past red to a bluer colour. He struggled for breath. The blue colour could have two meanings. He was de-oxygenating. But he could also feel a kind of pain increasing all over his body. Too fast to be Nero, but something was attacking him.

He slid towards the floor, and as he did so, a couple of the neatly arranged cooking utensils also crashed down alongside a large cooking pot.

He couldn't speak.

He couldn't breathe.

He couldn't see.

There was another crash, and he felt a sharp pain in his chest.

Useful nanofibre pressure suits

Denny had booked some tickets on the Hypersonic out of LAX. It was a regular route, if somewhat pricey - what with enviroset taxes added to the ticket price. It didn't have the comfort of the V-Blade that Makatomi had arrived on, but as the Mach 6 speed meant the journey only took around 30 minutes it was worth the annoying pressure suit.

Suze and Denny were both frequent travellers, and both had nanofibre pressure suits of their own. They could go through the business check-in wearing the suits which would be tested on the diagnostic before they boarded. It was a lot less irritating than having to use one of the suits provided by the airline.

They decided to go hand luggage only. Makatomi had given them a decent amount of upfront money, so even if there were no separate expenses, it was still worth it for the convenience.

Denny packed a small box with some gadgets and dropped them at Fed-Ex on the way to the airport. They'd receive the items at an address in London later.

The flight was being called as they arrived and after the bios scans, checks of their cartridges, declarations that they hadn't been in contact with the Tract for the last 30 days and the pre-diagnostics for their suits, they boarded the flight.

A head-up display forced its way onto their vision. It was a feature of the suit and forced them to watch the pre-flight safety instruction. Danny referred to the suit as 'boil in a bag' on the basis that if anything were to happen there'd not be much left of anyone, except whatever it was would be entirely contained in the armour proofed pressure suits.

A few more minutes and the HUD flipped to a news channel. It could be adjusted by eye movement, but Denny just watched the programme, which was giving updates on a few political situations, a couple of scandals involving a movie star who'd been in the porn industry and some football results. Next up was a pop video, but as it started, the screen cleared. They'd landed and were in London.

The combination of the HUD, the pressure suit and the cartridge modification during flight meant that the entire sensation of take-off, flight and landing had been replaced with a somewhat intrusive video show.

Denny felt the suit pressure release, having not noticed it tighten at all during the flight. The haptics were designed to bring passengers down to reality again at the end, and he could feel circulation and pulse for a few seconds as the suit ran its post-flight diagnostics of his blood pressure and pulse.

He's joked that suits had a mind of their own, and in a way they did. They'd stay inflated and rigid if a passenger was suffering adversely from the flight, or indeed if there was any security concern when they'd been run through the passport and customs processes.

Thankfully for both Denny and Suze, the suits de-pressurised and returned to a skin-layer level. Denny pulled a tee-shirt over his head and Suze wrapped herself in a jacket.

"Let's go," said Denny, "We've some tracking to do".

Suze nodded. They had been awake since 4 am LA time, and after the flight against the clock it had turned back into the London evening.

Charlie's titanium SIG

Charlie heard the crash from the kitchen. First a small one, then a larger metallic one and finally a scraping and a thud. She was in the bedroom and reached into Scrive's bedside cabinet to bring out a SIG pistol. Titanium, lightweight and with minute rounds, it could fire as fast as many machine guns.

She flexed and moved fast and silently towards the kitchen. She could see Scrive inert on the ground. Scrive was on his back, arms upturned, but still breathing. She could see the plexi and the blue, almost black, blood display.

"Scrive - stay with me - this is Charlie," she called, "this is a nano crime". She glanced around and slid back to the bedroom, returning a few seconds later with a small handheld wired to a little T shaped connector.

She lifted it above her head and smashed it down onto Scrive's arm, smashing the plexi and the cartridge. She held it there as black blood oozed onto the floor. She was holding in two buttons on the device and kneeling in the slow ooze that was dripping from Scrive.

The T connector glowed blue, and she could see it was processing Scrive's blood.

Ten minutes passed. Charlie looked down at Scrive. The thin slick of black slime on the floor by her knees was changing colour. Scrive's face was also evolving from a grey colour to one that was notably redder. She could hear him breathing very quietly. She gently removed the unit that she had slammed into his arm. She stood and hurried to the freezer, selecting a polypack of frozen vegetables. She ripped the packaging with both hands, allowing the small chopped vegetables to fall to the floor. She took the packaging and wrapped it tightly around Scrive's wrist. She could see his eyes moving rapidly under his closed lids.

Then he shook violently, and with a sudden and sharp gasp he sat up.

His eyes opened.

"What's happened?" he looked at Charlie, "Something has gone wrong."

"Yes," replied Charlie quietly, "I think someone has just tried to kill you."

Scrive looked at his arm. "I was adding a cartridge; the last one was defective."

"Maybe...", replied Charlie," But I think the new one was contaminated. Deliberately".

She looked again at the liquid on the floor. It was now a blood colour, having been black a few minutes earlier.

"Ew," she said, "Kind of messy."

"Someone had added a payload to your cartridge", said Charlie, "I've seen this effect when I was working with the nanotech. Someone has added nanobots to the cartridge. I think they were intended to mash up your inside."

Scrive looked around and spotted the handheld device on the floor. "You used your experiment on me?" he looked at Charlie.

"This time, bad science has a good outcome. I saw your black blood, typical of a nanobot incursion, I reckoned that my device would finish off any normal nanobots and it seems to have worked. I inserted a huge block of nanoreductives into your bloodstream - it worked because even the blood spill has been processed. The zappers half-life is one hour, so we'd better keep an eye on you. What's interesting is that the zappers have been so thorough that your blood has reverted to red. Not yellow or orange. There's something else weird happening here, normally nanoreductives restore balance but are not powerful enough to completely neutralise tropus."

Scrive pulled himself up using the edge of the kitchen counter. He did it slowly, aware that his blood level was a little low.

"Lay down, you've lost some blood" said Charlie, "and where do you keep the first aid kit? I don't think you've lost that much. It looks worse than it is. I'm going to guess less than half a litre. That's less than a blood donor session."

"Weak tea with sugar and a cookie then?" asked Shrive. He was aware that his reaction times had slowed. He seemed to be running at normal rates. He wouldn't push it at the moment until his cardio had stabilised.

"I'm a little bit worried that whoever has done this might want to come back and take a look," said Charlie. "I think we may still need to fake your demise".

She slid across the floor and retrieved the SIG pistol. There was a quiet click as she replaced the safety catch.

Non-linear cubism

Denny had gone non-linear. He was strafing various global systems to try to find any patterns that would help trace what had been happening in London, LA, and wherever Makatomi seemed to be taking his presence.

He'd brought a Cube with him; it was a small offboard processor that he could use with a regular handheld to boost the power and number of connections. He'd brought them both in his carry-on luggage as well as a somewhat cumbersome looking mains adapter so that he could run his system in the UK. It wasn't the voltages; it was just the over-engineered plugs and sockets that the Brits seemed to prefer.

Suze was also browsing online, but at a more leisurely pace. They'd checked into a central London hotel and needed to run their operation without attracting attention. She was gently reprogramming the network around the hotel so that Denny's activities wouldn't draw undue attention. He was hitting the system so hard that any schoolkid could probably spot the activity. Suze was creating an electronic cordon to stop it being detectable.

Denny glanced up.

"Makatomi is a real spinner," he muttered, "One minute he's in London, then LA, then Tokyo. He's carrying Arusen around with him on that V-Blade, but there's another electronic presence that seems to skitter around even faster."

Suze nodded," Yeah, I saw that too. Holden. He seems to turn up everywhere. I can't tag him properly; it is like he's somehow in the system. He's also been to Norway and Arizona."

Denny nodded. It must be evident if Suze had picked up on it too. Their work division was unbalanced, and he'd been doing most of the heavy tracing. Suze was quietly folding some of the quaint but expensive grey hotel stationery into the shape of a swan, with her spare hand. She was already wearing the colourful courtesy gown and had now pushed two of the chopsticks into her hair, making an instantly more Eastern look.

"Was that the influence of the room service?" he quipped. They'd ordered Japanese as a sort of homage to Makatomi and been enjoying maguru tuna sushi with nori seaweed. Suze had spotted a pineapple dessert, but neither of them had expected the laser cut slices laminated with microlayers of a ginger flavoured wasabi.

"Yes, it's auto suggestive, I think," replied Suze as she flipped another firewall. "The ginger and pineapple must be talking to me."

Chinese wake up

Guangdong Province, China and Shenzhen Ruby were due to play an important match. Den Xiapau had tickets to the Shenzhen Stadium for what promised to be the Super League match of the season, as far as he was concerned.

But.

Now he'd alerted everyone about that hacker attack, which seemed like two different sets of people on the same mission, he was notionally chained to his desk.

The station commander had called for a lock-down. No-one in or out. Sure, he could get a bowl of noodles from the canteen or spend half an hour playing some table tennis, but he was fundamentally locked in until they'd got to the bottom of whatever was happening.

There had been an initial burst of system scans apparently from all over the world. Den Xiapau knew it was typical of an advanced hacker - probably a tracker - who was trying to find out something important. It looked like a coincidence that the second series of probes had appeared but the second set (which seemed easier to trace back to London), had also been shooting probes into Biotree.

He wasn't sure what to make of this. Was China being challenged, or was this some corporate protestor trying to dig into Biotree's vaults?

The main reason for all of the escalation was because of the sophistication. Two sets of almost simultaneous probes with Chinese corporations and governments as a target.

After the first alert, they'd decided to inform the US and European Governments. If this was someone playing silly games, it was better to let them know that they had been discovered. The longer they left it, the more the West would get cocky about such things.

They spent a little longer deciding whether to inform Biotree. Still, because they also had a sizeable Biotree manufacturing plant right within the province, it seemed like the right thing to do.

The challenge now was that both the Americans and Europeans had escalated it within their jurisdictions and Biotree's Chairman had been on the red phone to the Chinese President.

It was all causing something of a meltdown.

Then, after the initial attacks, everything had gone quiet for a couple of hours. What was interesting now was that a new series of high-intensity probes seemed to have started. From London, although someone very sophisticated was running a cloaking operation on them. It was fortunate for Den Xiapau that he'd spotted the source and knew where to be looking. Otherwise, the cloaking would have worked before he'd been able to get a fix.

5

And all I need now is
intellectual intercourse
A soul to dig the hole
much deeper
And I have no concept of time
other than it is flying
If only I could
kill the killer

All I really want – Alanis Morissette

Bodø

Sheri was originally Canadian, although she had studied in the USA, as well as a short spell in Switzerland and was now into her second year at Biotree's facility in Norway.

The Bodø environment was surprisingly familiar, a mix of her childhood's Vancouver waters and the nearby ski areas, where she had spent winters skiing as well as getting something of a reputation around Whistler for her freestyle snowboarding.

The cold end of the Pacific had first raised her love of nature. She would still think of times spent with her Grandfather out to look for whales with their tail splash, fishy snorts and the rippling radiation of the water as they would dive near to the boat.

The Pacific had also stimulated her study of marine biology and the organisms that maintained the ecology. Then her time at Harvard where the study of very small things had eventually led her to Biotree. Harvard had taught her how the organisms worked and then CERN in Switzerland had taught her how to build them, ironically by first showing how to smash things apart.

Now she was working with mechanosynthesis, construction an atom at a time. It was beyond a watchmaker's precision, to know how to bolt the atoms together to make the tiny machines that formed the basis of the Biotree business model.

She'd learned how to build these tiny structures, how to make them operate, which parts would simply refuse to work together because of the still only partly understood and apparently tiny forces between them. Forces she knew were big enough to destroy the machines to which they were attached if they were not coupled properly.

She sometimes thought of it as being inside God's head. If a God existed, the God would need to know this stuff really well.

It was her work in the USA had lifted her profile considerably. At Harvard she had gained extra letters after her name. She had also met some of the super-scientists that worked in her field. They had told her about the opportunities at Biotree, but initially, she had remained sceptical.

Then she'd worked on ultra-transformables, which were a branch of the science that could help significantly in healthcare, the machines having a squishiness which meant they travelled well inside humans.

The spell at CERN had been mainly using the accelerators to smash a few things apart and see the effects. There was something mysterious about the power needed when humans tried to do these things, compared with the weak forces that were apparent in the nano-machines and which could do exceptionally more powerful things if assembled incorrectly.

Back to God's head, it was like His way of saying, "No, No, don't do that."

Inevitably she'd also run into nanotoxins as part of the research. Still, to people in her community, there were some basic rules about what to attempt and mix, and most of the 'No-no's" were very obvious. It was more the effect of a constructed machine and its erstwhile operating system that became the challenge and the thing that led Sheri to Bodø, Norway.

She'd been working on nanoparticles to improve foodstuffs and found that the addition of inert machines as a way to deliver medicinal payload didn't work very well.

The human body (or any other living organism for that matter) detected and destroyed the nanobots on the way in. If they couldn't be destroyed, they were at least neutralised although this could leave residuals in the body.

What was fascinating was that the residuals were stored in almost homeopathic quantities.

Sheri had worked out that an average human adult could eat nano-processed food every day of their life. Unless the human system changed the form of handling, the effect of the residual "neutralised and stored" would still only amount to something which in homeopathy was called the 60X formula. This wasn't one sixtieth, it was ten to the power of minus sixty. Something like the equivalent of a single pinch of salt into the Pacific Ocean. This level was so far below the 24X considered to be the limit of any homeopathic remedy, that the little broken machines couldn't pose any threat at all.

Of course, that assumed that the body had done its 'repel all invaders' thing and broken the machines down and expelled them.

It was the very power of these tiny machines that fascinated Sheri. They were already being packaged and consumerised by Biotree, and she knew there were many more practical and positive uses.

When she'd left for Bodø, it was with the idea of spending a couple of years, to make enough to live well and then move back to the West Coast. What had been seductive about her time was both the work and her discovery of Nathan, a fellow

Canadian worker, with whom she now lived on the extended Bodø complex.

There was also the feeling in the Biotree Bodø R&D facility of being in the core of the core. It wasn't just in the Ellipse, Bodø was the inner sanctum of how everything worked. And there she sat, in the Advanced Technology Area, right at the centre of the centre.

Sheri knew that both she and Nathan had found something worthwhile and challenging. They'd both talked recently about settling longer in Bodø, and with her approaching birthday, she wondered whether Nathan was getting ready to ask her a big question. She smiled to herself as she knew the answer already. And it would give an excuse for a trip back to Canada.

V-Blade departure times

From their London hotel room, Denny was convinced that there would be a way to track the other suspicious person that might be following this assignment. He was sure that something had happened around the time he had run the last trace.

He was still hitting the Chinese sites and the Biotree locations but was now interested in tracing back Makatomi's steps.

"Suze let's see what happened inside Biotree this morning". He looked across at Suze, and they both laughed. Was it really the same day?

Suze was testing a few links around Canary Wharf. She found a tourist weather cam monitoring the general view. She jacked into its archive and ran back to the morning period. In reverse, a purple flash appeared over one of the buildings. She stopped the rewind and hit a button.

"That's the 'out' point", she said and continued to run the video backwards. Another purple flash, "and that's the 'In'," she added," Now we can see when Makatomi arrived and left."

Denny nodded. Suze had found the arrival and departure times of the V-Blade. There wouldn't be many of these crafts around, and a direct docking with the building was still relatively rare. They both knew this would be Makatomi's ride at the headquarters.

"Now we have a time range, we need to work out where he's meeting his visitor", said Suze," I've got the building directory here. It is the one used for visitors to the headquarters. Here we are, floors 60-70 seem to be the ones for the special meetings."

Danny looked at the list. There were a couple of boardroom floors, some training areas and three floors with individual meeting rooms, including two levels with ultra-secure screening.

"It will be one of these," he said, pointing to the secure facilities. Makatomi won't want to take any chances."

Suze nodded. "Let's play with the elevators". She flicked into a few more screens and then a few more.

"This isn't working, there's no access", she said.

Denny picked up his handheld and tapped a number. He was calling the building's foyer. "Hello, I'm a guest in your building. I seem to be stuck somewhere between floors 58 and the top." He hung up immediately.

The foyer receptionist punched another number.

"Gotcha," said Suze, "watching the number ringing through and tracing it to Westinghouse, who had a facility in the Canary Wharf area. They have people on hand to manage the elevators in case of problems.

"Now I know where you are, I might just need to borrow a couple of your documents," she said as she dragged a couple of diagrams onto her own machine's desktop. They were high-level plans of the elevators, with the network number for the various individual shafts.

"Okay, now to find their camera feeds". Suze tapped a few numbers and soon had three TV pictures displayed on the screen of her computer.

"Now I need to run the archives". Suze tapped some numbers and three pictures simultaneously wound back to the time of the V-Blade landing. Then she ran them forward at ten times normal speed. They watched as one floor became busy, but the other two had no visitors.

Then suddenly a lone individual appeared on floor 63. He walked to the reception and was met by a third person. It wasn't Makatomi.

145

"It's him," said Suze," I know it is."

Contamination

Scrive looked towards Charlie after hearing the safety click from her weapon. "You found my pistol, then?"

"Old habits," replied Charlie.

"What happened?"

"My handheld, the one I told you about. Complete with my failed blood reprocessor - the one that destroys nanobots. That's what I used on you. I could see your blood. It was turning black. Someone has contaminated you with nanobots.

"It looked like they were attacking your blood. It was clotting, instead of flowing. I managed to smash into your circulation through the cartridge and to release my little App. It is the first time its failure has been useful. It caused a signalling failure amongst the 'bots. Whatever they were doing stopped.

"It looks to me as if they were attacking via your cartridge. Someone has contaminated the tropus. "

Scrive looked around. The kitchen was a mess. He was a mess.

"Thank you," he said to Charlie, "I think that could have finished me."

"Yes, and I'm not sure whether whoever did this will be back?"

"And they don't know about me at the moment", said Charlie.

"That's a good point," replied Scrive. "We should keep it that way, no sense in showing all of the hand."

"And maybe we can throw them a scrap too? See if we can draw them out?" Charlie grinned.

"Okay," said Scrive, "Maybe I need to disappear for a while, make them think that I've gone."

"And not show them that I'm around either?"

"...Or we do something more reckless?" Scrive pulled himself up, "Maybe I need to carry on for a few days as if nothing has happened? They won't know when I'm exchanging the cartridge; they may even know that I'm a little lax on such matters. I'm going to carry on normally for the next few days.

The difference will be my traceability, and you can help with that."

"Sure," said Charlie, "But I think I'd better move away. It's better that they don't know about me at all, and it will be a lot easier if I'm somewhere else. And from one tracker to another, don't even think about tracing me."

She was already walking to the bedroom. Scrive could hear the sound of a zipper bag and realized that Charlie was already planning to move out.

"You'd better take this," he said and handed her the high fire rate SIG, "I guess you only found the one," they both smiled.

"And I'll be listening out for you", said Charlie, "Let's just agree on some signals." Scrive tapped a series of numbers into his handheld and then pressed a few keys. The numbers transferred to Charlie's handheld. They now had a private key between them, which could be used for tracking and tracing.

"And we'll use the transit station as a drop," if we need it. By the left-hand side of the entrance. Use a marker. I'll find it."

"Daily," said Scrive, "But don't tell me where you'll be".

Scrive knew that he and Charlie could operate a hidden analogue protocol between them. Charlie could track him, but he wouldn't know where she was. If she needed to exchange information, they would use a physical location, which Scrive would check every day. Charlie would not go there herself but would use an intermediary if there was to be anything placed there. If Scrive needed to pass information to Charlie, he would use the tracker to signal a location, leave the material and then continue. Scrive knew that he was now on an electronic leash, which was managed by Charlie.

Camtran mission

Suze and Denny continued to watch the replay. Suze was intently watching for the return of the visitor to the elevator. Some 20 minutes later, he arrived again, still accompanied by the same person. It was difficult to make out what they were saying, the sound channel from the elevator monitoring was faulty, and the wide angle meant they were both shown tiny.

"That was a short meeting," said Denny. Suze nodded. "Maybe he's not getting paid well as us - that can't have been much of a negotiation?"

Suze was referring to the negotiation they'd run with Makatomi, once they had realised that money wasn't a problem to resolve this case.

"Okay," said Suze, "Now let's see you leave the building", they flicked to another camera view from the ground level and saw Scrive exiting towards the transit station.

"Go in, go in," said Denny, willing the image of Scrive to enter the Tube. He did, and Suze and Denny smiled. We'll get him at the gate. Scrive passed through it as it automatically opened. Suze tapped a few buttons and moments later retrieved the cartridge RFID for Scrive.

"Radio Frequency Identification - Thank you for some old technologies," said Suze.

"We have you now, Mr Mallinson," she said, as the RFID sequence yielded its information. And you seem to have good health records too, Mr Mallinson of Chelsea Bridge Wharf."

Denny calculated that Scrive Mallinson's home address appeared to be less than three miles from their hotel in Central London.

A visit would be necessary. There were two ways to do this. Overt or Stealth. Denny ran some further scans to try to find the back story for Mallinson, but it wasn't straightforward to trace more than the most perfunctory information.

Denny thought this added up. He knew that a similar scan for his own ident wouldn't yield much, so the sequence of events seemed to form the right type of trail. Mallinson visits the office of Makatomi. He has as a meeting, leaves and then within a couple of hours there's a series of scans being run on China and also on Biotree. Checking on Mallinson yields little. Denny was pretty sure it had the hallmark of another tracker.

"Suze, I think Mallinson has the other half of our contract." said Denny.

Suze nodded. "Yes", there's a pattern that looks strangely familiar. And now we know where he lives. I don't think we should try to deep scan though, if he's as good as us he'll notice it in seconds.

"Do you fancy a ride in a London taxi?", asked Denny to Suze. "I think I know someone we can visit."

"Now about tomorrow morning?" answered Suze. "We'll need to be sharp." She pulled the chopsticks from her hair.

"You stay here", said Denny, "I'm going on a little mission with a camtran. It would be good to keep tabs on Mr Mallinson." He flipped open his hand luggage and retrieved a couple of small camera transmitter devices.

"I'll see you in about an hour."

Denny slipped from the hotel and took a taxi across town. It was one of the black cabs that could go anywhere, although their route seemed to be along the major streets. He was dropped outside a large apartment block, next to a hotel complex.

Denny looked around and then reached into his bag. He identified the entrance to the apartments and set up a small camtran monitor across the way. It showed the main entrance and part of the thoroughfare either side.

He looked across to the adjacent hotel to the apartment buildings, then crossed the street and made for the reception. Ten minutes later, he returned with two cardkeys.

He and Suze were about to become Mallinson's neighbours.

Norway

Sheri was at home with Nathan. She looked out of the window, across snow towards some distant hills. Beyond them were mountains. She had grown to love the Norwegian scenery. The water, the sparkling ice and snow. It was like every cliché she'd heard about the place, an extraordinary land where bad vistas were not permitted. It made the already enjoyable work even better. She had a good location, good job, good money and most of all she was now sharing it all with Nathan.

Although she and Nathan both worked for Biotree, their roles were very different, and they didn't see each the during the working day. The campus was vast, and they would usually go to work separately, and because of the distance and security inside the facility, it was best to stay out of contact throughout the day. There were ways to communicate, but it was much the same as if they worked in different towns.

At the moment she was reading a report on her handheld. It was related to engineering advances in India and the possibility of some breakthroughs in molecular design. Sheri could sense immediately that this wasn't a plausible article. There were holes in the logic, and the approach was one she already knew to be flawed.

Nathan was preparing some food in the kitchen and called through from time to time to inform of progress. She could generally tell by the variety of hissing sounds, aromas of onions, garlic and the tell-tale sound of a bottle cork being extracted. The evening meal was almost ready.

Sheri knew she had the more demanding and specialised job of the two of them. Her work was at the (almost literally) cutting edge of the design of the nanomachines. Originally, there had been a set of standard assemblies that worked well together. Most of the incremental designs were based around these pieces.

When she explained it to others, she likened it to a car. Four wheels, one on each corner, some seats an, engine, steering and brakes. The nanobots had a similar basic construction kit.

At the small sizes of the machines, it was the use of protein as a fuel and the same effect that makes creme in coffee eventually spread through the liquid that created for a bot a power source. It also provided a significant physical limitation to the small machines and their deployment. The 'coffee-cup' Brownian motion made everything shake dramatically at this small scale. Nothing was every static and the trick with the scientists was to harness this motion as a power source.

The building blocks that Sheri used were similar to the components of the car. There were components for movement, components for sensing, components to join things together - the so-called fixtures - like the chassis of a car and elements to provide grip and contact between the machines - the end effectors.

Then, as Nathan referred, "JASMOP" - or "Just a small matter of programming" to create the operating systems for these small devices. Just a small matter was an interesting point. The technology of Scanning Probe Microscopes used to view the assembly work had never really scaled itself and relied upon clean, secure environments and mega-voltages. It was not surprising when a speck of dust would be like throwing a planet at some of these machines.

Sheri's work was within the so-called 'exotics' division. As expected, there were pictures of palm trees and Pina-Coladas stuck to the walls inside, but fundamentally this was the area where Sheri tried to outdo her maker.

It was the place where new elements were designed. Original elements to create the missing shapes of matter needed to extend the constructor kit of parts for the nanomachines. The pieces that

God forgot. There were practical physical limitations to how they could be used. Apart from atomic forces that would blast structures apart, the continued jittering from Brownian motion and the protein fuel consumption of the tiny devices, there were still some basic components that were proving impossible to construct. It was like the car but with only a few degrees of steering and no gears.

Sheri and the team were attempting to build the new shapes. The missing piece parts that would extend the nano constructor kit.

Nathan entered the room, triumphant. "Dinner is served!", he quipped and gestured towards their dining table. They would still eat together whenever possible because the nature of the work often meant irregular hours, and this would give a chance to spend some time chatting. There was an inverse luxury to 'dining in'. Most of the time, workers in the facility would avail themselves of the vast eco-system of restaurants and cafes that had established around the complex.

Pretty much all cuisines were catered for, from fast-food Americana to the fanciest French or Japanese food. Most evenings they would eat out, sometimes alone but often in company with others from the facility.

Being alone in their living quarters was an excellent time for decompression, even if Sheri had started the evening with a scientific journal article.

"I can't believe it's nearly two years that we've been here." started Nathan. "I know it will be after your birthday that its officially two years for you and about three weeks later for me."

Sheri alerted herself as Nathan started this line of conversation. A meal at home, talk about how long...would this be leading to a discussion of 'them'? She decided to see where it was going, but Nathan moved in another direction.

"I hope tonight's 'dish of the day' is okay?" he inquired, "I had to scratch around for some of the ingredients".

Sheri relaxed. She was keen enough for a talk about their future, but tonight it didn't somehow seem to be the time. She was just too strung out on the current work. A few tonal changes were creating some new upsets. Makatomi's business plans were at odds with Sheri's personal beliefs. Instead of the Biotree being about healthcare and the future, it seemed to be moving towards more ominous goals. They had recently brought some contractors into Sheri's department who seemed rather more lackadaisical about their approach to safety systems.

"I've been working on some new secure perimeter systems this week," called Nathan," It looks as if Biotree are getting even more paranoid based upon the recent share prices and business news."

Nathan worked in another area of high technology, but rather than being progressive and forward-facing, like the pure R&D that Sheri conducted, this was more related to the protection and security of the Biotree complex. Beyond obvious physical defences, there were rings within rings of security measures that could both give an impression of a relaxed environment but at the same time could become extremely strict in moments if something inappropriate was detected.

Nathan worked on the improvements to this world. A guardian role that also meant he spent more time around the whole complex that Sheri.

They had initially met just after Nathan had joined. Sheri had been out for a weekend skiing in the adjoining mountains, with a couple of new-found girlfriends when they had run into an 'induction team' part of which included Nathan.

Sheri was snowboarding at the time and noticed that Nathan also seemed pretty accomplished, and they'd broken away from the group to try a particularly exciting route. At least that was what Nathan had said and - on reflection - Sheri had also thought the course unexpectedly delightful.

They'd been together ever since that first encounter. After a short time, they had decided to move into what was considered one of the better apartment areas. Their facility looked out to the sea on one side and hills and distant mountains on the other side.

Tonight, Nathan had placed candles outdoors in the Norwegian tradition, and Sheri could see a distant twinkle from boats on the sea and stars in the sky.

But no, tonight wasn't the one to have deep conversations about the future.

Backtrace

Captain Taylor had a problem. He'd almost singlehandedly scrambled the U.S military to a state of high alert. All based on what started as a routine intercept in China.

He had seen some routine tracing by a hacker; it had tripped his high-intensity alert. He'd selected the trace, and watched it hop about between Biotree and SuzGene, a Chinese biochemical producer. Then he'd seen a second trace. It looked as if it was doing something similar. Taylor worked out that the traces looked like they were coming from professionals. London and, more worryingly, Los

Angeles. The LA one was a problem because if it was left undeclared, someone might challenge it as a state cyber probe. The kind of probe invoked before a cyber-attack.

Taylor knew there was no such thing on the horizon and thought he'd better call it in. That's when everything disappeared and seemed to go back to normal. Except, it looked as if a Chinese listening station had intercepted the activity and was now sending a few quiet probes to try to backtrace to the source of interference. He could see that the Chinese were running their monitoring from Beijing, and he thought it highly likely that it originated in the Chinese Ministry of State Security (MSS). The event was troublesome because it could easily pop up as a diplomatic incident.

He worked out that the president would already have been alerted to the situation. Taylor was old-school, from before the Great Leap, when most comms was still stuff with dials and buttons, rather than something one gestured to or voice activated. He'd paid extra to have his automobile fitted with a facsimile retro radio, one that had a rotary volume and push buttons for the channel selection. He knew that behind the covers, it was all solid-state, but it somehow felt better to dial things up.

Taylor had a secret habit. He was one of the people who ran low dosage from the tropus cartridges. Taylor didn't sell on his excess tropus, which meant that hardly anyone knew about his habit. He'd discovered the phenomenon by accident after a boating injury, that depletion of tropus made him feel somehow sharper. He could also remember more. He doubted, now, that he would remember about the analogue stations if he was on full dosage.

He'd still had to deal with the shadowy worlds of sifes and Tractwalkers though. He knew that the standard cartridges produced logged usage reports which could be monitored. He'd arranged through dealer connections for the fitting of a cloned cartridge holder, which somehow reported normally, despite his unconventional usage. He'd even paid over the odds to get it fitted because he didn't want to be linked to a dealer to whom he would supply his surplus tropus. It was another link in the chain that he'd prefer to avoid.

Taylor knew he could still fire up the old listening station and with the improved access from an array of satellites plus the old links created when Camp Lejeune, NC and Naples, Italy were still front-line monitoring stations, he might be able to uncover some further information. A few of the old links were worth re-activating

Outside was heavy rain. A squall from the Pacific had whipped into the harbour area, and there was a grey blanket across everything. Taylor was wearing a weatherproof cape, and a walked at an angle of forty-five degrees towards the four-wheel drive. The usual transit rail system was available in the main town here, but he'd be trekking into the forest and paying a visit to a couple of smaller buildings seldom used nowadays.

He booted up the four-wheel drive and reversed onto the road. Then along to a lane and then to the end of a road with a gate and wired fence.

He pressed an access pad in the four wheel's cab. Two large metal bolts slid open in the gates. Perimeter lights lit and a series of green spots briefly twinkled. He had disarmed the perimeter field, which would otherwise prevent his progress. He drove through the gates and into the area, which was buried in the forest. Then further along the track and sharp left. Two buildings, overgrown with what he'd have called kudzu or foot-a-night, back home in Tennessee, but here it was some other kind of vine. It did the trick though, and the two buildings were almost absorbed into the forest and undergrowth.

He tapped a few more access codes and hopped from the vehicle. A splash from underfoot, despite the now more distant sound of the wind and rain. The trees provided a groaning shelter in this part of the forest, although he knew that the weather further afield was still savage.

Now he entered the first building. He reached to the side of the door for a still familiar monitor light. Flipped it on and heard a countdown sequence. He had 60 seconds to disarm the building and punched in the access codes. 3-2-7-0. He still remembered it, despite the years of disuse. This facility had been a staple in the older days when picowave interception and traditional listening posts were still the order of the day. Now the remnant of the facility might give an unsophisticated way to access what was happening in Beijing. He really was going 'under the radar'.

6

What you see is what you get
You've made your bed, you better lie in it
You choose your leaders and place your
trust
As their lies wash you down and their
promises rust
You'll see kidney machines replaced by
rockets and guns

Paul Weller – Going Underground – The Clash

Follow me

Scrive was walking towards the transit station on his way back to his apartment. It was time to check for any update from Charlie. They were using a purely analogue protocol so that they could not be tracked by listening in through phone links or similar. Scrive knew that if anyone wanted to, they would probably now have access to his RFID and could be tracking his movements. The main thing was to make it all look normal as a way to reduce suspicion.

He'd patched his arm from Charlie's 'smash and grab', but it meant he couldn't use tropus again until he got the cartridge's plexi fixed. That would require medical attention which would signal that he'd already taken one of the doctored cartridges.

He'd be using the cocktail of his blood's residual tropus, any remnants of the hostile nanobots and the hacked concoction that Charlie had forced into his bloodstream. His blood was already running red from after Charlie's intervention, and now he simply didn't know because of the lack of a tropus fix.

Yesterday he'd used a pin to prick the end of one of his fingers, to see what colour emerged. It had been red. He'd been taught this meant danger, and it had made him feel unexpectedly queasy at the thought. Then he'd rubbed the finger, the blood had stopped, and since that point, he'd tried not to think about it.

Now he certainly felt okay. He felt better than he'd expected. He felt sharper with a kind of clarity and freshness. Today, it was beyond his ability to rev his thoughts to a higher speed. This feeling was offset by the sense that part of his mind was awakening that was usually dormant.

He took his routine walk to the transit and already had in mind the point he would approach to check for any marking from Charlie. It was only a day, and he didn't expect there to be anything yet. As he approached, for the fourth time he saw the slim girl he had noticed previously. She was walking across in front of him. He saw the tattoo. She was singing quietly to herself as usual. 'Follow me', she was singing. "Follow me, follow me, follow me Scrive. Follow me Mr Mallinson."

He looked startled.

Then he decided to be as deadpan as possible. Was this something from Charlie? He doubted it.

It was too much of a coincidence to have seen this person four times consecutively. But there had to be a link. He thought quickly. He'd seen the girl before he'd been to Makatomi. Before the threat to his life. Before he'd made arrangements with Charlie, but this had to be related.

He decided to follow.

Around the street corner was a small pavement cafe. Busy with local well-dressed people sipping small coffees and tapping into various handhelds. His guide showed him to a table in the corner. An athletic-looking and tanned man was sitting there.

"Mr Mallinson?" he inquired, "My name is Lars, and this is Carolin. We think we can help you."

Scrive looked at them both. He noticed Lars looked weathered in a way that wasn't very common. Then he realised, Lars was from the Tract. He looked back at Carolin. So was she. He hadn't picked it up when he first saw Carolin; maybe he was looking at, well, other aspects.

"You're both from the Tract, what are you doing here?" he asked.

"The same thing as you, "Mr Mallinson," we are looking at what Biotree is trying to conceal. We know it is not about a Chinese plot, and that the story has been put out to help explain the share price drop and the strange activities within the company."

Scrive was tallying this new information. He'd only been involved with Makatomi for a day, and already someone had tried to kill him, and now he was being intercepted by a couple of Tractwalkers.

"Okay, say I go with this," replied Scrive, "what else can you tell me that would make me want to work with you?"

"The main thing we have to offer is immediate access to someone working inside Biotree, close to where Makatomi operates. But before that, I should tell you some other things."

Lars began to explain his background, that he was from Norway, that he lived close to Bodø, near to the Biotree R&D complex. He stated that he was one of the first people discovering their immunity to the Nero toxin. He had been forced into the Tract, along with others that were also immune.

He lived close to Bodø and seen the growth of the R&D facility and the influx of scientists.

"But the thing I need to tell you about is that Biotree has been working on its second-generation business. Nanobots. Before that it made its money from the tropus and cartridges."

"Now it is working on a third-generation business, and that's the thing we need prevent."

Scrive knew that the original business model for Biotree, along with several other large pharmaceutical based companies, had been the creation of the tropus that had formed the basis of the inoculation against Nero.

He also knew that the pricing for this had started high because of patents, but that global governments had forced a rapid change in order that the tropus could be manufactured on the industrial scale needed to provide it for large parts of the world population.

Everyone in the Ellipse took the regular medication of tropus through the cartridge system, and it had grown to be a basis for other services, based upon the addition of the radio links and secure identity capabilities.

Of course, Scrive also knew that this had effectively given everyone an electronic tag, based upon the need to use cartridges permanently and that the cartridge support clip was mainly where the tracking, wallet, comms, telemetry, health and other functions were held.

Scrive had also been noticing that his own system didn't seem to be affected negatively despite his lack of tropus. He had never been designated as immune and wondered how long Nero took to have an effect.

"You're both immune to the N3Ro?" he asked, "I can see that you don't have the plexus, so I assume no cartridges?

"Correct," said Lars, "but that's one of the things you should know. The Nero story has been convenient misinformation for the last several years. The cartridges that are in use now are for another purpose."

"...and what might that be?" asked Scrive.

"To stop you from seeing", replied Lars. "To hide what is happening".

Scrive looked quizzical, "To hide what?" he asked, "to stop us from seeing what?"

"You'll have to take what I say on trust," continued Lars. "We've no way of proving this here, although we do have other things we can show you later."

Scrive said, "It's already been a helluva week. I'm prepared for just about anything at the moment." He absentmindedly scratched at the place on his arm where a bandage covered his broken plexi.

"This is what we think has been happening," continued Lars,

"The Biotree corporation are being employed on several missions. They are one of the manufacturers of the tropus that all of you use to protect against the N3Ro virus. That has been a great continuous source of revenue for them and allowed them to create the facilities to build their other businesses."

"The main source of new business now is the Nanotechnology, although they seem to have a hit a wall with their R&D and at the same time there's a rumour that the Chinese have cloned the technology."

"We think that's why Biotree has employed you, to track down if there's a leak to the Chinese. We don't think you'll find one though, we think that the Chinese will be as surprised about this as anyone."

"How can you say that?" asked Scrive," You don't appear to have the resources, especially being based in the Tract."

"It is because we are from the Tract that we think we have an idea about what is happening.

"We believe that the Tract is the source of the new nanotech and that there is someone building products to compete with Biotree. In the Tract, we hear of things by the old-fashioned ways. Some of it isn't as reliable, but there are too many stories of people in an area deep in the Tract where this work is being done.

"If that's the case, how is it we haven't spotted it from the Ellipse?" asked Scrive, "I can't believe that anyone would be able to do this without someone from the Ellipse knowing what was happening.

"Normally I'd agree, said Lars, "But I think there is a reason, part of the way that the Ellipse has been engineered means that there is a huge blind spot for what happens in the Tract. It is as if we don't exist."

Scrive thought for a moment. It's true; he knew the Tract. Aside from the warnings to stay away and that they may be carriers of the Nero virus, he had little idea of what else went on.

"What? Is it like a return to the 'flat earth'? When people used to think of the earth as flat, before they discovered it was round, then the corners of the map would sometimes be printed with 'Here be Dragons'?" asked Scrive.

"It is a little like we've returned to that concept." continued Lars.

"Except we do all know that the world is round, indeed that's where we get the Ellipse term. There are still some areas that don't ever get mentioned by Ellipse dwellers. It is mainly an area south of Japan and China, an area we still call Australia."

Scrive replied, "But there isn't anything south of Japan, it is the exclusion zone, where the Nero toxins wiped out everything and where there is still a huge risk to anyone that attempts to go there. Part of the process of creating the Ellipse was to block off the remaining toxic zones. That's really where the terms of the Ellipse."

Lars nodded, "Even the Tract dwellers knew there were still some areas off-limits. The Ellipse dwellers had such advanced technology that they could fly just about anywhere, but the safety systems in the craft would ensure that they did not stray into dangerous territory. The Tract dwellers didn't have this technology, which limited their ability to move to all but the edges of the Ellipse. Without technology, Tract dwellers would not have access to the Exclusion zone, even if they wanted it."

Lars continued, "The last 30 years have seen a formidable rate of increase in technological progress compared with any period before. The nanotech, the transit, the handhelds, the tropus are all examples of the changes. I know it's called 'The Great Leap', but it does sometimes seem kind of far-fetched that so many changes happened so quickly."

Scrive thought, there was superb sophistication of technology and rapid advances in many things, all within his lifetime. The eradication of Nero by use of tropus cartridges created what media referred to as 'The Great Leap Forward'. A rate of unparalleled technological advancement, creating newer and faster transits, better media, a plethora of new devices including the ubiquitous handheld and the majority of what had become the secure networks and RFID based access systems.

A modern citizen could walk around safely and securely within their designated zones. By a simple application, they could visit other areas, but the system was well regulated to also keep crowds and supply and demand for goods and services under control. People with higher status (he included himself in this category) had greater freedom and the ability to travel more widely. And it had all been created without the politics and controls of a Big Brother state. The modern Ellipse citizen considered themselves pretty well off.

Carolin added, "We think there's a code word for where many of the secrets are held. It is called 'Australia' and we believe it is an area somewhere within the exclusion zone."

Scrive shook his head, he didn't recollect hearing of Australia.

"What or where is Australia?" he asked.

"That's one of the things we hope you'll be able to help us find out", answered Lars.

Analogue Tracking

Taylor found the inside of the tracking station remarkably familiar. There was a clinical look at complete odds to the run-down, camouflaged appearance of the outside. He had walked through the double entrance chamber, and by the time he had closed the access doors, there was a cool charcoal filtered air-con smell permeating the building. He knew he'd soon get used to it, with the slightly boosted oxygen levels to keep anyone in there sharp.

He flicked on a few of the displays and waited for the technology to settle. Sure, it was from before the 'Great Leap', and so some of it was a little dated looking, but he twisted a couple of the satisfyingly analogue controls, knurled surfaces with a real tactility missing from the modern devices with their flat screens, HUDs and haptic feedback.

He started with a probe to Beijing, mainly to see whether anything still worked. Sure enough, he was able to access a clean picture from a conference room inside an important building in Beijing. There was no-one in the room though, so he thought he'd try jacking into some of the other video links. He soon had access to some camera phones and a further and larger conference facility. It was all quite easy, but he knew that was because he was using the modern-day equivalent of listening through a wall with a glass beaker. It may not be possible to scan for individual devices, but, still, a basic cup could be a useful spy aid in the right hands.

The lack of any activity to watch made him wonder if the Chinese had been smart and that he was now watching a doctored video feed. Maybe they had tied these links down, and now there wasn't anything left to view.

He flipped a few dials to see whether there were any other live feeds still running. He found the continents menu and switched to the USA. It would be interesting to see if he could get back into the Maddox meeting undetected. In this case, there was nothing, so it looked as if someone decommissioned the link. He flicked back to the menu and noticed an extra entry at the top.

Australia.

He had never heard of Australia before. Yet there it was on the menu.

He flicked to enter the menu structure. A little series of towns appeared. Was this a test environment, maybe.

He clicked in.

Adelaide. Nothing
Canberra. Nothing
Darwin. A signal, but a blank screen.
Melbourne. Nothing.
Perth. A scratchy signal. A bad picture. There was something on the screen. It looked like a storm, although there were some large cylindrical structures running across the view. It wasn't easy to make anything out clearly.
Sydney. Nothing

Two more options. Woomera and Yulara. He wondered whether to bother, or whether to flick back to Perth to try to make out more.

Instead he clicked Woomera.

Sixteen squares appeared in his view. 16 cameras, 12 clear ones and four that had blank or static.

He opened the first one. Sound as well. He had a full monitor signal from this place. If it was a test site, then it was pretty impressive.

He studied the picture. A blue/green coloured scene, with what looked like some almost molecular structure in front of him. There were small red flashes in the image as well, which he initially thought were interference, but were tracking the shapes of the molecular structure.

It was difficult to scale the picture though, and he couldn't tell whether he was looking at something substantial or if it was a scale model of some kind.

He flicked to another screen, and then another. Whatever it was, the people who had set up the monitors had wanted to get a good view of it.

He bookmarked the page and hit the recording system in the control booth. He'd run this onto disk so that he could relay it later. He wasn't sure whether the links would stay reliable and whether he'd just struck lucky with this viewpoint.

He selected a few more of the screens.

They showed different external perspectives on the same structure.

Apart from the molecule shaped item, there were tubes running in various directions. They looked like pipes - uniform and machined. It was like a very large oil installation or something similar, but he could not see any fractionating towers or flames or any of the other tell-tale signs. This was a very clean installation and looked as it if it didn't need human intervention.

He kept each feed running for several minutes, partly to look for any signs of activity, but also to ensure he had something committed to his recording.

Then he decided to flip to the last spot.

Yulara

Yulara

Captain Taylor had never heard of any of the places in this area of the system, and he began to wonder if they were tests, a secure facility somewhere or even 'off-world'.

As he flicked to the Yulara system he was again greeted by sixteen small screens, although on this occasion only three of them had a signal. He immediately saw that there was movement.

He tapped the screen to zoom into one of the pictures and recoiled as he saw the detail of what was in the feed.

Looking like similar pipe and molecule structures to the earlier Woomera feed, here was a system that seemed to be handling a viscous liquid.

He let this run and he could see that the process was probably something that ran for several hours, or perhaps even continuously.

There was clearly audio on the link, but no signs of human voice just a background ticking and clicking sound.

He eventually flicked away from the sight, after dutifully recording around 20 minutes of what appeared to be a section of a compound being reduced to its core constituents.

He decided to flick to the next screen. It showed a similar scene, but this time he could see that there were more of the same processes. It was like a processing plant. He didn't know how large.

He ran the recording for ten minutes and then flicked to the final active feed. A different scene. Red flashes mainly, some kind of glass structure. He didn't know what he was looking at or whether it was real or some kind of interference.

Again, he recorded it.

This camera had an extra set of numbers along the bottom of the feed. He recognised them as GPS co-ordinates. -25° 20' 51.90", +129° 51' 12.93" .

He had a fix for the camera. He already knew it was deep inside the Tract. Off the radar. In terms of the Nero toxin, this was a deadly area. He started to think it was deadly for other reasons.

The monitoring station he was in didn't have the level of communications needed to contact the Pentagon securely. He realised he would need to leave and make his way back to his main station to be able to explain in detail what he had discovered. Nonetheless, he thought he'd better send an update so that by the time he reached the secure facility they would already be prepared for the discussion.

He decided to send a short message:

"No further activity detected on Sparrowhawk. Another development. Complex called 'Australia' / 'Yulara' in the Exclusion Zone has relevance. More when back inside Brookings Main Complex."

He read the message back. It was suitably basic for a forward alert. He pressed the button. It was gone.

He carefully made a copy of the disk onto which he had recorded the video, and then made a further copy onto a removable unit, which he put into his pocket. He'd use that to transmit his findings from Brookings Main.

He left the complex switched on. The monitoring for Yulara would also stay running. For Beijing, he would need to make a further visit to see whether any of the screens became active. He somehow doubted it. It looked as if the Chinese had blocked the view and were sending back dummy pictures.

Outside it still rained heavily. Taylor moved back to the four-wheel drive, revved the engine and started the short journey back to Brookings Main. He would upload his videos to show the content of Yulara.

Ailartsua

Scrive looked across to Lars. "I'll try a few search terms now," he said, "I want to see what I get on a basic search."

He flipped open a small computer.

"This is a clean environment", he explained, "I keep the image on here to look like a factory specification machine. It is usually better to look like an amateur that's just trying something for the first time, rather than a calculated tracker."

Lars nodded.

Scrive selected a search engine and typed "Australia". There was a long pause while the search spawned other searches cross a wide range of systems.

He tried all capital letters. Alternate capitals and small letters.

Nothing.

Scrive tried another search 'Australia'. And another 'Aust*'

Now he had 'Austria' which immediately returned thousands of results.

He reversed the term 'ailartsua'.

Nothing.

He would need to check the code word. Something was wrong. Somehow, he recognised the name. He was fairly certain that "Australia" was the key to something.

He repeated this process with several other search tools and on several systems.

Still nothing.

Lars looked at his watch.

"I guess I'm boring you", commented Scrive.

"Not at all", came Lars reply, "Carolin and I had arranged for another meeting here today. They are due to be with us in a few minutes."

"How did you know I'd go along with this?" asked Scrive.

As he did this, a single word came up on his screen. Woomera. He blinked. He tried to run himself at hyperspeed. It didn't work. He decided it was the lag from lack of tropus.

Woomera.

It reminded him of something that had once been in his mind. Australia. A country. He couldn't remember how he knew about it and why it had disappeared from his thoughts so completely.

It seemed to be something to do with the sharpness he'd found since the tropus dose had worn off.

He could even remember that Woomera was famous for something. Travel, planes, space travel. That was it. Australia was a big country on the lower part of the planet. He thought it was probably outside of the Ellipse now.

That's why he couldn't' remember anything about it. The television maps of the planet didn't show it, and there was no reference in books or online.

He began to wonder if it was a made-up place, but somehow, he was sure that it was real. Canberra. Melbourne. Sydney with a harbour. Woomera, where they tested rockets.

He thought of Tajikistan. Plenty of people wouldn't name that as a country. Or know its capital — Dushanbe, which used to be the main market town.

He flicked to blank the screen on his handheld. He flipped a bookmark to Charlie. The first time, the only time, he'd broken protocol since they had separated.

"We didn't", answered Carolin, "We didn't know you'd go along with this." Those in the cafe were entirely unaware of the search result that Scrive had seen, his thoughts and that he'd now effectively concealed his finding and signalled it to Charlie.

Carolin continued, "We had to make some assumptions though. We thought that you'd be impressed if we told you what we already knew. We also realised that even if you were the best tracker, you'd probably have difficulty finding anything without some further help."

"What do you mean?" asked Scrive, he looked concerned.

"It is okay; it is not another tracker - you won't be sharing trade secrets," answered Lars.

"We've done better than that," added Carolin," We've found someone with access to what happens inside Biotree."

Scrive looked questioningly," You are not just expecting me to trust you - you're now expecting me to trust a Biotree employee as well? All of this seems wrong."

"Okay, at least meet her," replied Lars, "she, and her friend will be here in a few minutes."

Scrive considered, "Okay, but I'll want to talk to them first."

"Not a problem," answered Lars, "...and by the way, they have seen a picture of you from the ones that Carolin took over the last few days."

As he said this, the cafe went quiet for a moment. The door had opened, and Scrive saw two good-looking women enter.

One was dressed conservatively as if for work, the other had a gold metallic micro-skirt and a white tutu. She appeared to be carrying an umbrella which looked suspiciously like a wand.

"This is Janie and Chantal", introduced Carolin, looking up and down Chantal's outfit. There were several others in the cafe doing the same. Chantal wiggled onto a chair, and Janie sat beside her.

"Hello again, Lars," started Janie, "...and hello also to you, Mr Mallinson, or should I call you Scrive?"

"Scrive is fine," said Scrive, "You both seem to believe in making quite an entrance."

Scrive couldn't help admiring the remarkable impression that Chantal was having on the others in the cafe. She had stopped conversations. Scrive noted that they were both very attractive women.

"Let's just say that everyone will remember we have been in here this evening," said Chantal. "We want our movements to be very noticeable at the moment."

Carolin nodded, "This is the situation. We've told Scrive about what we think is happening; we are sure that the investigation he is on has more to it and that it affects the Tract.

"We believe that there's something to do with the Tract hidden somewhere with a code word and have said the word to Scrive. He has already run searches but not found any links. We believe that he will need to go into the Biotree systems to get further. That's where Janie comes in. She can help Scrive get access because of the area that she works in and her access to codes and security idents."

"What were you looking for?" asked Janie, "Maybe I already have some ideas."

"Okay to tell?" asked Scrive, and Lars and Carolin nodded.

"The codeword is 'Australia' or some variation of that spelling."

Janie looked blank. Chantal looked up. Scrive stayed straight-faced.

"I know Australia," Chantal said, "Or rather, I know someone who says they were once from Australia".

She looked across to Janie. "It's one of my acquaintances from the - er- fundraising."

Janie looked back. She knew that Chantal was referring to the illegal trade she did with the tropus. Chantal's little habit meant that she got to know some rather unconventional people.

Janie said, "Look, we are getting into this quite deeply. I only brought Chantal along to give me some backup when I was meeting Lars. I didn't want to get Chantal involved further."

Scrive was interested in the Australia comment. It could be more of a breakthrough than rummaging around inside Biotree. He'd prefer to take both options, and he certainly wouldn't mind working with these two women for a while.

"Okay," ventured Scrive. "I'd appreciate your help. Both of you actually; Janie to help with the Biotree systems and Chantal to introduce me to a friend from the Australia Project".

"Actually, Australia isn't a Project," answered Chantal, "I'm pretty sure it's a place. A town in the Tract somewhere, I think."

Chantal continued, "You know what, I'll - we will both - help, BUT I would expect Mr Mallinson to find ways to compensate for my other possible loss of income."

Scrive smiled. He was dealing with an unexpectedly ad-hoc group of people. He was used to working with hard-nosed professionals who would set a task, agree some parameters and then leave him alone.

This situation was different.

The people he was working with seemed to be making it up as they went along. He guessed that Chantal would have no idea how much was in play, although he suspected that Lars would have a more realistic idea.

He surmised that Chantal was a tropus dealer. He noticed all of the bangles on her wrist around where the cartridge would typically be. She was probably a Sife. Cutting her tropus doses and selling on the residuals.

It was good money but dangerous to do this. Scrive had experimented with this, not for money, because he wanted to get a sense of effects of tropus deprivation. He was getting that experience big-time at the moment because of the damage to his last cartridge by Charlie when she saved him. If anything, he felt the lack of tropus was surprisingly good, and seemed to be clearing areas of his mind and thought. He had not expected that.

He spoke to Chantal, "Okay, I'll pay you for your help. There is one thing though; you'll be responsible for your safety as we move this along."

"Okay," answered Chantal. "Let's see; my fees will be the equivalent of a two thousand sales of tropus, with half up front...and the same for Janie. That's 20000 tropes now and 20k at the end," Chantal dropped into the street slang which treated the cost of tropus as if it was a currency.

Chantal was trying to get enough cash to mean that she didn't need to sell tropus anymore. This would be the equivalent of several years' worth of sales.

Scrive blinked. He didn't know how much the tropus sold for, but it couldn't be that much compared with his usual fees. He'd accept the deal but haggle slightly to ensure that Chantal thought she was pushing him.

"Okay, but I'll do half upfront, then a quarter when we've done the work and the last piece two weeks later."

Chantal looked at Janie. Janie hadn't expected this to turn into a commercial haggle in any case. Janie nodded to Chantal.

Chantal said, "Okay, we'll accept, but the first money is due immediately." Chantal was delighted. The immediate payment of 10,000Ts was 4 or 5 years work in one hit. And more to follow.

Scrive nodded. "Okay but remember I'm a tracker. Any funny business from this and I'll be on to you." He tried to make the threat sound both realistic but also friendly. He would prefer the simplicity of them being on-side with him rather than having another conflict to handle.

Janie nodded and looked to Chantal. Janie briefly held Chantal's hand, as if talking to a child. "You heard what Scrive said, Chantal. We need to play this straight."

Scrive assumed that Chantal could be a random element in many situations and that Janie was the best chance to tame her. In reality, he'd consider the payments to them would be small change. A lead that helped him move forward would be great, but he'd not worry too much if they both legged it after the initial interactions.

Scrive and Chantal both clicked their handhelds and placed them on the table.

Scrive said, "You request it, and I'll make the payment."

Chantal pressed a few buttons. Scrive noticed an amount displayed upon his machine. It wasn't much at all. He tried to keep a serious face.

Chantal looked across, "We're ready," she said.

"Okay," said Scrive and pressed a couple of buttons. The money transferred.

Chantal smiled, briefly jumped to her feet and clapped her hands together very lightly. Then, as if remembering she was just finishing a negotiation, she looked at Janie and said, "Great, Janie, now let's see how we can help Mr Mallinson.".

Tokyo

Makatomi was back in his office in Tokyo. He'd found the little trip to the UK and LA somewhat irritating because its primary purpose had been to find out about the leak affecting his business.

It was all so negative. But also, a chain reaction.

Someone had started a theft which he was now being asked to clean up. He'd had to hire two sets of people who were on the edge of legal. He'd then found one of them creating ripples which had upset his boss. He'd been forced to use an extreme measure to remove that person from the investigation.

Then he'd had a call from Holden.

The person running the task with Mallinson had told Holden that Mallinson had somehow survived. The indirect approach using a tampered version of the tropus hadn't worked.

If it had, they could have used the nanobots to clean up any evidence. Instead, somehow the 'bots had been eliminated. Mallinson was not to be messed with.

"Use a Trigax," Holden had said, "Make it fast and remove Mr Mallinson. Use one of the Biotree units. They are at our test facility," added Holden. This was a whole further dimension of escalation.

Makatomi knew the Trigax was illegal for aggressive use within the Ellipse and that it was only used for peacekeeping in the Tract.

He also knew that the Trigax would be effective and leave no trace. Makatomi knew the Trigax as a finalising device although the technology was still not fully understood.

He'd assumed that his 'no questions asked' assassin would have ready access to such technology, which he considered to be almost alien. Instead, he was now having to provide the unit as well. This was really getting out of hand.

The Trigax units had a global range and were individually tuned to a specific target. They could be fired from anywhere and the beam that they asserted was efficiently scrambled until the point at which it reached its target. It used quantum principles and a focusing of the wave using discrete photon focus.

Most people had said the technology was impossible and poked a cat's paw at great physicists like Bohr, Bohm and von Neumann, but the results had spoken for themselves.

The devices were now licensed and maintained for Tract management and scientific experimentation. If used, there was no evidence that they had been fired, because of the wave dispersal of the energy.

It was like a perfect weapon.

"You'll have to use it from Bodø," said Holden, "You will have one chance".

Makatomi nodded. He knew that Holden would remove him if he didn't remove the mess he'd inadvertently created. On the other hand, if he fixed it, then he stood to gain exceptionally from the expected change in fortunes of Biotree.

Chantal

Chantal's penchant for the low dosage form of tropus had led her into some fascinating communities. They were people who regularly ran the risk of redding their blood and to some extent ran an alternate if somewhat privileged lifestyle.

It also meant they had access to some things that were not at all in the mainstream. It was as if the reduced tropus gave them abilities to see things that others could not. They could also remember things from before the time of the Nero toxins.

Today's outfit had been Japanese manga and Chantal had included combat boots. It worked to her advantage because there were no inconvenient heels. Useful around the stairs and cobblestones of this old part of London.

Chantal took Scrive to the door of the club. It was an old railway arch from the 19th century. There was a small door, she pushed it open, and it led into a sort of cave.

"There's miles of this around here", she explained. "They were originally built under the old railway systems in London and used to be a kind of retail space. Then as the Transit was introduced, they became bypassed with the new generation of retail environments. Now they are vestiges of an older London."

She continued, "Look - when we meet Crispin, don't tell him that you know he is from Australia. He might not co-operate. Ask him about Australia instead as a concept. Let him decide how he wants to talk about it."

Scrive replied," I'm ahead of you on this. I kind of know when I'm dealing with secrets that it is easier to have them fall out than to try to push them. Like that Chinese finger trap. The more you pull, the tighter it gets."

"Just don't say that around my friends," said Chantal, suppressing a smile.

She showed the way through the labyrinth to a dimly lit area.

Candles flickered in between several people sitting together.

Despite the candles they had power as was evident from the powerful workstation that a couple of them were using. "Hi Chantal," said one, looking up, "You've brought some more tropus?" he asked.

"Yes," replied Chantal, "plus a friend who'd like to ask you something."

"Is he cool?" asked the same person.

"Crispin - He's fine. As a matter of fact, I think he can help us, but we will need to help him as well. You know the Vaults? I think they would like to take a look for something."

"Hi," said Scrive, "I've tried the reddening way too." He held up his arm from the smashed cartridge. He'd had time to tidy up the fragments from the attack, and it now looked as if he was mainlining on red blood instead of the usual tropus mix.

Crispin looked at his arm.

"Jeez – That's messy – and unusual," he grimaced, "you look as if you are completely red? I've never seen a plexi manipulated like that – it looks awful. It looks as if the telemetry is still working, but I can't see how you'd ever get another cartridge to be accepted?"

Scrive looked at the mechanism. He'd play it hard. "Yes, I've broken the tropus injector. If I don't get surgery, then I'll be completely red in a couple of days. It doesn't seem to affect me though, if anything, it makes me see things more clearly."

Crispin looked at Chantal, "Whoa hardcore - you do hang out with some crazy people, Chantal. So, your name is Scrive. How can we help you?"

"Other way around, "said Scrive," I want to help you- but I have a few questions first."

"We are told you have preserved a lot of the old ways," said Scrive, "That you have ways to review old files and information from before the time of the Nero toxin."

"That's correct", said Crispin, "but you'll have to ask us to find what you need. Ask us, and then leave us to trace it."

Scrive wrote down a few words on ordinary paper. Australia. Woomera. Where and What?

Crispin looked at the paper," I can do that." he replied, "And I think I may know something about it too. Please leave now. Wait outside. We will find you."

He turned to another person working the workstation. "Look Lucas," he said, pointing to the paper.

The second guy turned back to Scrive and Chantal. "We can get you this, but Chantal, your friend looks as if he might have some fees for us?"

Chantal looked at Scrive, "I haven't discussed this at all; this is all freestyle," she commented.

Scrive replied, "Look, I won't kid you both, I need this help, and I will pay for it. I can also be dangerous, but I'm a friend of Chantal, so I want to do this the right way. You both understand me. I'll pay, but please, I need to know about this project 'Australia'."

Chantal answered for Scrive," He'll give you the equivalent of 100 units of tropus. I know he will. I think that's his limit."

Scrive nodded. "Yes, Chantal knows my limit. I can pay you right now, handheld to handheld, but I want to see the information first."

"He's good for it." said Chantal, "And he won't trick you. I will vouch for him."

Scrive looked across to Chantal. She was doing more than her fair share of handling this. He decided that she'd got emotionally committed to the situation.

"Okay, we'll do it", said Crispin. "Lucas, help me with this." They pulled a couple of boxes together, and all sat around.

RFID

Suze had been pleased with herself since she'd found the RFID for Scrive. His Radio Frequency Identity. She had his address, his transit chip identity and could easily follow his movements around. She'd seen him take a walk from the apartment to the transit and had been about to follow him when he changed course to a cafe.

She'd seen him spend time and assumed it was a meeting that would lead further towards the answers to the various questions.

Who was trying to kill him?

Why?

Was Makatomi or Biotree involved?

What about the Chinese?

Suze was also suspicious about whether Scrive was operating alone. It was quite normal for trackers to work by themselves, but they'd often have some kind of safety system, particularly if they were on a bigger quest. If Scrive's pay was anything like theirs for this, then he'd have an accomplice somewhere.

Suze discussed this with Denny.

"I think we may want to pay Scrive's place a visit, when he is out on a long journey, said Suze.

"I agree," said Denny, "We'll probably need half an hour just so that we have time to check for any safety precautions he may have put up around the place."

The little cameras they had installed gave an easy indication of Scrive's departures and return and he didn't seem to be taking any particular precautions.

There had been two other visitors they had seen accessing his premises since they started monitoring. Both had a key. One had been wearing a hooded jacket and had only stayed for around five minutes. They didn't have any idea who this was, and the other was an attractive woman who had been in and out of the apartment a few times, but since her last departure had not returned.

They had no idea who the people were and had not had time to set up any form of monitoring.

This time they decided that after Scrive's next departure, they would attempt to break into the apartment, but using the fine equipment in Denny's holdall, which should not leave a trace. Of course, a tracker could probably work out what had happened, but they would be careful to leave no mark of their entry.

The hotel they had moved to was just across the road from Scrive's. It was a modern location and overlooked the River Thames. The chimneys of Battersea Power station were also close by, as an embedded part of a south of the river luxury shopping and entertainment complex.

This helped because there were plenty of people around the area, so the movements of Denny and Suze would easily blend in.

Denny had left the tracking systems running as Scrive had left and then taken a transit across to the area around London Bridge. Even if he took a taxi, it would take him twenty minutes to return — enough time for them to make their move and break into Scrive's apartment.

"Okay, we'll be looking for memory blocks, idents, Hitech and signs of who the other visitors are," said Denny, "We'll need to work fast and not take anything away."

Suze nodded, she knew this well, they had done other 'information gathering' sessions together and speed and a very light touch were what was required.

Denny carried a couple of small devices. One was an e-burster. This created a small electronic pulse that sensed all of the electronics in a room. It would inventory them and provide an exact location. The devices were available domestically for locating remote controls and missing keys, but this version was a military grade device that could pinpoint any form of technology. Its second function, not available on the domestic ones, was to be able to read the content of a device and store it. The third function, chillingly, was that it could destroy the device, both silently, and destructively. Denny was only planning to use the first two modes, find and copy. And to do this selectively.

The images copied would not necessarily be readable straight away, because of possible encryption, but that was something they could worry about later, back in the comfort of the hotel.

The second device was simply a form of basic self-defence. A needler was device that could generate high volume sound that would disorientate an attacker, and which could also fire small electronic probes which could then deliver variable voltages. The technology was based upon an older wired technology called taser, but in this version the darts had the power charges attached and could be separately triggered at a selectable threshold.

Suze and Denny both carried these devices, which were also silent in operation but very painful to any recipient. They had never been in firefight situations with them but were both aware of the need for some self-protection in their line of business.

They both inserted ear systems which included personal communications as well as filters for the sound wave defence. Denny made sure they had tuned it to the device he was carrying so that the cancellation effect would work if they needed it.

"Okay, let's go", he said. Scrive was over in London Bridge, in the tunnels and vaults to the south of the river.

PART TWO

7

As the verses unfold
and your soul suffers the long day

And the twelve o'clock gloom
Spins the room, you struggle on your way
Well, don't you sigh, don't you cry
Lick the dust from your eye

Life's a long song
Life's a long song
Life's a long song

We will meet in the sweet light of dawn

Ian Anderson (Jethro Tull)

The long song

Crispin started to speak, "Sometimes, people make fun of the way I speak; I pronounce a few words differently from most people. I have some extra words in my vocabulary. It's because I'm originally from a real place called 'Australia'. Australia isn't a Project, Scrive. It isn't even a town. It's a whole country. Or rather, it was.

"I'm from the Tract originally, and my parents had me when the Nero virus was at its height. They were both immune and so am I. We lived in the country called Australia, in a town called Darwin. When the virus was at its height, Australia was the original centre for it and the whole country was quarantined. We'd had the Flames a few years earlier, and so much of Australia burnt to the ground.

"The Flames was through climate effects, we'd seen the wildlife progressively eradicated over a few years, because the huge bush fires kept coming back. The fireys just couldn't keep up with it. It was relentless, year after year, like the fires in Southern California now.

"It was a modern-day tragedy, a side-effect of global heating. Most of the livestock and about a third of the population were killed.

"It made Straya a very dangerous place to live. The old joke was that The Northern Territories (which is where I'm from) was filled with nasty critters. They were all out to kill and eat one another or passing humans. Freshies, Salties, jellyfish, sharks, spiders. You name it, they'd kill and eat one another.

"Now add to that the Flames and then the viral attacks which led to the introduction of tropus. I guess the decimation from the Flames left many places with unsafe water, which created some of the contagion. The evolution of the Australian virus ran away from the engineering of its vaccine. They couldn't keep up with the variants. Some said it was because there was a clone vaccine introduced from China. I don't know.

"What I remember is that people went a sort of black colour when they caught the virus. There was no way to stop it. Their blood didn't run yellow or red, it went through a blue colour and then to black.

"And despite the death of so-much wildlife, there were still the buzzards, vultures and the rats which seemed to thrive.

Lucas chipped in, "What I remember is that the whole landmass was horrific, like something out of a disaster movie. But it is strange. Only people that were actually on the landmass seem to remember it. It's like it never happened to everyone else."

"Did people try to leave?" asked Scrive.

"You couldn't go in or out of it. I'm not talking about a small landmass here. I'm talking about something the same size as North America.

"Biotree had been trialling their newest versions of tropus and nanobots in the territory. Speculation was that they were trying to cover up for something. It was hard to get accurate news because most of the comms infrastructure was down too.

Then we heard that quarantine restrictions were to be boosted. We were told that Biotree was helping the effort to instigate the new processes. It turned out they were implementing a series of geostationary satellites, which were nicknamed 'The Bracelet'. The Bracelet applied an electronic border around the landmass. It seems ironic that they had to shoot things into space to do this, after all the fuss about global warming.

"How come none of this was in the news?" asked Scrive.

"This was like the End of Days," said Crispin, "The politicians and world leaders opted for discretion to avoid a world panic. It was thought better to contain it than to let panic set in globally."

"I'm not so sure though," said Lucas, "The Chinese were open about that Wuhan virus, and it probably saved lives because it gave the rest of the planet a chance to prepare."

"Yeah, I agree, and it showed how some of the plans were quite piecemeal. They ran out of protective clothes; the facemasks were not to the right filtration; Planeloads of possible contaminants shipped offshore," added Crispin.

"Pressure was put onto Biotree to come up with a resolution. I'm guessing it was desperation which led to the Bracelet. The Low Earth Orbit monitoring system for the boundaries of the Australian zone. Then they added the so-called 'charms' to the Bracelet, which provided the enforcement.

"I've not heard of either of these things," said Shrive.

Crispin continued, "You wouldn't, out here in the Ellipse; it is only Tract dwellers and anyone still in Australia that needs to know about these things."

Lucas added, "The charms operated with a railgun. It was a sneaky way around space-wars legislation because the railgun is not technically classed as a weapon. There's no explosive warhead or anything."

"I know about railguns' said Scrive, "they can be pretty lethal. They fire a massively high-speed projectile which can cut through just about anything."

Yes, that's right- the exit velocity is about 3km per second. Enforcement of the territorial edges of Australia was via the Bracelet and charms. Typically, a breach would be spotted, triangulated and then three railgun cannons would be deployed to stop the escape. There was even a Biotree branding for the technology: Trigax."

"Ah, I've heard of Trigax," said Scrive, "Biotree put out some seemingly jolly marketing videos about this."

"That's right," said Crispin," And also about their final clean-up systems."

"They didn't come up with a pretty-sounding name for this piece. I think the Brits invented it and called it something like APKWS laser-guided rocket."

"APKWS?" Asked Scrive.

"Yeah, Advanced Precision Kill Weapon System, "answered Lucas.

"These were standardised laser-guided rockets, which fired from anything from a hypersonic pursuit vehicle down to a regular drone. They were handed out to the cops to put next to their tasers. They would have the handset, lock it on with a bluedot and ka-boom."

Crispin continued, "I was eight years old when the quarantine restrictions came down, and we had no chance to leave. The country was also in the middle of a vast area of sea and so the idea to leave by, say, a small ship was impossible. And the exclusion zone around that was built up around the country was intense.

"When a few people tried to leave by ship or plane, they'd be detected and destroyed. The argument from authorities said was safer to keep the virus in one place on the planet than to have it spread. It's another reason why there was such a news blackout from the region.

"What about wildlife, birds, insects, migration?", asked Chantal, who Scrive noticed was taking this story in for the first time as well.

"We used to call it the Glimmer," said Crispin. "There was a sort of sparkle that you could see from the seashore and sometime in the night sky. We used to think it was somehow magical, but it was the perimeter systems destroying anything that was flying or swimming out of range."

"If there were so many defences, then how come you are now on the outside?" asked Scrive. "The way you describe it doesn't make it seem possible to leave."

"Correct," answered Crispin. "There wasn't any way to go. Basically, those of us that were not affected by the Nero were effectively prisoners. We had a small amount of sea edge, then a cold zone and after that was the exclusion area that effectively killed anything that entered it."

"That's some pretty big weaponry," said Scrive.

"I know," said Crispin, "I used to wonder how we'd created the technology for such a thing, but it all happened at around the time of the Great Leap when the planet's technologies also accelerated. Of course, I didn't know that at the time, because the Australian communications systems were destroyed as well. We didn't have television, radio, computer communication or phone. It was like one of those EMF pulses that you hear about that destroy electronics, except in this case it was communications but not other forms of technology. Cars still worked, for example.

Crispin looked across to Scrive, "We then saw a period where the technologies in Australia accelerated almost as fast as they have done in the Ellipse. It went on for a while and for the survivors wasn't so bad. The weird thing was that the people affected by the virus didn't hang around like in zombie B-movies. They seemed to disappear almost within minutes of dying. Faster than the vultures or rats could handle."

He paused to think about this.

Scrive noticed that Lucas had been watching as well and nodded a few times during the description. Lucas seemed to know as much as Crispin while Chantal looked on, fascinated at what they were hearing.

Crispin continued.

"Those of us that survived couldn't get to the bottom of what was happening. Most stories were word of mouth, but it sounded as if there'd been some kind of riots in another town quite a long way to the North of us. You'll need to remember that Australia is - was - a vast country with not so many people. There was also quite a lot of desert land, and the reduced infrastructure meant most people stayed in the areas they knew to be safe.

"We heard that this area to the South near to a wild area called Uluru was where there had been the riots and a lot of people killed. They were not killed by the virus, but by the fighting that took place. We never had a chance to find out though because that's when Lucas and I managed to find a gap in the "Glimmer".

"As kids, we'd play dare games with one another. We used to take the small boat out to the edge of the safe zone. It was to where the air started to get cold. We could see the area where you couldn't go further and sometimes, we'd throw things into it to see them spark.

"One day we'd been onshore, and there'd been an extra wave of new bodies die and disappear from the virus. I was around twelve by this point. There had been some big rumbling sounds which we thought were some kind of hurricane or earthquake or something.

"We cycled as fast as we could to some high ground in case it was a big sea or something that could harm us. Our thinking was that if the virus wouldn't get us then we didn't want to get struck down by a wind or a flood.

"It turned out that it was an earthquake. The buildings shook, and we could feel the world moving underneath us. It was a pretty scary feeling.

"Then we looked around and could see some geese flying away from what we assumed was the source of the 'quake. We never actually saw the 'quake ourselves.

"The geese flew towards the Edge (where the force-field starts). As kids we were waiting for the sparks as a whole flock of birds were vaporised.

"But they flew on. They flew past the Edge. We looked at one another. We both jumped onto our bikes and shot down the slope towards the town. There was almost no-one around. The official warning system was sounding, which meant people had gone to shelters.

"We went down to the harbour and picked up one of the larger fishing boats. This was a deep-sea boat for catching sharks. Metal hulled, big engines and very fast. Even at our young ages we knew how to skipper those boats.

"We gunned it out to the Edge. No coldness. We took the harpoon guns from the front of the ship and fired one into the Edge. We expected it to vaporise. It just kept flying through the air.

"We took another one and did the same. Same thing happened.

"We looked at one another. Crispin looked at Lucas now. We asked each other whether to risk it. We were going to take the boat through the Edge.

"We trickled the engine and headed for what we knew would typically be the point of vaporisation. We threw everything overboard in front of us as a test. But we just kept going. We headed north west for another 100 miles. Then the boat's radar suddenly started working again. We'd never seen the radio communications working so this was a novelty. It was a pretty cool system too, with flat panel displays and maps of the sea and land. We could see ahead of us a large belt of island, behind us was some sea and then - nothing. The place we had come from had blanked from the system.

"We worked out that the Edge must have started working again. We'd managed to get through a gap, probably caused by the earthquake. It had taken us about three hours to get to our current position, and it was only when the radar came on that we could tell that the Edge was back surrounding Australia.

"The radar showed us various islands, some of which were huge, but we could see that our best chance was to use the fuel we had to get as far as possible. We charted a course that threaded through a belt of islands and eventually wound up in Indonesia. This was around 800 miles from where we'd started!

"What we didn't realise was that we'd navigated from the Edge through the Tract and landed at a place that was within the Ellipse.

"It was mainly luck, but by doing this, we'd avoided the areas where if we'd landed, we'd have been stuck there for good. The lack of infrastructure would have prevented us from going any further. It was simply the fact that we'd had a boat from inside Australia, where there was still fuel and that we'd then passed the desolated areas and arrived on the

Ellipse with its super high technology infrastructure.

"We were both used to living by our wits, so we brought the boat in by night and let it drift the last part of the way. We snuck ashore and effectively became two more of the shadowy people on the edge of the systems. We've lived via the economics of trading tropus and other street skills ever since.

"The strange thing is that no-one here has ever heard of Australia. It is as if it has been wiped from people's minds. We don't think there are many people who did what we've done either and managed to escape."

Lucas added, "Although scattered around the city and in other parts of the country are others like us but from other places usually at the edges of the Tract.

"They are the ones that have managed to get inside the Ellipse but are not citizens.

"None of us has the cartridge but selling the tropus creates an economy to keep us alive.

"How did you get from Indonesia to London?" asked Scrive; he was still trying to assimilate this story.

Crispin picked up the story, "As we said, most big cities have a few people like us. We live in the underbelly of the city and so eventually we find one another. There are a few routes to move us around, mainly between the big metropolitan centres. We usually have to stow-away on the big planes between centres. Strangely enough, since the security became so tight it is easier for us, because the main security relies upon the transit tags that everyone has in their tropus cartridge. It's very easy to find anyone in the wrong place if they have been tagged.

"It's a lot less easy if you don't have any identity. Stowing away usually requires someone to create diversion when we go through the airport scanners. It can take days to get through an airport, but trust me, it's possible. The main thing is to not be too impatient. And the other thing is to look for flights that don't seem to be too busy.

Chantal interrupted, "So you've come from Australia (which none of us have heard of), through the Tract in a boat and then snuck into the Ellipse from where you've stowed away in planes to get to London?

That's about the sense of it, replied Crispin.

"And now you make your living dealing in tropus?"

"Yes - you'd be surprised how many city types pay for boosts. They say it takes away the pain. For us, we say 'no pain, no gain'. " Crispin and Lucas looked at one another and smiled.

"We can jack you into the Vault system to see if there is much more information. There is some, because we've looked at it previously. It is part of how we pieced together our route from Darwin to London."

Alert

Holden had been alerted. There was more network traffic than usual checking the sources of the domes. There had been radar and lidar pings to the Bodø location as well as additional fly-bys of the location.

There was unconventional analogue activity on a series of locations in Australia, including the largest one in Yulara. The US Desert locations had also been probed.

Holden understood the ways that the domes were connected. That one could interconnect with another and it was this powerful set of linkages that exerted some of the power which was often referred to as the Great Leap.

Holden was uncertain what was causing this level of activity. Unless it was the trackers that Makatomi had invoked. They were having the opposite effect to that intended. They were drawing more attention to the domes and creating new forms of activity.

Holden decided to track down Makatomi. Perhaps Makatomi was losing his grip on the situation?

Makatomi was back in London. He had put some miles on the V-Blade running around the planet. Maybe he should try Holden's approach? So much simpler.

Holden called Makatomi.

"This is getting out of control. They are probing some of the domes. That includes the Biotree complex in Bodø. You are letting this slip away from you."

Makatomi answered, "No, I have a couple of trackers working on this. They are finding the source of the problem. I had to use Scrive as bait to force a sighting."

Holden's voice shifted to a softer tone, "Your explanations are wearing now. We cannot afford any more mistakes. Consider this a final warning. The next time you will go like Scrive. Get this fixed, as we agreed."

Makatomi bowed his head slightly towards the monitor. He hated to bow to these passive aggressive screens like a Nam June Paik installation.

He felt something like the fingers of a pressing across the top of his head. He knew it was from Holden.

Punching out

Lucas flipped the workstation screen so that they could all see it. He tapped a few access codes and was soon browsing secure sites. They were not those inside Biotree but places that were part of an American defense network. It showed some basic Information about Australia through something called the CIA Factbook, dated in the early part of the 21st Century.

"This will give you a sense about Australia," said Lucas, "and you'll see there's way too much for it to have been something that we prepared earlier today."

He found the map and showed them the whole of Australia. "Here's Darwin," he added pointing to the top. "Here's the ring of islands and here's Singapore. You can draw the Edge of the Ellipse by Singapore, then the Tract to just off of Australia and then Australia itself in what is now the missing part."

"I can understand that from a geographical perspective," said Scrive, "But I can't understand it from a memory point of view. Why don't people know about Australia? It is not as if it disappeared thousands of years ago. Maybe 20 years which is well within living memory."

"This is something we don't understand either," said Crispin. "But when we test people on this, no-one shows any recollection. It's as if we dreamed the whole thing."

"But we didn't," said Lucas. "I am Australian."

He emphasized "am" not "was", "am".

Scrive pondered his next steps. He asked Lucas to copy some of the data onto a memory block that he could review later. Lucas flipped a small card into the side of the machine. "I'm using a non-rewritable stick," he said. "It will burn this image on but once it's there it can't be erased. I'm going to copy this whole site for you," he said, and his fingers flipped a few select software constructs as he piped the content of the secure vault across to the memory block.

He pressed a mechanical catch, and the block slid out. He held out his hand. A small block the size of a gaming dice. "It's all on here," he said. "You can read this on most systems. I've encrypted it. The password is 'Australia'," he smiled, "not very original, but you'd have to know it to find it. Heck, it's not even a forbidden word; the password scanner didn't even flag it as weak."

He passed the block to Scrive. Scrive nodded his appreciation. Chantal smiled. "Scrive, I think Crispin and Lucas have been incredibly helpful." You should give them their money, and when we walk away, you should promise not to see them again."

"I'll do that," said Scrive.

They exchanged electronic money. Scrive added a huge extra sum to that which they had requested. Lucas and Crispin smiled at the thought of their improved economic status.

Scrive and Chantal walked back outside into the street, with Scrive still holding the cube.

"You know what", said Scrive, "I'm going to trust you some more. Don't try to scam me on this, but I'm going to hand you the cube. It's better that it's separate from me. We both know the story, and we both know what's on it. Keep it somewhere safe."

He handed her the cube. They walked along towards the nearby transit. "Thank you, Scrive, "said Chantal.

Scrive started to reply; as he did so he looked down.

Three holes appeared in his chest.
Perfectly circular, each the size of a fist.

Chantal stepped back; there was a crackling sound, like sparks, she watched as Scrive's body appeared to be sucked into the three holes.

Then she ran. As fast as she could manage.

The combat boots helped her speed. She still had the cube in her hand. She'd need to get inside. Call Janie. Figure out what was happening.

A quiet stopover

Charlie had been tracking Scrive ever since she'd left his apartment. She thought that this trip to London wasn't at all how she'd expected it to be. A quiet trip to Geneva, with the London stopover to see Scrive had turned into something altogether different. Still, the money was good. Scrive had already paid her a third of the fees, and with that, alone, she was already substantially better off. She'd worked out she now owned her apartment in New York and had enough to buy another one in London, if she wanted.

Her new hotel was close enough to Scrive; she'd decided to hide in plain sight, rather than to move a long way away. That way if she needed to intervene, it would be easy. Scrive wouldn't expect her to be almost next door, and the Portuguese themed hotel was enjoyable.

She'd dialled to get a penthouse room and could see the river, the power station entertainment complex and even an area where people seemed to be exercising dogs. She'd asked the concierge about this and been told it was a home for stray dogs in London. Something she'd never thought about in New York, but that the Brits seemed to like doing.

Charlie had made sure Scrive was wired for sound as well as tracing when she'd left. It was pretty easy to do, based upon the accidental suffering she'd imposed after smashing his tropus cartridge when she was rescuing him from the nano toxins.

She'd inserted a small transmitter and had sound, but no video, as well as the RFID tracking. It was enough to have a pretty good idea of what she was hearing. She was sure that Scrive would know she'd done this, although they'd not talked about it and had followed the silent process of splitting up without agreeing to any specifics that would allow one of them to betray the other if they got caught. It was a one-way situation though because Scrive would be the one caught, and he didn't have a clue where Charlie was.

Charlie also recorded the movements of Scrive onto a Geosystem and bursts of conversation; buying a baguette at the local store, the meeting with Carolin at the transit, the cafe session with Lars and the introductions to Janie and Chantal.

Charlie had also seen Scrive meet Chantal for the second time and visit London Bridge.

The sound reception from the arches was poor. They were underground and in a damp area where radio frequencies were finding it hard to penetrate.

Charlie had a broad idea of what the meeting was about but although the tracking device worked well enough, the sound was awful.

After around twenty minutes Scrive had obviously reappeared at street level and he could hear him talking to Chantal.

"You know what", said Scrive, "I'm going to trust you some more. Don't try to scam me on this, but I'm going to hand you the cube. It's better that it's separate from me. We both know the story, and we both know what's on it. Keep it somewhere safe."

Charlie could hear them walking, "Thank you, Scrive," Chantal was saying, as the sound disappeared, and then the signal from Scrive.

Charlie looked at the systems she was using. They were still working.

She reset the communications; She rescanned for Scrive; she tried a transit link as if polling to book a journey. Nothing worked. Scrive had gone from the system.

She knew what this would mean. Scrive had been terminated.

Charlie felt nausea overcome her. She wasn't used to this feeling, even in combat situations where things could get pretty robust. But she'd been with Scrive. Right in his room across the way. They'd planned together for the mission. Scrive should be invincible.

She snapped herself together. Think - Either Chantal had murdered Scrive, or possibly they had both been killed together?

Charlie knew she'd need to erase Scrive's presence from his apartment and that it needed to be fast. Mainly to remove the electronics and to check them at her own pace. If he'd been killed there would likely be people showing up at his apartment.

Charlie mentally considered her presence of mind to be staying so close. She could be into and out of Scrive's apartment in ten minutes. She knew which devices to take. Scrive had plenty of technology, but there were only a couple of critical small units that contained the information that mattered. It would take anyone else an hour to locate and then remove the technology, and even then, they would have a long task to sift to find the important stuff.

She picked up the pistol and pocketed several silver devices about the size of a small fuel cell. They fitted easily into her hand and had a flip-top safety catch. Each was a stun grenade that used a combination of sound, smoke, EMF and potentially ballistics to create a defence cordon. There was a large arrow embossed on the front. It pointed away from Charlie. Charlie knew that at the time it was deployed, she needed the arrow to point towards the hostiles because the device was radial 270 degrees. The person using it should be in the 90-degree shadow.

She'd decided they would be a last resort, but one was ready to prime in her hand.

She crossed to the apartment and let herself in.

Immediately she could hear a sound. There was someone already inside. She felt for the grenade and could feel the raised arrow pointing away from her body. She looked around the corner towards the main room. Two people were frozen. One was holding a metatazer. Then she noticed the other one. Also holding a metatazer. They could see she had the stun. It was stalemate. If they hit her, she'd fire the stun, and they'd be blasted, assuming she had it set to ballistics. She didn't.

"You know Scrive?" asked the woman.

"Do you?" came her reply.

"We all do." said the man.

"We're trying to help him." said the woman.

"How did you get in?" said Charlie, "I live here, it's my apartment." she lied.

"We've seen you come in here. You haven't been back for two days," said the woman.

"You know why?" asked Charlie. Her arm was beginning to ache, holding the stun grenade forward.

"Do you?" asked the man.

"Someone tried to kill Scrive," said Charlie. She'd worked out that if they were professional assassins, she'd be dead by now. They were probably clients of Scrive. Not friends routinely armed like that.

She noticed the technology that the man had scattered in front of him.

"You're trackers." Charlie realised. "You're tracking Scrive."

She decided that they didn't know he'd been killed. But their appearance here couldn't be coincidence.

"Look," she said, "Let's put down the armaments. I think we are doing the same thing."

She moved her arm down slightly but didn't take her thumb off of the top arrow on the grenade. It made her look more peaceful rather than fundamentally changing anything.

She realised that the pistol would take too long to reach and fire, so the grenade was her only chance if they got nasty.

The woman started to lower the metatazer and looked at the man.

"Okay," said the man, "let's talk."

"How can I trust you?" asked Charlie.

"You can't," said the man, "Look, my names Denny and this is Suze, we're working for Biotree, and we think Scrive has been doing the same thing."

"Okay," said Charlie. She pressed the safety catch back onto the stun grenade.

"One more thing?Tea or coffee?"

Charlie had to decide how much to say to Denny and Suze. they didn't seem to know that Scrive was dead. They presumably didn't know about the other people he'd been meeting, but they were pretty good because they'd been able to find Scrive.

Charlie wouldn't give too much away about being a tracker herself, but the small arms she was carrying were a pretty big hint that she wasn't quite like other local people.

"Okay," she started, "If I'm going to tell you anything, you'll have to tell me what you know first. Scrive will be back soon, I can alert him, and you'll never see him again, or you can tell me enough that I reassure him that all is cool."

"Here's the deal," said Denny, "We think Scrive and maybe you have been given the same task as us. To find out who has leaked information about Biotree to the Chinese. We are supposed to trace the leak and report it back to someone in Biotree."

"Who?" asked Charlie. This was a good test of how much they knew.

"Makatomi, and a guy called Arusen," answered Suze. "They met us in L.A yesterday and briefed us and then offered us a deal."

"Did they say anyone else was involved?" asked Charlie.

"No," answered Denny, "But we suspected that Makatomi would want an insurance policy in case something went wrong. Then we noticed someone else on the grid searching for Chinese secrets and around the Biotree site. We are almost certain it is Scrive. We tracked him back to the Biotree building a few hours before Makatomi flew to meet us in L.A."

"Neat," said Charlie, noting that these must be pretty good players and wondering why she didn't know about them. She didn't want to ask too many specialised questions, though, or they'd realise her level of involvement.

"I'm Scrive's girlfriend", she lied, "We've been together for a couple of years".

"There's not much sign of it here," said Suze, looking around.

"This isn't Scrive's main place, and I live in New York," embroidered Charlie, "Scrive was using this place for the current project."

"Okay," asked Denny, "So what do you know about what has been happening?"

There was a ringing sound. It was the entry phone to the apartment.

"This is getting crazy." said Suze. She looked over to Charlie.

"Is this anything to do with you?"

"Nothing, I swear - er - it's probably Scrive," she lied, "He'll probably let himself in but is letting me know he is back."

Suze walked to the entry-phone.

She put her finger over the camera.

She lifted the receiver.

It was another woman. She looked like a Japanese cartoon character. Somewhere between stylish and absurd. She also seemed quite distressed.

"Hello, can I help you?" asked `Suze.

"I'm a friend of Scrive," answered the person. "Can I come in, please?"

"Ask her what her name is," said Charlie, "If it's Chantal, let her in."

Suze relayed the question, "Just a second, what's your name?" she asked politely.

"I'm Chantal, a friend of Scrive," she answered.

Suze looked at Denny, who nodded, "Let her in".

There was a buzz and then a few moments delay as Chantal made her way through two sets of entry system and reached the front door of the apartment. The regular front doorbell rang.

Denny opened the door, while Suze and Charlie remained seated. Charlie had a hand reaching towards her pistol.

As Chantal walked in, she burst into tears. She was shaking. Suze stood and walked over.

"There," she said and lightly touched Chantal's arm, "Sit down, take your time."

Suze looked at Denny, who had been ultra-vigilant as Chantal entered. He relaxed slightly. Charlie was next to speak.

"It looks as if we all know Scrive one way or another. I guess Chantal was the last person to see him."

"That's right," said Chantal. Her appearance was still of bright colours, in an outfit that looked as if it had been outlined with a neon pink pen. But her expression was anything but bright. She looked decidedly ashen, and her skin complexion reminded the others of a Tract person. Denny had already looked at her arm and seen that she did have a tropus cartridge, but he wondered if there was some illness affecting her.

Chantal spoke, "I was with Scrive when he was killed. About half an hour ago. We had just left a meeting and he kind of turned into a vapour. I've never seen anything like it before.

"One minute we were talking and the next he had holes in him and then sort of vaporised."

The others looked at one another and then Charlie asked something.

"Did you see who did it?" she asked, "who killed Scrive?" She was angry that someone she cared for had been removed without trace. In her line of business, she had heard of this kind of thing happening, but never had any first-hand experience. It didn't look as if Denny or Suze had seen this either.

"It was so fast," said Chantal, "and very selective. I was almost next to him when it happened. I heard a crack, like a spark, saw three holes appear and the next thing I remember was that he had gone. I just ran away as fast as I could."

Charlie remembered the conversation before the signal had dropped. She had to decide whether to ask deeper questions, with the risk that she'd show more of her hand. It looked as if Suze and Denny were trackers, but Chantal seemed to be a regular person that had been pulled into the situation. Either that or she was very good and throwing them all off of the trail.

"Did you find out anything from Scrive, or did he give you anything?" asked Charlie.

"Yes," replied Chantal. "That's why I've come over to Scrive's place. I have a memory cube that may have some answers, but it needs to be played in one of Scrive's devices. Otherwise it doesn't work."

Cube root

Chantal fumbled into a side pocket in her outfit. It was zippered but somehow made to look like a lightning flash.

"Here, I know I've got to trust you. Scrive gave me this after we left the meeting with the people in the Vaults"

Charlie knew what Scrive had done. The cube would have two information partitions; a public one and a private one. Anyone picking up the cube to casually browse its contents would get the public version. The secret content would only work in a machine devised by Scrive. Charlie was also pretty sure that Denny and Suze would know how this worked.

"Okay, we'll handle this together," said Denny, "I guess that you two - Charlie and Chantal - are now both in danger from association with Scrive. At the moment Suze and I have covered our tracks pretty well, although Biotree and Makatomi know about us. It doesn't make any sense that Makatomi would set us on a mission and then send someone straight after us to kill us. I can't think why he'd do that with Scrive though, yet he appears to have done so.

"I can't think that anyone would be onto Suze and myself yet - we have moved so fast to get from L.A. to London so that probably Scrive's place would be the last one on the planet anyone would be looking for us."

Chantal said, " Look - I'm not supposed to be involved with this. It's only through a friend of mine - Janie. She asked me to help and to meet someone who, it turns out, wanted to give Scrive some help at getting into Biotree."

Chantal explained how she'd accompanied Janie to meet Lars. How Lars had led Scrive to them, via Carolin. How Lars wanted to help Scrive get into Biotree. That Lars knew Janie's work colleague Karin and she had also disappeared. But mostly how Chantal was only involved because she'd known about Australia.

"...And Scrive paid us too, it was 20,000T at the start and another 20,000T at the end," she knew she was taking a chance.

Charlie Suze and Denny looked at one another.

"3x7s?" asked Charlie.

"Okay," answered Denny.

"We'll cover Scrive's money; we'll give you 21,000 tropes," answered Charlie, "If you stick with us."

Chantal nodded vigorously. Eight years' pay, in total.

Charlie had heard all of the conversations about Australia, but Suze and Denny were hearing for the first time.

Chantal explained how Australia was outside the Ellipse and even outside of the Tract and that it had somehow been erased from memory.

"I don't know how they could do that," continued Chantal, "Two of my friends said they escaped from Australia in a boat. Australia had an exclusion zone around it. My friends are both red. They don't use tropus, although they are both dealers. The reason I know them is because I have a bit of a habit myself. She looked at her arm and showed them the depleted cartridge.

"You cut your tropus doses", said Denny. He realised that it would also account for Chantal's different complexion from most people in the Ellipse.

"Yes, I deal", said Chantal," I'm trying to make some money so that I can move away from London. And you know something, I feel better and sharper when I don't use the tropus."

Charlie interrupted, "That's what Scrive said too. He'd lost his tropus delivery system after someone tried to kill him a day ago. His blood was turning black until I destroyed whatever was attacking him. It was a nano culture of some kind. Because of the smashed cartridge, he ended up with blood that was turning red, but he also said he felt sharper with the red blood. He was a little concerned about the loss of Nero immunity, but otherwise felt fine."

"That's what Lars said," added Chantal, "When Janie and I met him, he told us that the Nero toxin was nowadays a hoax. Misinformation put out to keep us scared and needing the tropus."

Get your coat, you've pulled

Taylor had arrived back in the main Brookings complex.

He'd saved the information from the old monitoring station in a way that meant he could access it from his central systems. He wanted to find out if there was anyone else that knew about Australia and Woomera. The nature of his monitoring meant he could easily check for this as a correlation and his own systems could dig deep into secret files.

Taylor was thinking how useful it had been to get some additional information from the ancient monitoring systems.

He was bypassing the gatekeepered modern ways to obtain information by simply referring to older systems 'frozen in time' in the way they looked at things.

Taylor remembered the old stories about concreting the gun emplacements, but that it meant you had to know which way to expect the enemy.

On this occasion the systems had been pointing the right way.

Back onto the modern connections he now had a variety of information to use to help him find more depth. Within ten minutes he'd found a link and the name of someone who seemed to have a connection.

Bruce Henderson. He was a retired ex-marine Captain who nowadays lived on Cape Cod. Taylor smiled at the cliché of this. He'd seen those old movies where a black multi-role vertical lift arrives to extract a one-time military hero for just that one special mission. He envisaged that would soon be happening to Bruce. Heck, Bruce even had the right first name.

Taylor realised he needed to pass the information to the Sparrowhawk gathering at the Pentagon. If he went any further himself, it would create problems.

He decided the fastest way to alert them was by sending a short message to Colonel Maddox.

"Sparrowhawk, relates to earlier Yulara files sent. We have now located assistance. Captain Bruce Henderson of Cape Cod. He attached an electronic ident for Henderson to the message."

The uploaded files covered an area of land that was not normally visible to any of the US surveillance systems.

Maddox had a team of National Security Agency experts review the material as a high priority. They described the location that Taylor had recorded as within the land formally described as Australia. Technically this was now part of the exclusion zone and regarded as off grid.

They had also checked for experts that would be able to assist with this and following Captain Taylor's lead they also identified Captain Henderson, who had been on black ops missions to the southern hemisphere.

A military Levitor was sent across to the airport at Otis Base on Cape Cod. At the same time a call was placed to the National Guard based there and a small h-Rover was dispatched to pick up Henderson. The h-Rover had its full complement of weapons on board and the riders looked alarming enough to scare most people, although Henderson hardly blinked when he saw them.

"Guys," he said, "Welcome, but I'm guessing you've come to get me for something."

Henderson could still handle himself but realised the arrival of fully armed National Guard in a high-speed hover transport could only mean that he was to be accompanied somewhere.

"Let me get a coat," he said, at the same time priming a few switches on his desk console.

He then left quietly, wondering what was creating the fuss. Henderson had been through mind conditioning as part of his Marine role so most of what was happening now was for him, relatively routine, even if there had been a gap since he'd left the service.

His preconditioning also meant he was able to withstand severe torture and questioning. He wasn't expecting anything bad though, he'd kept a straightforward and low-key existence since he'd left the Marines.

Like many, he'd suffered from jitters once he'd left the service although he'd found, against prevailing advice, that he was able to steady it better by not using the tropus in the way that most people did.

He self-administered a reduced dose, realising he could be adding a different danger, but at the same time knowing that he felt better on the lower dosages. He knew other people that did this and that they were generally considered part of an alternative lifestyle and that they often sold the spare dosages to those that wanted a different kind of buzz. He didn't do this, preferring to wash away any surplus and at least stay the right side of part of the law.

The ride in the h-Rover was strangely soothing. It was a new model and didn't look as if it had seen any active service. The seats were relatively plush, still with the metal grid that was uncomfortable to sit on for long journeys, but overall the speed and comfort were slightly better than he remembered.

The same applied when they arrived at the airport. Even in the military he'd often spend ages waiting to get through various controls as well as all kinds of weapon checks to be performed.

This time it was through the gates and across the airstrip to the waiting Levitor to take him quickly to Washington.

The Levitor had both passenger and freight capabilities and the h-Rover drove straight into the back of the unit.

They disembarked and walk through to a stairway and up about ten stairs to what looked like a medium class airline seating area.

"Buckle in," said the steward who was waiting for them. You'll get some refreshments when we are airborne. This will be a short flight and we are not expecting any turbulence.

They all clipped in and the plane rose vertically before firing forward on what was a levitation rail. The predefined parts of the route gave the craft speed and accuracy.

Henderson felt the handoffs from the Lev-routes as the plane switched on what was the equivalent of invisible rails in the sky, while it made its way rapidly towards Washington.

Around thirty minutes later they were positioning for a landing, and again they used the stairs, back into the h-Rover and away to one of the complexes on the edge of the Pentagon.

Henderson was again surprised at the lack of security as these processes took place and as they drove through the final gate into a building, he realised they were entering the tunnel system, to the north-east of the Pentagon. Henderson knew about this area and also that it was a highly secure part of the base.

He looked at his watch. It had been around 90 minutes since he'd first spotted the incoming h-Rover back at his home. For Maddox, it was still less than two hours since he'd heard from Taylor about Henderson.

8

"Whether you take the doughnut hole as a blank space or as an entity unto itself is a purely metaphysical question and does not affect the taste of the doughnut one bit."

— Haruki Murakami, A Wild Sheep Chase

Holden doughnut

Holden knew he had a reputation that he lived in the wires. That he was reclusive. It was a convenient story.

Holden knew just about everything driving his mission and its link with the domes. He secretly knew more than anyone about the domes and how they linked together by micro-hysteresis.

A slight change in one dome would send tiny magnetic ripples to the other domes. The tiny granularity of the field changes meant that enormous amounts of data could be exchanged imperceptibly.

Holden thought of it like gently washing the world.

And that was how Holden preferred to work. Stealthily, imperceptibly.

And now, through links to the multiple sites where research was conducted, he could keep track of all developments.

Holden knew about other so-called secret developments around the planet. Some were laughably public.

A prior meteor incursion had landed in the Groom Lake salt flats in Nevada. The Americans had gone for the old trick of hiding it in plain sight. They named it R-4808N, as a flight zone close to Coyote Alpha. They could not stop there, though, and went on to call it Area 51, which attracted plenty of sci-fi nerds who thought there must be something else happening there.

Holden knew the mundane truth, that the Americans wanted somewhere to test captured Russian aircraft and for years flew dogfights of Russian MIG-17Fs and MIG-21Fs across the area. Have Drill, Have Doughnut; the missions were code-named. The foreign planes were not claimed in a superspy sting. No, they were simply residuals from defecting Israeli Airforce pilots.

And then there was the recent super bolide which hit Chelyabinsk. It was a small piece flaked from the larger 2012 DA14 asteroid. Like an accidentally detached car wheel on a freeway, once it was off the vehicle it could accelerate away and surprise earth 16 hours ahead of schedule.

That was in the times before the Great Leap. Such events were waxed by what came later. Curiously, no one had made any connections of the behaviours of the historical meteors compared with those forming the Ellipse.

Holden held the data and the process capacity to out-think most of the occupiers of earth.

He could see attempts to use Great Leap thinking, but only in the most basic of ways.

For example, he knew that Makatomi was using the quantum effects of the Trigax as the way to eliminate Mallinson. The Trigax. A great Leap, but now being reduced by humans to being little more than a murder weapon.

That second attempt on Scrive was still much better than Makatomi's first botched attempt to use a sabotaged cartridge to kill Mallinson.

Holden had monitored Makatomi while he took a V-Blade all the way to Norway from Tokyo to set it up. Holden considered it blind squandering of resources.

Then Makatomi used Arusen to acquire a fixer. Double blind handling of the request. Arusen had handled the fixer for the Trigax too.

For Holden it was just a flash along the wire. But it was easier to let the real people perform these acts against one another.

Holden worried that Makatomi's actions were getting less dependable.

He dialled into Makatomi's biosystems and ran a trace. Makatomi was stressed, but still functioning well. There was no need to intervene.

Apartment 123

In Scrive's apartment, Denny, Suze, Chantal and Charlie sat around a table.

Denny spoke next, "There is a pretty high chance that both of you are known to whoever has killed Scrive. We're not known at the moment and I want to keep it that way. We can help you get new idents which will help keep you out of view, but in return I'll want to know if there's anything else that you know."

Charlie wasn't particularly interested in this type of deal. She'd spent enough time on the road to know how to look after herself. She'd also acquired quite a lot of new money from the deal with Scrive, where he'd already passed her part of his share at the start of their working together.

"I'm okay," she said, "Don't get me wrong, but I can look out for myself." She looked down to where she had clipped the small stun grenade to her belt.

Denny and Suze knew immediately what she meant.

They looked at the data cube that Chantal had been given by Scrive.

"Nice," said Denny, "This is a very high-tech device. If we access it wrongly, it will still give us information, but it will also destroy the part where the valuable stuff has been stored."

"I can help you," said Charlie. "I've worked with Scrive and I'll know how to find what is on it."

"Back to our early questions, how do I know I can trust you?" asked Denny.

"Let's just say I'm also motivated to see this thing through. Two reasons, firstly for Scrive and secondly for money."

Charlie didn't want to mention the machines she had stored in the hotel.

Denny asked, "so you know Scrive well - do you think you know how to access this cube?" He held up the data cube that Chantal had produced.

"Sure," said Charlie, "Let me have it for a few minutes. I'll find the right system, and access."

"Remember if you get it wrong you will wipe it," said Suze.

"Not a chance," said Charlie confidently and clicked it into one of Scrive's decks. It was the machine he used the most. She knew she'd need to use a code sequence to read the cube and pressed a sequence of keys. It was a sequence they'd used together in the past. She knew it would work and immediately a small blue light appeared inside the data cube.

Seconds later the cube had offloaded its contents into Scrive's deck. It was going through a decryption process and arranging itself into a series of hyper-walls. Each wall was a set of archive materials. The ones that had originally been downloaded from the Vault by Crispin and Lucas.

"It's going to take a time for us to search this," said Suze.

Not if we type in "Australia", said Charlie and started a search based upon what Scrive had sent to her.

The cube was starting to give up its secrets.

Cube

Denny and Suze watched as Charlie manipulated the Cube using Scrive's technology. Charlie had worked with Scrive on enough jobs that they could both work through each other's patterns, and they had frequently stored safe codes to help one another break into each other's technology.

"Scrive must have really trusted you?" said Denny, watching Charlie at work.

"The trust was total and the same from me," replied Charlie, "I'm doing this for Scrive."

"...and the money." thought Chantal, but she didn't say anything.

"Okay... Here's what we have," continued Charlie. "Australia looks for real, and it seems to be outside the Tract. We all know about the Ellipse and the Tract. The Tract seems to be a barrier layer protecting what is a third layer. The main part of this

Third layer seems to be in the southern part of the planet. It's as if we've all somehow stopped noticing a whole piece of the world. I can't work out why none of us even remember it?"

"You know something," said Chantal, "I have this very faint recollection. It is like something from childhood. It's so strange. We all grow up, and despite living intensely through our childhoods, there are large swathes of it that none of us remembers. It's a bit like that with Australia. It is like a childhood party I attended that wasn't very good. Not bad enough to remember because someone fell in a pool or we got chased by a clown, but on that edge where if I think really hard I can just about remember something... Kelly," she said, "Somebody Kelly, a folklore robber."

The others looked at one another. Charlie said, "What is even stranger is that even while we are doing this, I'm thinking that I won't be remembering this tomorrow. It is as if there is something erasing part of my mind even while we are having this conversation."

Denny and Suze looked up. They were having a similar thought. They could remember Scrive clearly enough, but already the name of the place was starting to fade again. Denny had written it down. It was in his handheld. But what had he filed it against?

"There's something extraordinary about all of this," said Chantal." I'm not getting that same feeling. I remembered that two of my friends claimed they were from Australia. They told me that months ago. I haven't forgotten it."

"We'll still need to move fast on this," said Denny, "I suggest we start the process with Lars to get inside Biotree. If we can contact your friend Janie, we could try to obtain some improved access codes, and that may increase the effectiveness of our search."

Chantal looked up, she agreed this was the best thing to try next. She just wasn't sure about bringing Janie into the middle of all of these new people.

"Let me contact Janie alone. I'll need to explain to her what has been happening. Then I can see whether she is still prepared to help. She didn't meet Scrive, but she knows that Karin disappeared as a result of helping Lars and Carolin. I'm getting worried that this could start to happen to all of us."

Chantal stood as if to leave. "You know what," she said, "I'm a little concerned that you are all going to forget some parts of this."

Charlie nodded. She also felt that the aspects associated with Australia were already becoming less clear.

"You're all going to have to trust me on this," Chantal said decisively.

"I'm going to take Scrive's system and the data cube. I'll also upload it to Wolkerech - you know that

German cloud system. Purely for safekeeping. I've got money riding on the outcome of this. I don't want you all to forget where you've placed the system or something."

They looked at one another in the room. Denny gestured to the others. "Okay, I can see why you are saying that. I'm also concerned about the way this information is slipping away. But we won't forget who you are, Chantal, nor Janie, so please remember that. If there's an attempt to be too smart, we'll have a way to find you. "

He put on a menacing look. Chantal's own expression overrode it. She was treating Denny like a comic playground hero when she'd already discovered smoking and boys. Kind of "yeah, right."

"Like I said, I want this to work." She moved to the door. Her manga cartoon outfit somehow seemed stronger to the others.

Search

Chantal left Scrive's apartment and made for the street level. She would get a taxi back to her place and then tell Janie what had been happening. The death of Scrive was huge news, plus the disappearance of Janie's friend Karin were both big alarm signals that all was not well.

Chantal was also worried that so many people were now getting involved. It had been a whirlwind couple of days.

She called ahead to check with Janie that she would be indoors and sure enough, Janie picked up the phone.

"There will be a lot to explain" began Chantal.

Thirty minutes later she was back at home and started to tell Janie what had happened. She also felt that they needed to decide who they could trust because it still wasn't clear whose side people were on.

Janie was also cautious, "We've said to Lars that we would help him get information for Scrive, does that mean the mission will also automatically transfer to these other people? It almost seems too convenient?"

"Well Charlie, who I met, seemed to have a genuine affinity for Scrive," said Chantal, "I think I trust her based upon the conversations today. It also looks to me as if Denny and Suze have been asked to do the same task as Scrive. I wonder why Makatomi asked two teams to look for the information?"

"Maybe for exactly the reasons we see now, where Scrive has been killed. He might even have been a decoy for all we know," speculated Janie.

"Tomorrow, I will go to work as if it's normal, but I will also try to find the codes or searches for what people are trying to access."

"Great," said Chantal, "Although I think we need to tell Lars some of what is happening. He did ask us to let him know as things move along."

"Do you think Lars is on the level?" asked Janie, "I am less certain of whom we can trust by the minute."

Chantal responded," I think we should assume that Karin was already working with Lars. She then disappeared. That all seems consistent.

Lars already knew about Scrive and was trying to approach him to get Karin and now you to provide access to some of Biotree's secrets. The other team of Denny and Suze seem to be an insurance policy by Makatomi - or if as you say, Scrive was a decoy. I somehow doubt it though, he was too good to be expendable in that way."

Chantal didn't mention Charlie. She was upholding her part of the deal to keep Charlie a secret from as many people as possible. It had been the deal with Scrive, and she thought that she owed him, - them - that much at least.

Janie contacted Lars, and they arranged to meet again that evening, in a different location and this time without Carolin.

Chantal was interested that like Scrive and Charlie, Lars was putting distance between himself and Carolin. She decided it was part of the way these types of teams operated - maybe with the exception of Denny and Suze.

Chantal similarly realised that such an approach wouldn't work with herself and Janie because they were already sharing an apartment and it wouldn't take anyone more than about five minutes to make the connection. But on the other hand, neither Chantal nor Janie had any previous connection with this type of activity.

The cafe they had arranged to meet in was in the west end of London, in a busy tourist location close to Trafalgar Square.

Lars arrived at the cafe just after them. They were seated on the pavement, at round metal tables, closely spaced and on the edge of the theatre district. The swaying area was crowded, mainly from early evening theatre goers.

Janie explained to Lars that she would help but needed to be told what she was to look for.

Lars had explained that it would be information firstly about the manufacture of tropus. Then it would be information related to the nanomachines and their design.

There was also a couple of projects; code names seemed to be "woomera" and "australia."

Chantal had already told Janie about Australia 'the place', and they all now assumed it might be something to do with the location rather than a specific project.

The way that Janie would need to try to discover anything was to type these searches into a highly secure system and to see what happened.

If the system itself could be located, then Denny and Suze would be able to drill into it securely from afar. The challenge was to know what they were looking for. It was far easier to discover this from inside rather than to try targeting everything from outside.

Lars said Janie might strike lucky and get to some actual secrets, but it was far safer to find the right system and then to let Denny and Suze take over.

Janie was to use another data cube which would provide trace recording of what she did. It would give the system addresses that Denny and Suze would need.

Lars asked Chantal if she believed Denny and Suze were working for the same side.

"I don't even understand what the sides are," replied Chantal.

Chantal added, "Denny and Suze seem to be on the level as much as anything could be over the last few days."

Chantal decided not to mention the little matter of the fees she would be accepting from Suze and Denny, although she would do right by Janie once this was over.

"I think tomorrow we should link whatever we find through to Suze and Denny," said Chantal, "that way we bring them along and also have capabilities similar to those from Scrive."

Lars nodded in agreement.

"We should split up tomorrow," he said, "Janie will go to work, you, Chantal, will go to Suze and Denny and I will coordinate."

Like they had all agreed, Chantal had kept Charlie out of the story. Scrive and Charlie had decided to keep Charlie involved but separate, and it was an excellent ongoing plan.

Chantal took the Transit system across to Scrive's apartment where Charlie, Denny and Suze waited.

Janie's next day was a regular working day, and she would be back at her main offices. Suze and Denny decided to accompany Janie on her route and to wait in a nearby WorkSmart location, which was a managed office facility, with high bandwidth communications and coffee.

Janie worked in an area close to the facilities that Makatomi used when he was in London. Makatomi travelled the globe and so was more usually a virtual presence.

That was nothing compared with Makatomi's boss Holden, who was never seen in this office in person. Holden had a large suite on one of the top floors, but even when people attended for meetings it was usually supported by telepresence and through the agency of another person who would stand in for Holden during the session.

None of this phased Janie, who was used to the way of the modern and heavily virtualised workplace.

She arrived at her workspace and began what looked like a typical day. She would create a situation where she needed to go to the area that Makatomi usually worked and needed to create an issue that would warrant a visit rather than just a call or email.

She decided to use some further information about the Chinese and adapted some numbers in a report which implied even faster erosion of Biotree's financial position.

It was a clumsy adaptation, but enough to mean she needed to visit Makatomi's floor directly. It was the type of sensitive information that would usually be treated with the highest confidentiality because of its potential impact upon share price.

She made her way up to Makatomi's floor. As she arrived, she was aware that the V-Blade deck was occupied. There was a V-Blade on the building. She hadn't noticed it when she arrived, but it probably meant that Makatomi or Holden were actually in the building.

Janie thought this slightly unusual. Makatomi had been around half the planet in the last couple of days, and it would need to be something special that that had caused his return so quickly to London.

She carried on along the corridor with the special report she had manufactured and was able to get through to the area where Makatomi worked. It wasn't an exceptional feat; the reason Lars had selected her was that she had this access.

The area was deserted. If Makatomi was in the building, then he was elsewhere.

She could see a workstation in the corner off the room. If Makatomi had left it switched on, she would be able to bypass the security screen and get into Makatomi's workspace.

As she walked towards the terminal, she caught sight of a reflection in the nearby glass. It was the glow from the terminal screen. It was switched on. It would be more straightforward than she had hoped.

She used her access code to bypass the screen security and then flipped into Makatomi's area of the system. As one of the trusted people in the team, she had generic access to many of the privileged areas.

The difference was accessing the systems from Makatomi's physical system. It automatically gave her a better status of access. She clipped the small data cube into a port on the workstation and watched a short blue light pulse. The cube that Denny had provided for her had found its way onto the network. Now she could record everything that she entered along with the responses from the system

She brought up the search screen.

Australia.

Nothing

Woomera.

A response came back immediately.

"Access to this area is restricted. Physical presence in Biotree's Research and Development facility required. Access from Bodø Only."

9

I am not free,
because I can be exploded at any time

Jenny Holzer, Tate Modern, London 23 July 2018

Jog-shuttle

The memory cube quietly captured the response and Janie could tell that it was running further analysis based upon the code from Denny.

She assumed that her typing of a few words was somehow filling up the cube with various types of useful information.

Janie reinstated the workstation and removed the cube. She was toying whether to leave the faked report when she heard the door to the office slide open.

"Hello" she called. "Is that Mr Makatomi, I have a report for you. It's rather confidential."

Makatomi looked startled. He crossed the floor towards Janie.

"Hello," he said graciously, "I'm slightly surprised to see you in my office alone. Did someone show you into here?"

"I'm Jane Southern from Advanced Analytics, and I thought I'd better bring you this analysis without alerting too many people." She handed him the eSlate with the information. He flicked his way through the first couple of pages.

"If this were true," said Makatomi, "Then I think we'd have another serious issue to deal with. You say you are from the Advanced team? There seem to be some basic flaws in this analysis. I'd have expected you to have spotted them very easily?"

Makatomi pressed a circular control. Janie looked at it and thought that it was an ancient way of accessing some kind of playback system.

"You know what," said Makatomi, "I decided not to have the old systems replaced when I move into this suite. This jog-shuttle control is a quick way to wind back through the video recording that is built into this area. Let's take a look, shall we?"

He twisted the control anti-clockwise. Sure enough, there was a video projection which now ran along the back wall of the room. It was displaying four images, each a metre across. In three of them, Janie could be seen walking in reverse, and then a few moments later she could be seen at Makatomi's screen intently typing.

"This is interesting," said Makatomi, "Ms Southern, you seem to be using my system? I don't recollect giving you that authority."

Janie was holding the small data cube in her hand. She felt it get hot. Almost hot enough to drop. Makatomi looked more intently at the screen.

"I think you'd better hand over the data cube you installed," he said as he aimed a microcordon at her, "I'm going to need to hold you here."

The cordon snaked from Makatomi's small pistol-like device. Janie felt the electrics pulse as it surrounded her. She was captive.

Charlie could be a stunner

Denny had been monitoring the cube's system all morning from the WorkSmart location, since before Janie had arrived at the office. He was waiting for any sign from the cube that Janie had accessed the system.

Sure enough, at around mid-morning, there had been an alert, and the channel to Makatomi's office had opened up. Denny hadn't told Janie, but the cube had several functions. It was a recorder, but it would also drop a small payload into the Biotree systems. It would give him some direct privileged access so that he could work fast without waiting for Janie's return.

He kept a monitor screen running with Janie's image as she worked while he dropped a few more small packages of code into the Biotree environment.

Then he noticed the entrance of Makatomi. He flicked to the surprisingly dated monitoring system for the suite and noted that Makatomi was challenging Janie. Makatomi had found the cube. This was not good.

Suze was also working and had followed the link back to the Bodø system, based upon the original search created by Janie.

"It's a tough one," said Suze, "there is only one way to access the Bodø environment, and that is from Bodø. It's completely cut off from all of the other access routes. They looked at one another.

"So how will we get to Bodø?" asked Denny.

"Makatomi's roof has a V-Blade on it", said Suze. "But we need someone who can operate it."

"That would be me, then," said Charlie. "I worked with these with Scrive, when we were in the middle east. I have a licence to fly the military versions. Makatomi's is a luxury model by comparison."

"All we need to do is break into Biotree, rescue Janie, steal the V-Blade and fly it to Bodø." said Denny.

"We might as well kidnap Makatomi while we are at it," added Charlie, who was counting out some stun grenades.

Sky fire

Captain Henderson took the short flight to Washington. He was led from the h-Rover and escorted through another couple of corridors. He expected to be taken into something resembling a cell or a white room. Instead, he entered a room which looked comfortable. Leather sofas, military pictures on the wall, a coffee pot and some fine porcelain cups. Not a standard intel room. It looked like the Pentagon had money.

"Captain Henderson?" asked a serious-looking uniformed man, who turned from a seated position across the room. He had been in discussion with two other people and also with a video wall.

"Yes, I am Captain Henderson. You've brought me here on some sort of military matter, I assume?", he decided to stay unruffled, as much as he was capable.

"Correct. My name Colonel Maddox, US Marines. I know you recently retired from the Marine Corp, and now it is information we are requesting, and it's the sort that I think you will freely give. We are trying to understand something that is happening and think you may be able to take us further. We'll re-commission you for active service and provide significant years served pension increase if you'll help us."

"I was just about done with fishing, anyway," said Henderson.

Maddox proceeded to explain what he had heard from Taylor, and how Henderson's name had occurred during the various searches.

Henderson nodded while he was being told the story and decided it was better to come clean on everything.

"I worked on an assignment in a country which used to be called Australia." he began. "We were there as part of international peacekeeping and running quiet exchanges of information about rocket propulsion technology. I was a part of an active monitoring unit asked to validate specific claims made by one of our allies. The technology they were using didn't seem to be possible, according to the scientists and so they wanted to check a few secure areas to see what was behind particular closed doors. My team were part of a black operations mission to find out what was happening.

"Frankly, that was routine, and we were just waiting for our chance. Compared with what else happened there, this was an almost irrelevant diversion.

Maddox listened suspiciously to what he was being told.

"We were at the site during what turned out to be small meteor showers. They had been forecast and were vectored towards our location. The scientists said they'd burn out in the upper atmosphere, so I wasn't' too worried about it. We were all thinking about how to get the doors open on our mission."

"This was maybe 20 years ago. There was a kind of sky-fire as the first meteors streak across the sky. It looked a little like the trails from a modern-day V-Blade actually. There were several more, but they all seemed to burn out.

"We assumed it was the tail of a vast comet somewhere much further out in the solar system. The early reports made the news and the science community was quite excited. At the time, the individual showers didn't make it through the earth's atmosphere. Like most things thrown at earth, they were burned up on entry."

Then a larger item was spotted, on a different trajectory and a course for earth. This one was different though because it seemed to have steering. No -one could work out how it changed course and speed as it approached the earth and it then took a path that allowed it to glide in, to where it landed, which was in the middle of the Woomera rocket testing ranges in Australia.

"So how have I not heard of it?" asked Maddox.

"It is part of what happened," continued Bruce Henderson, "And it is something that only a very few people are aware of now. Australia is unknown, the Woomera ranges are unknown, and the landing is also unknown"

"The meteor, or whatever it was, landed in the middle of the test range. The Australians took this kind of thing very seriously. There was a significant base of the former Joint Defence Facility at a place called Nurrungar, which was about 15 kilometres south of Woomera. The planes from there were in the air long before the 'meteor' hit.

"I should explain that the test area around Woomera is huge. About the same size as the state of Alabama, or the whole of England, as a matter of fact.

"This facility, and another one, the one where I was based, was administered by the Department of Defence. I was based at Maralinga to the far west of the Woomera Testing Range, on the edge of the facility. We had planes too, but we were also on special instructions to evacuate if anything untoward were to happen. To be honest, we'd all worked here for years, and it was mainly quite a sleepy place.

"But on this occasion, we had the Aerospace Operational Support Group of the Royal Australian Air Force appear over the horizon like a swarm of bees.

"They escorted us into the air in fast fighter planes and told us we would be permitted a non-intrusive fly-over of what was happening. We took an SR72 with all the spy gear fitted. We were to use this to brief about follow up action.

"Several crew flew the Lockheed and the rest of us took an Australian chauffeured ride in fast planes back to the site of the impact.

"The strange thing was that the site of the incursion was almost antiseptically tidy. Instead of a huge hole in the ground or a long scar, there was an elegant teardrop shaped glassy looking structure on the ground. It had a slight movement from within, like light, but that was the only sign that there was anything active.

"My immediate reaction was that it was like an egg or spawn or something and that we'd better stay clear of it and create a cordon. By its landing in the middle of a rocket testing range we already had a head start. My plane was the one on the outside of the formation. We flew at a half kilometre wing separation but did a vertical bank over the structure. We were also to look at whether there was anything else unusual in the desert.

"We returned to the base. It was a typical scorcher of a day with temperatures up around 42C at the middle of the day. I remember stepping out of the plane and being hit by the heat.

"Then we regrouped inside the facility and started to compare notes. There were a few things we'd noticed, ahead of getting the telemetry from the SR72. The flights lower over the structure had sighted some red trails moving along its surface. Thin lines that wove around. I didn't see this. There was no sound and the area around the structure looked undamaged. It looked more as if the structure had been built there rather than had somehow crashed or landed there.

"We also tried a replay of the structure's incoming flight path. There were a couple of adjustments on the way in that looked more like flight corrections than something that could happen by chance. It was also a very fast entry; beyond anything we'd expect to land without a massive impact zone.

"Of course, we were on the communications link about this, and it had also been picked up by plenty of other satellite tracking systems. The Americans, NATO and most of the super-powers were on our case about what had occurred. The Australian Prime Minister had also been alerted and had said he would allow the situation to be treated as a global one, rather than through just the resources of Australia, but that it would stay under Australian command.

"The opportunity to get anyone to us quickly was low, except for a couple of American stealth planes which were on the ground in Nurrungar within a half an hour. It is one of the times when everyone realised that Australia is quite large and quite a long way from everywhere else.

"I can still remember that one of the American-marked stealths was a Chinese design, J22-Dragon or something

"We had various cameras and radar on the planes, but we are talking about using the technology from before the Great Leap."

Henderson looked at Maddox, "Of course, now we know that this was one of the reasons we could have the Great Leap."

Maddox was looking at Henderson with an uncharacteristically softened expression. "I'm not sure about any of this. You seem to be telling a true story, but frankly, it is all so far-fetched I'm wondering if your mind is altogether stable?"

Henderson looked back, "That's the irony, that is exactly the problem that the landings started."

"You said landings", said Maddox," Are you telling me there are more than one?"

"Yes," replied Henderson, "The one we found was one of several outliers. It turned out that the main landing was in Yulara. The way it worked was a kind of teardrop shaped scattering of six separate impacts. It took us several days to realise this, though, because of how the structures worked.

"Yulara, how far from Woomera?"

"About a thousand kilometres, north west, 12 hours by land transport. Australia is vast. The Gibson desert is to the West of Yulara, it's about 60,000 square miles. But it's even bigger really because it is sandwiched between two other deserts - The Great Sandy and The Great Victoria. The Great Sandy is over 100,000 square miles and the Great Victoria is more like 160,000 square miles. We are talking about a deserted spot in a desert within a desert.

And that's within a continent that no-one has ever heard of?" interrupted Maddox. "Like the lost city of Atlantis, or Eldorado? - only as big as the United States? I don't think so."

"Let me continue," said Henderson. "It will be difficult to prove any of this directly, but you will need to know if there is any chance for us to change anything."

"The various authorities decided it would be better to clamp down news about the structure until we knew more of what was happening. This was standard protocol for us in any case, so we had already been running everything encrypted and secured."

"The story to the world was that we'd had another meteor shower that had burned up in the atmosphere. We'd had all the fires earlier too, which only added to the mystique around everything.

"A few people had seen the flashes, but we said it was the burn up. Some of the civilian astronomers asked more questions, but we created an explanation which also covered the apparent changes of direction. Sunspots, I remember, came into it."

"Because we were based in 'deepest Australia' it worked to our advantage when we were explaining any of this. I think the conspiracists thought we'd let off a rocket or missile that had somehow crashed in any case."

Bruce sipped at the coffee. He ran his finger around the pressed-bamboo lid and fidgeted with the small hole through which he could drink. With a fingernail, he was absentmindedly counting the corrugations in the holder.

"Of course, that was before we realised that scale to which the structures would develop. We couldn't approach them at that stage and Woomera and the Gibson Desert made automatic cordons to prevent people from getting nosey.

"By the next day, we had our own monitoring systems in place. Secure cameras, telemetry and a side presence of serious military strength."

"That's also about the point when everything changed..."

Illicit Trigax

The Bodø facility where Sheri worked had some of the most cutting-edge technology. The rest of the site referred to it as the ATA, which was supposed to stand for Advanced Technology Area, but most people called it the "alien technology area".

The Trigax was one of the most secretive devices available. It was intended to be for use in atom separation as part of building new nano structures. It could operate with extreme power and could select individual atoms for isolation. Such was the nature of the device that Sheri used to think of this as a 'god device'. Although having a local range which they used for experiments and building, the boosted calibration could deliver the same power and capability anywhere on the planet and also probably as far as the moon into space. It was simply a matter of getting the coordinates set.

There were various safeguards included that limited its range to a minimal area designated within the R&D facility and the levels of failsafe were such that it effectively had a huge electronics and software guard to prevent it being aimed anywhere else. The technology was classed as munitions, and the current peaceful use came with stringent conditions.

Sheri wasn't sure how the original design had been created. It was something to do with Holden, who was now in a top company position. The science within the device was still beyond her, despite her ability to use the machine with high precision. But, she rationalised, she didn't know the details of how Transit system engines worked either, but she still used the Transit.

This time she had arrived for work and gone directly to the lab. She was surprised when she noticed that the system for Trigax had its coordinates adjusted. Apart from her, there were only three other people with routine access to this device, and they wouldn't interfere in the middle of one of her experimental protocols.

Not only were the coordinates changed, but they were also outside of the guard rails. She looked again; the access had somehow broken the deadlocking system that prevented the Trigax being re-calibrated to other locations.

She pulled up a second screen image, this time a planet model. She punched in the coordinates that the Trigax had as its focus. It wasn't even in Norway.

They were pointing to London, England.

Then she noticed that the Trigax had been deployed, and on a high-power setting.

It looked to her as if someone had used the Trigax as a weapon. It also looked as if they had done so on her watch and with her access codes.

Sheri tried to think who could do this. Other than the three other users, she could only think to ask Nathan. He didn't work in this area or have access. He would need to get through several sets of security, although that was his role. Managing the security of the site.

There was something highly irregular here, and she needed to take great care to find out what had been happening.

Sheri decided to call Nathan. She knew he would be on-site, but probably a long way away.

"Nathan, its Sheri, something's happened. To do with work. I need to talk to you. It is important"

They arranged to meet, but Sheri decided it would be best if they went back to their apartment. She told her department chief that she was unwell and that she needed to get out for a few hours. She made a point of saying that Nathan would be joining her.

Sheri arrived back at the apartment. Nathan's four-wheel-drive transport was already there. She walked inside, and Nathan was sipping tea.

"What's going on?" he asked," this seems pretty unusual."

"Nathan, I'll need you to keep this secret," started Sheri. "It's to do with work, but I can't let this go elsewhere."

"Hey, Sher, what is it?" asked Nathan, "This isn't like you." He looked concerned.

"I think someone has managed to steal some of my codes, my ident," said Sheri," They've used it to gain access to a critical piece of equipment." She knew Nathan wouldn't automatically know about the Trigax, and it wasn't something she'd routinely discuss.

"A special device for handling atoms has been tampered with. We use it for science, but it can be used for other purposes too."

"As a weapon?" asked Nathan.

Sheri knew that Nathan would be aware of the nature of some of the specialised equipment in her section. The whole of Biotree had many esoteric and potentially lethal devices, mainly because of the power that they were using.

"Yes, it is something that can be used as a weapon. There's only a few of them on the planet, and the Pentagon holds one. As well as its experimental potential, it can target an area and then send a huge pulse with an accuracy of a few centimetres. It could take out whatever is at those coordinates, which are measured in three planes. Effectively it can address any point on the planet.

"Whoa," responded Nathan, "So it is like a 'death-ray'?" he asked, "That does sound a bit far-fetched."

"It would have been before the Leap," answered Sheri, "To be honest even me and the people I work with don't understand what makes it operate. The Science of it seems to be almost too clever."

"Another piece of your alien technology?" joked Nathan. Sheri knew they had conversations sometimes about some of the things she worked with, which just seemed too good to be true. Even Nathan had found technology in his security line which seemed to be beyond anything he could have imagined, yet it all seemed to work and as if it had always been there.

"The machine is called a Trigax. It uses three types of energy as an output. When they combine, they create an exceptional power surge which we have been able to use to extract unusual atomic structures. Effectively it is building us atoms that shouldn't exist. The three pulses have to focus at a single point - the coordinates are set, and then the pulse travels like a wave through the air, but when it converges, it will take the source at which it points and de-materialise it. The resultant effect is like something out of Einstein - kind of E=MC Squared, but we are re-building the Energy from the matter.

We have been using the side effect of it to isolate the atoms we've needed. The energy seems to disappear somewhere, but we've still not worked out how that part works.

So, you are creating massive energy but then losing it? asked Nathan

"Yes," said Sheri, "it's as if it's all transferring somewhere very quickly, in a way that we can't trace."

"Another part of what Einstein described?" asked Nathan "- something to do with the speed of light?"

"Maybe," said Sheri, "we just don't know."

"Anyway. The Trigax has been primed and fired at a location outside of our controlled range. I thought it was impossible to do that because of the way the Trigax has been locked down."

"But I can see the Trigax has been fired, and it was pointed to somewhere in London, England."

"Now you want me to help you figure out what has happened?" asked Nathan.

"Please," said Sheri. "Everyone in my area will know that there are only four scientists with the access codes for the device. The triggering is showing my ident, and my codes have been used, but I know I haven't done it, nor have I told anyone-not even you, Nathan, about the codes."

"It sounds like you need me to take a look at this in a professional capacity." said Nathan, smiling, "This'll be a first!"

"You're sure you couldn't have done something to affect this?" asked Sheri. "Please tell me if you think there's a way that you'd give information to someone."

"No," said Nathan," I didn't know about the Trigax until a few minutes ago, and I've been offsite for the last two days when this is supposed to have been happening."

Sheri nodded, " Let's think of a more basic security leak that would give you a reason to be on site. I know. I'll say we've had a hack into one of the lower-tier systems. It would be exactly the sort of thing we'd call you over for."

"Okay," said Nathan, "I'll be nearby to ensure that I get the call."

Nathan left in his security patrol vehicle and parked across from Sheri's block.

Sure enough, Sheri called through the request for assistance and Nathan got the call because of his proximity.

Nathan worked his way into the area where Sheri worked following normal procedures. He didn't want it to look unusual, yet he did need to be in the secure area if he was to be able to trace back what had happened.

He had brought some of his security checking systems with him. Compared to the technology used by the trackers, he knew his own technologies were still rather primitive, but he did know his way around the Biotree environment and with his access codes had a head start on most people.

"First of all, we should check where the Trigax was pointed, he said, that will give us some extra information."

He looked at the coordinates and traced them back to London. Sheri assisted, and they found a particular location. It was by an old part of London called London Bridge. They zoomed tight and found the target.

Jumpy RFID

Nathan then zoomed using his own technology onto the same area. He was able to see the RFID of the person targeted. He looked it up in his directories and noticed that the code jumped around before settling.

"Unusual," he muttered, "...the way it is jumping suggests it is someone that didn't want to be found. A tracker probably, they all do this but the toolkit here at Biotree can get past that type of camouflage."

"A Mr Mallinson, Scrive Mallinson. But his trace has stopped after this point. It looks as if he has been wiped. I don't know how, except its exactly where your Trigax was pointed."

"Yes," said Sheri, "That would be the Trigax. An accurate tracking and then elimination. I have never seen it used at that range or in that way before. Its way outside of our safe tolerances."

He froze the grid reference and looked at neighbouring proximity. There is another RFID close by he said. It's got a signal; Someone else was very close by.

He dialled the codes. "Chantal," he said "'Chantal le Strang'. So, who are you Mademoiselle le Strang?"

He continued to work and noticed that Chantal's other known movements were around London. The tracing he was using was only at thirty-minute intervals and he could see that she had stayed in London for the last two weeks prior to the firing of the Trigax. He couldn't easily check her off against all of the other people she had met, it would take separate time and analysis for that. He decided to flip forward to now.

"My god," he said, "the trace for le Strang is showing from this facility here in Bodø. I'm certain that Chantal le Strang knows something about what has been happening."

"So how can we track her down?" asked Sheri, "If she was in London when the other person was targeted then she can't have been here also. But maybe she is part of a gang, and she's come to contact or collect the other members?"

"Perhaps," said Nathan, "or she was a friend of the person targeted. But in that case, I don't think she'd be able to find this place so quickly, let alone the Trigax."

"And another thing...the speed of her movement from London to here is phenomenal. She'd have needed to use a V-Blade to get here that fast. I'm going to check for flights from London in the last couple of hours."

He looked at the system, "It says here that Makatomi San has taken a flight from Biotree London to here in the last hour. The V-Blade is over at Dock Three. Do you have comcam in here?"

"Sure," said Sheri and flipped on a display. "Where do you want to look? I'm going to add my control layer onto it so that I can control the video," he said. He flashed some codes and the security system become operable from the comcam.

He flipped to Dock three, via a couple of preview screens. Then he flipped through five or six displays.

"There's no-one here, but that V-Blade is in cool-down. It's been on a fast flight in the last hour. I'm guessing it is in from London and that Chantal le Strang was on it."

He flicked to another area of the base. "This is the dock area. There's a route back to the main levels and a holding area for security clearance. I'm guessing that Ms le Strang won't have the right idents to get inside. I expect she is in the arrivals area somewhere."

There was a large and comfortable set of lounges for arrivals and departures and he ran a quick scan through the area. "It will be easy enough to check her ident again," he said and commenced a scan.

Within a few seconds, he had located her spot in the area. She was with several other people. He snapshotted their idents too so that he could start to trace who had arrived.

"This is getting very interesting," He said and started making for the exit. "I'm going over to find out what is happening. I can contain this group in a secure area whilst we decide upon next steps."

He was speaking into a handheld as he left, and Sheri realized he was getting a secure unit to take him to the arrivals lounge. She saw him clip on another level of insignia to his uniform as he walked out.

Bounce

Chantal couldn't believe the last couple of hours. They'd been in London, and then they'd been to Janie's office - she'd never seen inside it before. Somehow Denny and Suze had kitted the three of them plus Charlie with special idents that let them get to Janie's floor.

They'd taken an elevator to a high floor and as they exited Chantal had noticed the V-Blade docked to the side of the building. It looked pretty cool up close. She'd never travelled in one before.

Then Charlie had walked away from the group, with a rather serious expression. Chantal had heard a couple of loud thuds from inside a room and saw it filling with a greenish tinged cloud. There had been a crackling sound and Charlie had re-emerged with Janie, who looked totally horror -struck.

"Chantal," Janie called, as they emerged, "These people are lethal."

Charlie said to Denny, "We won't be able to take Makatomi with us – something crackled out of a wall and took him down. I think he was getting a little carried away with what Janie has been doing. Shew as secured in an e-cordon until Makatomi was fried"

They flipped a few controls and walked into the V-Blade area.

Glass panels opened; they entered the holding area. "Not a typical departure zone," said Charlie.

"This is just for individual execs. I'm pretty sure where we are going there will be a full-blown arrivals reception area."

They entered the V-Blade. It had ten seats in two rows, plus a frontal cockpit zone with two places next to one another.

"Strap in," said Charlie, "I'm going to fly this thing."

"Are you sure you know what you are doing?" asked Janie.

"I've flown these plenty of times, military grade, with Scrive. This is quite a luxury vehicle." responded Charlie. She was plugging in a headset and adjusting some of the controls.

She flipped a few buttons, asked Denny to take co-pilot and started a short countdown sequence.

"I'm going to fly this the military way," she said, "no niceties, so stay buckled in."

She hit the airwave, and the cabin pressure kicked in. Chantal felt as if she was in a bubble and found it difficult to move her arms. There was a juddering, and the lights went blurry. A slight sensation of movement and then a loud suction noise as the pressure re-balanced.

"Something wrong? asked Chantal, "What, more than everything else?" asked Charlie, "No - we've arrived. I said it would be a short flight."

"Where are we?" said Chantal, "I thought we were going to Norway?"

"We just did," replied Charlie, "These things are fast."

Charlie could again see out of the windows, which had some sort of polaglas, which had just resumed vision. It was a different scene. Snow, Hills, Mountains, a huge airport-like lounge ahead.

"Welcome to Bodø Arrivals," said Charlie. "Thanks for riding wingman, Denny."

"Now we've got to figure out how to get through their security. This may take a little time."

Chantal sat looking at the coffee table in front of her, wondering what had happened in the last few minutes, when a man in a uniform approached, smiling.

"Chantal le Strang?" he smiled, "We have been expecting you."

He held out his hand to shake hers and nodded towards the others seated in the area.

"My name is Nathan, please come with me, and I'll escort you through the system."

Chantal looked confused. How could anyone possibly know she was here? Even she didn't know a few moments before.

"I'm a friend of Scrive Mallinson," he added, "I thought you'd be along around now."

The team looked at one another. This was either very good or very, very bad.

Charlie fingered one of the stun grenades in her pocket. Denny looked around for signs of other security people in the background. To his surprise, Nathan appeared to be alone.

"Look," said Nathan, "I'm going to help you, but you will need to trust me. I am taking you all to a secure area and then I will take Chantal to a further area. We know about Scrive and think we know what happened to him. I can't talk about it here, so we will be creating a locked-down space where we can all talk."

Chantal looked around towards the others. "I'll only go if I can take Charlie with me," she said. "Otherwise we won't cooperate."

Nathan looked across. He looked at Charlie and then back to Chantal.

"Sure," he said, "I'm asking the rest of you to stay in one of our VIP lounges for the next hour. Then I'll be back - in person - and make sure it is me - to accompany you through security. Let's go," said Nathan, "I've someone else I would like Chantal to meet."

Sheri had been working on the Trigax whilst Nathan was away meeting Chantal. She'd noticed the firing sequence and the long-range setting which was something they were forbidden to use and also which she didn't even know how to override. They had always been told that the Trigax had been locked down. The thing that interested her was whether the longer range would give better signals to help identify the way that the device worked. Their routine use, which they deployed for stripping out atoms was a slow process, partly because the power range of the device was always set to minimum. It was like trying to listen to great music on a very low volume.

She analysed the outputs from the Trigax. She was interested to see where it was dumping the energy it had created as a result of the terrible thing it had done. If it had vaporised Scrive, then there would be a trace in some form, somewhere.

The amplitude of the deployment gave her a chance to check this. Sure enough, she found a signal from the Trigax. It seemed to have streamed the energy to a further co-ordinate. She tried to locate the position globally. It had a type of arc, like a pebble skittering across a lake, except the bounces seemed to defy normal logic. After the weapon had been fired there was a small arc from Norway to London and then a much larger arc from London to the other side of the world. The energy had bounced to the edge of the Ellipse, to a point almost opposite London on the earth at the extremity of the Ellipse.

Sheri looked more closely. It hadn't stopped at that point. It had bounced again. The next bounce was smaller than the one before, but it seemed to arc over the Tract to an area that shouldn't really exist.

As Sheri was thinking about this, she could feel the knowledge that she was gaining starting to go away again. It was as if she was forgetting something whilst she was still discovering it.

She wrote 'bounce, London, Japan, over Tract, further' on a piece of paper. She found herself picking it up and throwing it away.

She wondered why she was forgetting what she had just discovered.

At that moment Nathan re-entered the apartment, with Chantal and Charlie.

Charlie caught Sheri's movements as they walked into the room. It looked as if Sheri was acting oddly, but she wasn't sure why. Almost as if Sheri was trying to hide something.

"This is Chantal, and her friend Charlie. They have said they will help us. We'll need to tell them what has been happening."

Sheri started to explain what had happened, but it also seemed as if she was forgetting part of the story. Charlie and Chantal listened. Sheri tried harder to explain what had been happening, but part way through said," You know something, I think I'm forgetting some important parts of this. It's as if my memory is being erased while I'm telling you. It has something to do with the Trigax and something I found, but I can't remember what. This is stupid, I only discovered it a few minutes ago. I guess it wasn't important.

"Is this room monitored?" asked Charlie.

"Yes, regular cameras only in here," said Nathan.

"Can we replay them?" asked Charlie, "Just the last hour should be enough."

Nathan picked another small handheld from his bag and tapped some codes. Now he had a wall display showing their current room. They could see they were all standing together, until Nathan started to wind the display backwards.

He sped it up and ran it like a video shuttle, until they saw the points where Sheri had been analysing something and then wrote something on paper. They had been watching the video backwards and so they could see that Sheri had written on paper and then thrown it away. Nathan reached for the paper disposal. He opened the unit and the single sheet was still inside.

"I'm not sure why I did that," said Sheri, "to write something and then immediately throw it away."

Nathan read back the words - "bounce, London, Japan, over Tract, further"

"What does this mean?" he asked.

Sheri shrugged. "It's my writing, but I don't understand it"

"Bounce. Something bounced from London to Japan? and then bounced over the Tract?" suggested Chantal.

"There's some things I discovered with Scrive, and I think we need to talk about them. It will need to be here somewhere where we can't be recorded," said Chantal.

"Okay," said Nathan, "Let's move to the diplomat lounge. We can fine-tune security in there."

311

PART THREE

10

Norway...Pretty didn't do it justice.
I felt like we'd sailed into a world meant for
much larger beings,
a place where gods and monsters roamed
freely."

— *Rick Riordan, The Ship of the Dead*

Diplomat

Nathan showed Charlie and Chantal the way back to the Diplomat Lounge near to where the V-Blade had docked.

Nathan said, "Sheri, I think you'd better introduce yourself more fully."

"I work with the nanotechnology," she started, "We are building the new constructor kits here. - that's the components that the nanobots are built from."

Charlie intervened, "Before Scrive was killed with that ray, or whatever it was, something else happened to him, you know. Someone doctored one of his cartridges, and the tropus contained nanobots which sought to terminate him. There was something strange though, I injected his bloodstream with a big blast of nanoreductives, and it stopped the nanobots in their track. But here's the thing, the nanobot and nanoreductive also spread across to Scrive's spilt blood. It had turned to a blue-black colour but then went back to red after I'd applied the nanoreductives.

"Nanoreductives?" asked Sheri, "That's some trixy stuff you've been handling. Where did you get them?" She looked at Charlie in a whole different way now.

"It's a long story, but I've been places, you know,"

"C-beams glittering in the dark?" joked Chantal.

"Yes, kinda," said Charlie, "I had some time tinkering with simple 'bots, to use as trackers.'

"Okay, let's see if we can work out what happened with the nanocrime first," said Sheri, "I don't mean yours, Charlie, I mean the original cartridge swap."

"I assume Scrive had a standard plexi-cartridge?" asked Sheri, "Not some sort of booster clone?"

"Yes," said Charlie, it was a standard A-port, with all the digital engineering included as well. At least until I smashed it to get my reductive injector into Scrive's system."

"And your nanoreductives were relatively simple devices? I'm not being funny, but I assume you'd not been into heavy-duty nano-engineering?"

"No, that's right. I used basic nanotech using small molecules and proteins. It's what I call my failed experiment."

For the first time Sheri smiled," Yes, we call them nubots - they are a reasonably basic machine type. I guess you ran into problems with them not working and destroying one another?"

"Yes- that was the outcome. I thought of it as 'let the weakness become a strength', and that's how I learned the term "nano-reductive". The ones I built reduced the number of nanobots wherever they were let loose."

Sheri looked at Charlie, "The interesting thing is that they travelled so far and kept working - for example, into the blood spill. That is usually a feature of a more advanced biohybrid. You'd need to be making them in the kind of lab we have here in Biotree."

"Trust me, I only had a cooking lab, I was simply trying to place unique tracers into the cartridges," said Charlie.

"For tracking? That's mega-illegal, you know? Hacking a cartridge and then adding something to it."

"I know," said Charlie, "but I guess that's what has got me here, so you know…"

"It is the same with the boosters," interrupted Chantal," People will swap out their secure and safe A-port plexis for a generic, and then shoot boosted cartridges into their arms."

Sheri nodded, "I guess I get kept in bubble wrap out here at the ATA."

Nathan nodded too," Yes, everything that Charlie and Chantal describe happens around the unsecured edges of the site. Biotree is the stable end of a very ragged set of processes."

"Something I don't understand," said Charlie," Is that Scrive reckoned his thinking was improved after he came off the tropus."

"Yes," said Chantal, "We notice that too when we are selling it. There are two types of boost. Speeder and Kalm. Speeder, like its name implies, jacks the metabolism and certainly the thought processes of the recipient. Kalm is an altogether more mellow experience."

"Nowadays you can usually tell which kind it is by the cartridge markings. Chinese writing is for Kalm and English for Speeder. It didn't used to be the case. They both worked the same originally, more like Kalm."

Sheri nodded, "That would make sense. Biotree changes the formulation every so often. One of the changes was to optimise deployment. Biotree brought in some hackers, and they changed one of the mechanisms inside the nanobots, when we needed the new variant to try to solve the widespread virus in Australia.

"I remember when the packaging changed on the Biotrees. Something about "New, faster acting," said Chantal.

"Originally, Biotree had always built them fail-safe, with a kind of small valve inside. The difference is that the newer bots can replicate; the original design had a so-called Brownian ratchet inside which was like a little cog inside a clock. It made sure the machines could only run up to a certain speed. It was an elegant fail-safe which stopped people's systems becoming overrun with self-replicating nanobots. They ran slower than a body's metabolic speed, which meant the body could handle them without getting overloaded.

That's what seemed to happen with Scrive until I stopped it," said Charlie. His blood was clotting, and I reckon it was black from the incursion of nanobots."

"Yes, the second exploit, which was really to weaponise the nanobots and to force even greater speed. It was an exploitation of the Laplace-Beltrami theorem for narrow escape. Think of it like air escaping from a balloon. It meant the bots could speed excessively and the effect would be like that which happened to Scrive. In battlefield the bots could run riot for a short time.

"And you know something, Makatomi's last business plan? Weaponisation of the nanobots. His "idea of a way to save the company."

"That would explain there being two types out there now," said Chantal.

"Yes, the unconstrained variant from Biotree and the safely managed clone from the Chinese. The old economic model of the cartridges was to ensure that the tropus had a half-life measured in weeks and then you'd need to buy a new one. It lost most of its potency by around week four."

"So," said Charlie, "we've got a desperate Biotree that is building weapons and the Chinese trying to steal a copy?"

"If you want to put it like that," said Sheri.

Meteor disturbances

At the secret Mil-base, Maddox had been busy. He'd been following up on the meteor disturbances that Henderson had described. It meant looking into quite ancient archives, from around 20 years ago. Sure enough, there were a few reports' although none in the mainstream press. He'd called Henderson back to his room at the Pentagon.

"It's as if this thing you describe never happened," he said, "There's more news of B-List celebrities than of a major earth strike by meteors. But there's some information which seems to concur with your account."

"I had the guys track a couple of astronomy sites, including the crowdsourced eurekalert, which did feature the meteors. Yale scientist Denison Olmsted was referenced in an article, from 1833, which talked about a prior meteor shower and the need for tracking. Then much later there's the establishment of the KELT follow-up network with two low resolution small telescopes. These enthusiasts tracked the meteor shower you describe to its collision with earth. One of the amateur reports described them as jellyfish-shaped structures – a dome-shaped body and elaborate trailing tentacles. They are outside of all the military and government networks, which is, I'm thinking, why the records are still available."

"Here's the thing," said Maddox, "According to KELT, the meteors seemed to be flying under guidance, which bears out your story. Not only that, there's another couple of hits in the northern hemisphere, both in areas with low populations. One near Fort Resolution in Canada, the other near Bodø, in Norway."

Henderson smiled, "Fort Resolution is in the North West Territories. It's right in the middle of nowhere; I'm guessing that Bodø is the same?"

Maddox nodded, "Not exactly, Bodø is also the R&D centre for Biotree Industries."

"They're the ones in trouble in the city pages at the moment, aren't they?" asked Henderson.

"Yes, and they seem to be under copyright attack from the Chinese clone manufacturers."

"No smoke without fire. Do you want me to take a look?" asked Henderson.

"I've already cleared your path to take a small detail to Norway," said Maddox.

"Okay," said Henderson, "but I don't want to put heavy Navy boots all over this, the fewer people that know, the better."

"But you won't turn down a V-Blade and some 'accessories'?" asked Maddox.

"Thank you, but I'll still travel light," said Henderson.

Bodø

In Bodø, Nathan was leading Chantal, Charlie, Denny, Suze and Janie back through the corridors from the Diplomatic Lounge. He was arranging for each of them admittance to the facility under his supervision.

Of them all, Nathan noticed that Janie seemed the most shaken up by whatever had happened to them. He took her one side and asked, "Are you okay? - Let's get you checked over."

Nathan spotted the tell-tale signs that Janie had been caught in an e-grid or some other form of containment, by her occasional little tremors. Nathan hated the devices and wondered what kind of idiot would use one on Janie.

"It's been a helluva day," said Janie, she looked over to Chantal, who nodded back.

"I'm going to put Janie through some base screening," said Nathan, "Just for peace of mind. Chantal, would you like to stay with her?"

"No, go, Chantal, please go," said Janie, "I'll be fine."

Chantal realised Janie was keen to be left alone. Chantal could only guess what had happened to her in Makatomi's office, and then what had happened when Charlie arrived, no doubt guns a-blazing.

"It's a massive complex you have here," said Denny,

"Yes, it has its own public transit system around it," explained Nathan.

"The transit runs pretty much around the entire perimeter and crosses over the centre in a couple of places."

"Do you mind if we take a look?" asked Suze.

"I can do better than the transit system for you," said Nathan.

"I'll get one of the jetters, and we can do a quick lap of the facility."

"I expect you'll all want to come along for the experience, so I'll get a ten-seater"

He spoke into a communicator and arranged for a pick-up.

An almost silent craft appeared, and they all climbed aboard.

"This isn't going to be as fast as Charlie's piloting, is it?" asked Chantal.

"No, we'll keep to a low speed and make a pass over the site," said Nathan, "We'll start by heading back to the dock where you landed the V-Blade. Then we'll do a circuit.

The craft crawled forward, and they approached the landing docks. A shimmer on the horizon denoted the approach of another fast craft. It was a military specification V-Blade. United States.

"Looks as if we have visitors," said Nathan. He called a central control number.

"It looks as if they are here for similar reasons to you," he said, half-listening to his communicator.

"Does anyone here know a Bruce Henderson?"

Everyone looked blank.

"Okay, here we go," said Nathan as the jetter made for the runway.

"This is a bit more interesting than flying in a V-Blade," commented Chantal.

"We can see things as they go past."

The pilot banked the jetter over the site. It was immense, with a series of modern blocks and a few scattered outbuildings. In the distance was another long teardrop-shaped structure, surrounded by further fencing.

"What's that place?" asked Suze.

"It's the old NATO stores," replied Nathan. It is almost dormant nowadays and we use Robocarts to gain access.

"Why is that?" asked Suze.

"It still holds dangerous substances, to be honest, I think we were tricked into storing them in the first place. To get this land, Biotree had to do a deal with the USAF to take the store off their hands."

"It was supposed to be a mutually beneficial trade," said Sheri, "Biotree claimed to have the wherewithal to clear up the chemicals."

"Essentially it's a big DND nowadays," said Nathan.

"DND?" queried Chantal.

"Do Not Disturb," answered Charlie," So what happens? You still patrol it then?"

"Yes." answered Nathan, "although there's not a lot to see. It's a tin shed covering a bunch of old stores."

The plane banked, and they could see several small autonomous Robocart units moving around the perimeter of the shed.

"Let's go back," said Nathan, "I think you've got a feel for the site now."

Meet Henderson

The jetter pulled into a landing dock, and Nathan could see the Military V-Blade on which Henderson had arrived. It stood next to the one that the others had flown in on, and the differences were striking. The commercial version was altogether bulkier and had a surprising number of antenna and other external attachments. The sleek dark stealth of the naval unit alongside it, with its missile hangers and guns, illustrated it was built for battlefield deployment.

They walked into the lounges again. They could see Henderson immediately. He was kitted out in combat gear and had a couple of supporting aides at his side.

"Hi Captain Henderson, we're pleased to greet you here in Bodø. I'm Nathan Belanger, head of security on the Bodø base. To be honest, we didn't know you were coming here until you'd more or less arrived."

"Same here, Mr Belanger, the US DoD has sent me for a routine inspection of the ex USAF part of the base."

"You'll know it is the ATA now - that's the Advanced Technology Area, so we have some fairly high security to protect commercial secrets?' asked Nathan.

"Yes, I was briefed on the way, and again in this reception lounge. Now if you don't mind, I'd like to make busy with the inspection?"

Nathan nodded. He could see that Henderson was in a hurry. He was used to random US DoD people passing through the base and stopping to have a look at the US legacy.

"I'll arrange for someone to take you to the store area on a jetter; you'll be able to pick up an h-Rover when you are over there."

"That's great," said Henderson. "I'm hoping to see inside too?"

"Sure," said Nathan, "We'll arrange that when you get over there, although there is not much to see. Unless you like oil drums and pressurised coolant tanks. I'll come along too, if you don't mind."

Charlie interrupted, "I'd like to come along for the ride too, if that's okay? You'll have a spare pilot that way, too"

They made their way back to the flight deck and were soon airborne in a jetter.

This time they took a direct route to the storage facility. They flew over the main hanger area and Charlie could see several HUM-Z rocket planes parked in a tactical formation.

"What are they for?" She asked," Once a NATO base, always a NATO base," said Nathan. "You'd have thought that when Biotree bought the land, the armed forces would move out, but there's some deal with the Americans and in turn with half of Europe about keeping a few planes here. They do circuits and bumps every so often."

The pilot took them high over the store first time and then lower on his landing loop.

Henderson looked as the store block approached. It was huge and traced a path across what could have been the foothills of a mountain range. It was hardly the best position to build a storage facility. Henderson noticed the unusual shape of the facility. Why would anyone make it that shape?

They landed and Henderson, Nathan and Charlie left the jetter and were escorted to the h-Rover. They heard the maglev kick in and gently made their way to an entrance hatch for the storage facility.

"You can pick up the screenings of the interior from here," said the h-Rover pilot. "It is probably quicker than looking all around."

Henderson nodded, looked at the h-Rover's screen and then to a window in the side of the shed.

There were equivalent windows along the facility, each with its own hi-resolution display, showing the interior of the facility.

"With the screens, we can pull up the co-ordinates of any part of the store and know what it contains," explained the pilot, "All from the safety of being outside."

"Okay, said Henderson," can we stop at one of the windows?"

"Sure thing," said the h-Rover driver and they slid to a quiet halt.

"I'm going outside," said Henderson.

He walked towards the nearest screen. It was touch-operated, and he flipped the small control console, which revealed the labelled contents of interior drums.

"I want to see inside this," he said, "Past the screens, to the natural condition."

"Sure" said Nathan. "The pilots usually do the checks from fly-by, but you can walk about if you like. Don't underestimate the distances. "

The three of them left the pilot and moved into the building. Along the edge were a high row of drums and a couple of complicated looking processing machines.

They walked past the drums to a flat fenced area.

There they saw it. Henderson recognised the same glassy dome structure which he'd seen in fly-by when he was in Australia.

"We're leaving," he said.

Secrets

Nathan was on the comms back to Sheri's lab.

"We've found something," he said. "It's vast."

"What is it?" asked Sheri.

"I think it is something that they have been trying to hide, probably Biotree, certainly Makatomi."

The jetter had reached the landing dock again, and Henderson and Nathan climbed out. They made their way back to the ATA research block and found Sheri and the others in Sheri's lab, with some in a second room, separated by a glass wall.

"Denny, Suze and Janie are working through the data cube that Janie retrieved from Makatomi's office, " explained Sheri, "I put them next door in a data room, So, what did you discover?"

"It's like the situation I first saw in Australia, out in the desert, 'said Henderson. "Except there were several of them. Vast glass-like structures, which had splashed themselves across the desert. At the time we thought they were meteor showers and later the Australian situation was erased from records."

"What made you think there was another one here?" asked Sheri.

"I remembered that there were two additional reports of meteors; one in Canada and another in Norway. That's why I came to take a look.

"These stores were established about 20 years ago," said Nathan. "That's long before we created the Biotree facility here."

"Yes, it's the same time that the ones in Australia were identified. And it's around when Australia started to disappear from records."

"Yes, the combination of the Flames and then the virus, Australia was initially cut off from the rest of the world as a quarantine measure. "

"Yes, and then the protection zone was instituted."

Chantal looked confused, "How is it that I don't know any of this?" she asked.

Henderson: "It was news managed at the time. Such a terrible loss of life in Australia and a successive quarantine imposed. They didn't want people going for a look, in case they spread the virus further."

"Could it be something that the domes brought into the continent?"

Charlie said," The strange thing is, the symptoms of the virus sounded very much like the symptoms that Scrive showed when he suffered from that nanobot toxin."

Sheri spoke, "Yes, that's when Biotree started shipping a specific strain of the tropus cartridge to Australia. It was supposed to combat the virus."

Charlie said, thoughtfully, "Unfortunately, it seemed to have some other side effects. I'm wondering if it was accelerated like the one I built, and was, itself the cause of the deaths?"

Sheri announced, "Suze and Denny have been looking through the data walls that Janie retrieved from Makatomi on that cube. They are very fast and efficient - it must be a tracker trait - Their findings show there were several attempts to speed up the nanobots but at the expense of some of the checks and balances.

"I think that is what they are trying to hide," said Sheri, "Biotree tried to stop the original virus with nanobot re-engineering. But they cut corners to make the antidote work more quickly. The hired help didn't have the same stringent processes as we do. That's what I was describing with those accelerants that they introduced.

Charlie asked," You mean that's how they multiplied so quickly and polluted people's bloodstream? Just like the toxin sent to Shrive?"

Sheri looked severe, " According to the papers we got from Makatomi, it was worse. It was not just their bloodstream — everything organic. The 'bots could jump using the 'balloon' reaction, and therefore infect anything else they could process.

"And because the deployment was so rapid, with everyone refitting their tropus cartridges every four weeks, by the time Makatomi's people had discovered it, it was too late, and Australia was destroyed, or people were infected but didn't realise it yet."

Sheri added, "In another four weeks it had run through Australia like a plague - unknown to the authorities the cure was worse than the virus. And it was a time-bomb that they had already set ticking."

"But there were some people, like Crispin and Lucas," said Chantal, "who didn't seem to get affected?"

"in most forms of rapidly spreading virus, there are some people who don't' catch it. Like their systems are somehow immune. Have you ever been on vacation with someone who doesn't get mosquito-bitten?" asked Sheri, "it's one of those mysteries."

"Yes, but this seems to be a double whammy," said Charlie, "First the virus and then the nanobots? Could someone really be immune to both?"

"Yes, it is highly likely," said Sheri, "The original design of the nanobot defences would be to target the virus. It's as likely that the same biological key repelled both types of 'boarder'. Think of it like a key and lock. The virus has to be able to get the lock undone. So does the nanobot to chase after it."

Chantal nodded at this explanation, which seemed to satisfy her.

Charlie said," No wonder Makatomi was trying to keep everything locked down and secret."

"But what do we do about the domes?" asked Nathan, "and what do they have to do with anything?"

"I don't know if you remember, but The Great Leap happened around the time that earth passed through that meteor shower," said Sheri.

"We think that the domes brought some new ideas to the world?" asked Chantel. "It's pretty cosmic!"

Sheri added, "Yes - The Great Leap yielded a range of discoveries. But, in addition, it seems to have been able to manage minds and communications."

"That could account for everyone forgetting about Australia so quickly, it became a case of hidden in plain sight," said Charlie.

"Also hidden on a dangerous land mass, though," said Nathan.

"And protected there too," added Chantal, "Remember what Crispin said about the bracelet and charms?"

"Yes, they've found something about that in the Janie's data walls," answered Sheri,

"Apparently, Makatomi, under Holden's instruction, sanctioned the use of a set of Geostationary Satellites to police the Australian boundaries. They sensed movement across the boundaries like a regular burglar alarm, but then deployed a massive railgun to the targeted area of encroachment. In other words, they were using Trigax as a way to police the boundaries."

"So, the satellites had a separate set of ray guns to support them?" asked Nathan.

"No, the satellites were dual purpose. They contained monitoring equipment and also railguns - the Trigax," said Sheri.

"Tri means three, doesn't it?" asked Chantal, "I'm wondering if there's something else spinning around above our heads?"

"And I'm wondering if the domes brought the intelligence beyond our comprehension?" mused Sheri.

"Take cats. Their intelligence can count to about 4 to 6, to keep track of kittens and they can train their owners to bring food, but give them a larger sum or bigger task, and they don't have a clue. Well, that's what the domes could be like. Delivering raw intelligence beyond our capability to understand. A Great Stumble Forward."

Chantal laughed at this last remark," Cats! can't live with 'em, can't stumble without 'em"

Henderson was engrossed in his thoughts," This is very difficult," he said, "If I tell the US DoD about this, they will come over in huge quantities. Who knows what would happen next? They could try to blow up the domes or at least conduct experiments with them. "

"I was wondering too," said Charlie, "and the effect that the dome has had below the equator."

Sheri looked up, "We can't tell what kind of clock the domes are running. They could be waiting or signalling or even doing something that we can't see. Take the one here. No one has communicated with it, although it seems to have passed on a great deal of intelligence."

Charlie looked at Henderson, "Aren't we forgetting something? Henderson you mentioned that there is another one of these things in Canada. Surely that one hasn't been kept secret as well?"

Henderson replied, "Yes, I've got the location. It is close to a sleepy military base too; Fort Resolution - we do northern early warning from there; I can call them up to see what they know."

Nathan offered a comms link immediately. "I'm not sure where this place is, but we can muster a link."

A picture flipped up on to the Communicator in Sheri's office.

"Hello," said a slightly startled civilian at the other end of the link.

"Hi, we are from Biotree Norway," said Sheri, "We are trying to reach Fort Resolution, Canada. My name is Sheri"

"Well, righty, that's us. My name is Jed Munroe, I'm from Tourist Services here, " came the reply,

"Okay, hello Jed; we're looking into some strange things that have been happening here and wanted to ask a few questions."

"Questions, - you've come to the right place. We are the tourist information. Questions, about what?"

"The meteor that landed some years ago?"

"Ah, that'll be about the dome, then," can the reply.

"We get asked about it every so often. Usually by Americans."

"Well can you tell us anything?"

"Sure, it's a large structure which crash-landed here many years ago." It got buried in snow when it first arrived, and it thaws out during most summers. We've got geysers, volcanoes and lakes around here too, so it is just another one of the occurrences that sometimes tourists want to take a look at. I think there's another one in Russia somewhere. They've also got a big meteor hole over there, you know. Tunguska, I think the place is called. Come to think of it there's another one in Yulara, but I can't remember where that is; we've always had a picture of it hanging on the wall here."

"Has the meteor ever 'done' anything?" asked Sheri.

"What, the dome? No, it seems to be completely dormant. With the snow cover and thawing, most of the time it looks like a big black heap of mine extraction or something. You know this used to be lead mines around here, don't you?"

Sheri had been dialling up Fort Resolution on her search engine and it showed a snowy terrain with pictures of a runway and old mining equipment.

"Yes, we can see the pictures of the mine,"

"The mine closed many years ago, but not before we'd also found a few dinosaur relics. They are in the museum. You know, we don't get so many visitors out here though, it's a lot less well known than what the Americans did with that Area 51. I said we should call it Area 52 around here."

"Well thank you for that information, you have been most helpful," said Nathan, I wish you a good day,"

"Well, thanks, I think we are in for a spot of snow now, skies have turned real dark. You have a great day, now" said Jed.

Regroup

"Okay, it's time to regroup," said Sheri, "Things have been moving fast, and we need to take stock."

She led Nathan, Charlie and Chantal into the glass-partitioned office at the back of the lab, where Denny, Suze and Janie had been working their way through the data walls.

"What do we have?" asked Nathan.

Suze replied, "Unlucky Australia was first ablaze and then virus-riddled. Makatomi's Biotree were making antivirus nanobots for the Australian market, which didn't work as planned. The result was unpleasant and wholesale deaths in Australia."

As she spoke, a bullet list appeared on the screen, with her edited highlights.

Charlie added, "Deaths which, by all accounts, were covered up by a manipulated media."

Denny added, "We've also got crash landing meteors across the globe including Australia, Bodø here, Canada and the deserts in the USA."

Chantal mentions, "A cordon over Australia, with a menacing guard system, implemented by Biotree."

"Everyone forgetting about Australia like it didn't exist," added Chantal.

"Except for people who had been there and have somehow got out," added Henderson.

"Then we had the Chinese copying the nanobots but not applying the accelerant technology," added Suze.

"And not forgetting the Leap in knowledge following the arrival of the domes," added Nathan.

"And we've had strange lapses in communications and in memory," said Sheri.

"And the US military showing an interest," added Henderson.

There was a hush. They all looked towards Henderson. "You know I'm retired?" he asked, "They only called me back because I still remembered Australia. It seems that people who lived there always remember it. It's everyone else that has forgotten."

Then they all looked to the long list that had appeared on Sheri's meeting room wall.

"Time for a plan?" said Sheri.

11

"Tell me, what is it you plan to do with your
one wild and precious life?"

-The Summer Day, Mary Oliver

Wall chart

Sheri's office continued to make the sounds of a well-kitted technology environment. Sheri was pre-occupied. She'd drawn a diagram on the wall.

"It pieces together the time-line," she said.

She had written:

- The A-port cartridge delivery systems;
- the anti-virals;
- Makatomi's warped business model;
- The captive market;
- Accelerants, military capabilities;
- The domes arrive;
- Australia is destroyed and a deadly protection ring established.

Charlie and Janie looked at Sheri's chart.

"I think there's something wrong," Charlie said.

"I think the domes arrived sooner. Before the virus. Before the anti-viral. "

"Yes," said Nathan, "That would make more sense. The domes spread a virus across Australia? Accidentally?"

Charlie said, "But suppose the domes knew they had done this?"

"Maybe that accounts for the Great Leap? Sharing information to help us design an antivirus?" said Denny.

Suze interrupted, "That's a great thought. But how could the information have been spread?"

"There are more papers from Makatomi on that cube that I stole," answered Janie.

"Yes, there's something about Makatomi getting information from someone called Holden. It implied Holden had a team of scientists at work in the background,"

"Maybe we should get a meeting with Holden," said Nathan. "I can check him out in the company directory."

"I've never heard of him until today," said Sheri. "If he runs a group of scientists, then I thought I'd have at least heard his name."

"And how did the information about the protection ring around Australia stay out of the news?" asked Chantal, "There's some weird stuff around all of this."

Arusen

Arusen had been summoned to Holden's floor.

He'd realised that something was wrong with Makatomi and that Holden did not seem pleased.

"What happened to Makatomi?" He asked.

"There was a scuffle with one of the recent visitors. Makatomi was trying to hold captive a base visitor."

"Is Makatomi all right?

"No, he was terminated, Mr Arusen, you will need to take over the loose ends now," said Holden.

Arusen was annoyed that Holden could not even appear in front of him for this important meeting.

"What are the loose ends?" asked Arusen, who felt he had also not been fully briefed.

"Now that we have several visitors to the base, we need to be particularly careful. The plan to terminate

Shrive worked and was much better than Makatomi's half-hearted tropus attack."

Holden continued, "A side effect of the first attack failing is that we now have an inconvenient number of followers, including the US Military."

"We must shut down the investigation, stop them from finding out any more information or making any more connections," said Holden, "Maybe re-energising the dome will provide some new powers, like the first time."

Holden referred to the first time the dome had activated. It had produced a data cube of instructions to build many high-technology devices.

Arusen had examined the datacube with Makatomi's science team. There was the new antiviral, instructions for building better transits, a guard rail system and various communication jammers. With Makatomi's scientists they had built some of the devices.

Makatomi had been surprised at how many of the devices had been commercial successes. He'd risen to a well-known status and magazines wanted him for their covers.

The great disaster had been the antiviral. Makatomi had tampered with the instructions. He'd used a hired-in hacker team to build the nanobot delivery system. The bots were faster than the blueprints expected and didn't have the usual fail-safe included. They also used a pressure technique to be able to jump from one environment to another. This was the so-called narrow escape exploit and meant the bots could magnify the weak molecular forces to jump over large distances.

That had been a great disaster. Makatomi's people played around with the recipe provided and cooked a horrendous result. Unfortunately, the tropus had been consumed by all of Australia and necessitated the application of the all-enveloping bracelet and charms. A self-policing boundary which fired Trigax weapons from space, vaporising anything that tried to cross.

Arusen was already in deep but wondered what kind of monster Holden was, and the way he had run Makatomi. He was about to find out.

Additionally, Holden had become completely anonymous and wanted everything to appear in Makatomi's name. Arusen had a worried feeling that he was about to become the next Makatomi.

Ominously, Holden added, "It's quite simple, we will need to build a trap. Offer them something. And then take everything back."

In Sheri's lab, Henderson was grappling with a problem. How much of what he had seen should he report back to Maddox? If he fed the entire story, there would be a massive increase in activity at Biotree when the full might of the Americans appeared, under the guise of NATO.

If he didn't say anything, Maddox would become suspicious and probably send a further team along to take a look. Maddox had sent aides to shadow him, in any case.

Henderson was worrying about the other links that had been reported to Maddox from Captain Taylor's surveillance station. They had reports of meteor activity which included both suppliers of the tropus. Biotree, USA and Norway and SuzGene, based out of China.

"You know what," said Chantel, "We should chase down the Chinese end of this. It's the only way to balance the supply lines. On the street we get as much sife tropus with a Chinese origin as we do from Biotree nowadays.

Suze nodded agreement, "And it was the Chinese that we were probing as part of the original Makatomi mission."

"Yes," said Charlie, "Scrive was certainly tracking the Chinese, We'll need to be careful though. The diplomatic ripples need to be managed, which would keep things quiet - or at least slow-paced.

We've got Scrive's original cyber-attack, not the Chinese in any case," said Suze, "I'm sure he created a few ripples when he ran those probes."

"I think he did more than that," chipped in Charlie, "he will have dropped some probes into the Chinese systems."

"I knew it," said Denny, "I thought that probe attack was very short-lived. Just enough time to drop something into the Chinese system."

"Yes, and they probably have not spotted it yet, because we haven't tried to use it for anything."

"Well now is the time for a wake-up call," said Charlie. "We can use it to tip the scales somewhat."

"What are you thinking?" asked Nathan,

"Well, we need something noteworthy that will draw people into the open," said Charlie.

"How about the nanobot acceleration exploit?" asked Sheri.

"That would be playing with fire," said Charlie, "Remember the damage it has already created in Australia."

"Or, what about if we leak one of the Makatomi papers?" asked Janie. We could show the Chinese that we know what happened. That should cool down their enthusiasm to copy the stolen bots."

"That's a good idea," said Nathan, "We can contrive a situation where we allow them to accidentally get access to a relevant paper that spells out the terrible things that can happen."

"Maybe we should adapt it first?" Said Charlie, "Remove the horrendous sections, so that they can see that it works but have some of the 'how' missing.

Sheri looked at the documents online, from the data wall downloaded from Janie's cube.

Here's what we'll do. I can rewrite this one to show a way to make nanobots faster, but incapable of replication. That should be enough to attract their attention.

It was getting dark in Bodø.

"I'm going to hit the friendly skies again," said Charlie. "I'm taking one of the 'blades back to London. Who is coming? We can re-unite with our various sets of equipment.

Denny said, "Suze and I will be coming, and I'll ride shotgun again if you like; I suggest that Chantel and Janie come back too - after all, it is their home turf. Henderson had best stay here with the second 'Blade. In case we need some sort of military backup."

"It'll also be more reassuring for my friends in Washington if they see that the Marine V-Blade is still in Norway, on a NATO base. Otherwise, they might start to get twitchy," said Henderson.

"That leaves Sheri and me, said Nathan, "At least we are also in our home surroundings at the moment. We have the best access to lab systems and security from here, too."

"And together we are sitting on one of the domes," said Henderson.

"Okay, "said Sheri, "We'll need to repackage the findings to make our story plausible and legitimate to the Chinese. I can do that."

"Won't you need my failed experiment?" asked Charlie, "I have the injector gadget right here." She rummaged into her rucksack and pulled out the small device that had earlier saved Scrive.

"Thanks, but it's not needed," answered Sheri, "Rest assured that I've made plenty of that kind of 'bot myself over the years, although I must admit I've never made a deployment pack as small as that."

Charlie looked pleased, "Minimum carry weight," she answered, "Maximum impact with minimum effort."

"That's great," said Sheri, "I think I will take a look at the device after all, and we are going to need to further optimise the 'bots in any case."

"I want to add to them the accelerant effect, created by removing that Brownian brake. I think you might have achieved it by accident, but I can make sure we have it incorporated."

Charlie nodded in agreement. If her gadget could be made any better by a nanoscientist, then she'd be pleased to accept the changes.

"Then we'll need to reach out to the Chinese," said Charlie, "We can do this from an embassy."

"Yes, provide the paper as proof of our integrity," answered Sheri.

"What about in London?" asked Charlie, "Although neither of us is a British national? I'm American, and you are Canadian?"

"But I'm British," said Chantal. They all looked at one another.

"I thought your name was Chantal le Strang?" queried Charlie.

"Well, it is," said Chantal, "as well as Daisy Stone, my parents were free-spirited hippy types, and I changed my name when I moved away. I'm still Daisy in the passport. Chantal, in French, originates from stony and people think the name is strange. There we are. Chantal le Strang,"

She looked uncharacteristically sheepish, "and now you are about to see 'Daisy' become a business lady! I need embassy clothes and makeup."

"In for the long haul, then?" joked Charlie.

"Okay - but now we've got someone who can easily apply for a Chinese Visa in London, and can use the visit to drop off the paper," said Charlie, "You are okay about this, Chantal?"

Chantal nodded, "Well, compared with what we've been doing, I don't think this can be classed as dangerous! Not even the shopping."

Charlie and Sheri looked over to Chantal, still clothed like a Manga heroine.

"Just leave me a while," said Chantal, "From around Scrive's place I can easily go along to Peter Jones. They will soon fix me up with some proper 'business lady' clothes."

Charlie and Sheri smiled.

"Okay," said Sheri, "I'm going to be working on the paper now, using a combination of my lab's work and some of Charlie's innovations."

"And I'm going along to check the V-Blades," said Charlie," I might bring their systems up to date too like when Scrive and I used to fly them; we had a few tactical mods. Then I'm taking Makatomi's one back to England, to as close to Scrive's apartment as I can land it.

Inscrutable

Charlie decided against a spectacular landing of the V-Blade in Battersea Park, next to the Zen Temple. Instead, she hawed it across to the Battersea landing decks where it arrived as an exotic beast next to the scrappy executive copters, h-Rovers and other civilian planes.

"We can grab a black cab from her and be over to Scrive's apartment complex in no time," said Chantal.

Charlie didn't let on that she was staying in the adjacent hotel, by the side of the Power Station complex.

"I doubt Scrive would have minded us using the apartment as a base?" asked Denny.

"No, he'd be thrilled that you are following through on his mission, and I'm sure hopes you find his killer," answered Charlie.

"I'll be going back with Janie to our flat, said Chantal. Janie smiled; the effects of the e-grid had just about worn off now, although she still had the vision of the short firefight between Charlie and Makatomi in her head.

"See you all tomorrow," said Charlie. "3pm at Scrive's apartment."

...

Suze and Denny had the spare key fob to Scrive's Apartment. They marvelled at his collection of tracker hardware, some of which they had never seen before.

"Some of this European kit is pretty good," said Suze to Denny, as he switched on a small aerial drone unit, which flew a tiny dart the size of a dragonfly.

"Yeah, but it all needs special plugs and adapters to work with our gear, and Europe seems to have different standards in every country, answered Denny, "it's a bit of a nightmare."

The door phone rang, and Suze answered it. "I'm sorry I'm a bit early, said Charlie, "I've still got my keys, so I'll come on in."

Charlie let herself into the apartment. She could tell that Denny and Suze had been checking out some of Scrive's kit. She could see the dragonfly drone on the table.

"There's another drone in Scrive's collection," she said brightly, "it's called a pigeon. It's slightly bigger but with an enormous range. Give it some GPS co-ordinates anywhere and it'll fly there and then circle the area erratically. It'll send back a clean A/V feed too and is almost undetectable."

"It sounds brilliant, but the FAA wouldn't allow it in the USA," said Denny, "I'm surprised you allow it in Europe?"

"I'm not sure it is fully legal, actually," said Charlie, "but I'm not surprised that Shrive has one."

"Anyhow, I've been looking for the Chinese Embassy," said Charlie, "The Chinese have places all over London, and they are building out even more in the east of the city now."

"Their main consular services are at the Embassy in Portland Place. That's where we'll need to visit, along with Chantal - er - Daisy."

The entry phone sounded.

"Hiya, troops!" It was Chantal.

Moments later the doorbell rang and in marched Chantal, with Janie.

There was an intake of breath from the others.

"Wow!" said Suze, "you really look the part, heck you could be a boss's boss!"

Charlie grinned approval.

Chantal had adjusted her appearance to that of a fashionable city worker. Grey suit, small attaché case, black heels and the merest hint of diamond jewellery.

"Glad you like it!" she smiled, "I think my credit card company will like it too. I got myself one of those personal shoppers in Peter Jones. They were more than happy to assist!"

She flashed a tiny sparkling brooch towards them. A green dragon with purple detailing. "It's Michelle Ong," she said, "A playful dragon - I couldn't resist!"

"Let's hope they can't resist at the Chinese Embassy!" said Charlie.

"We've dialled up Sheri from Norway," said Denny.

"Hi everyone...Wow, Chantal, you look - er - stunning - I nearly didn't recognise you. Hi Janie, I hope you've recovered from yesterday's ordeal! Nathan was telling me about those e-grids - it sounds terrifying."

"Look - I've written the paper," said Sheri," It's a mashup of the one I wrote previously, but I've added in some things about the nanobot destruction and the specialised equipment - which is really Charlie's idea."

"Failed experiment," chipped in Charlie.

"I also added in some facts and figures from the material that Janie acquired. Just enough to whet their appetites.

"I've also looked at where we need to visit in China," said Sheri," That can be part of the request to the embassy." After all, they won't want to turn down business, and we can make it look as if it is officially from Biotree."

"We'll need to go Hangzhou, which is the second IT location outside of Beijing. It is where most of the IT specialists work and is the base city for several large IT specialist companies. It works differently in China, where the companies are there to provide some other service and then hire in IT people to make it all work."

I'm glad you are saying 'WE' said Charlie, "It'll make so much more sense to have you along for the visit, as well as Chantal, of course."

"Did you work out who is providing the cloned nanobots?" asked Charlie.

"Yes, I cannot be sure, but I think it is a firm called SuzGene. They perform nanobot research, provide medical solutions and have a vast base much more extensive than Biotree Norway, in Hangzhou.

"They work in protein domain dynamics and with ribosome biological machines, so have all the right credentials."

"So, if we turn up at the embassy ostensibly to apply for a visa, but actually to tell them about the research paper, there's a strong chance that they will bite?" asked Charlie.

"I think with the wonderful Daisy Businesswoman of the year turning up with a Chinese dragon brooch and an exciting paper about nanotechnology, they should be biting off our hands," smiled Charlie.

Chantal looked concerned, "But what if they start to ask me anything about the paper?" she asked," What can I say?"

"We'll rehearse this, but what you'll need to say is that all three of us require access to SuzGene in Hangzhou," said Sheri.

"Okay, but you'll have to tell me what the paper is about. What it means," asked Chantal.

"I've written a handy one-page summary on the front as well - I'm assuming that the people you meet in the embassy will be similarly lacking in specialist knowledge about this. By the time we are through today, I think you will sound like an expert!" said Sheri, grinning through the screen towards Chantal.

Sheri continued to brief Chantal over the link. Chantal seemed to be understanding enough for the embassy meeting. By Sheri describing everything via analogies, it meant Chantal could break down the description she would need to supply to the embassy.

Charlie decided to call Henderson in Norway, on an operational matter.

"We've got everything positioned. There's a way to approach the embassy and a story to tell them. We have also reworked the nanoreductive device, with plenty of input from Sheri.

"The thing is, I want to test it. It would be a shame if the Chinese tested it and discovered it didn't work. Can we set up a test in Bodø?"

Sheri paused from her briefing to Chantal as she overheard Charlie's request to Henderson, "We should have everything we need for a test," she said.

"We can access the dome, with Nathan's help. And we can inject the nanobots into one of the access lines to the dome. All of that can be done without attracting attention. In fact, we should not tell anyone else what we are planning."

Henderson nodded agreement. He'd kept everything from the US Department of Defense up to now; another 24 hours should not make any difference.

"How will you make this work?" asked Henderson.

"You will need to operate the storage facility console for me," answered Sheri, "Nathan should be able to rig up a comms link."

Nathan had created the necessary links for Sheri to use.

"I can't send you the code over the link to Scrive's apartment- it's too big. I'll have to send it via the German cloud system we used earlier. You can then load it directly into one of our nanoinjectors"

The blue monitoring light from Holden's surveillance system blinked again as Sheri sent the code across.

"Okay, we have it, said Nathan, "I've moved it to a stand-alone device," he said. "'There was something odd about it stored on one of the lab's main systems. It was as if something was probing it, or even trying to delete it."

"I'll try to give you a camtran as we try to load it, "he said.

They could see that he was walking briskly with Henderson towards one of the h-Rovers.

"Forget the V-Blades for this flight, he said, we'll jump-jet with a Levitor to the site and then use the h-Rover for the last kilometre."

As the h-Rover drove into the Levitor, Sheri said, "Remember, the 'bots have got that speedup hack included, you know, the one that is not supposed to be very safe!"

Nathan nodded and checked with Henderson. "We might need a hasty retreat from the site," he said.

Henderson said," Yes, that's why wanted us to come along in the Levitor. As long as we can get back to it, we can move very fast to any one of a number of preprogramed co-ordinates. These nanobots are not like straightforward cyber warfare, where everything is digital. We've actually got to tip the starter elements of the nanobots into the system."

The Leviton arrived, and the h-Rover was deployed outside. It drove the remaining short distance to the dome at high speed.

"Okay, this is us," said Henderson, looking towards Nathan. He climbed from the h-Rover and moved towards the dome. He could see the access panel as Nathan had described it. It was as simple as recharging an electric vehicle. He fired the nanobots into the dome from the handheld injector.

At first, all he could hear was the environmental controls, humming around the site. Then this background buzz stopped. Henderson was already on his way back to the h-Rover. As he climbed in through the access port, he saw the troubled face of Nathan.

"What's the matter?" he asked.

"I don't know," answered Nathan, "but we should get out of here."

A silence had descended, and then he could feel a slight vibration.

Nathan was manoeuvring the h-Rover back onto the Levitor.

"Hold on," Nathan called as the Levitor made its way through the air.

Then he felt a wave, a hard, jarring thunder and the craft was shaken in the air.

The comms crackled, and he heard a distant radio station break though. Something he hadn't heard for years. He felt his mind clear, like someone had just freed a whole series of memories, some of which were quite uncomfortable.

He looked forward towards the shed containing the dome. It was moving. More than that, the roof was collapsing inwards.

"The dome is shrinking," said Henderson.

"It must be the 'bots said Nathan, "They are having a similar effect here to the one that affected Scrive."

"Yes, except it is making the domes smaller,"

"And freeing the airwaves."

There was a shudder. The roof fell away. Nathan looked towards Henderson. "Sheri - Are you getting his?"

Sheri's comms crackled, "Yes, everything, and it has suddenly started coming through clearer too."

The Levitor arrived back at the main ATA Lab block. The h-Rover automatically started to unload and rolled forwards. Nathan clicked the ATA local comms.

"We'll be back at Sheri's lab in a few minutes," he said.

"The Charlie and Sheri modifications work. The dome has kinda imploded. It may sound strange, but we seem to be getting some of our memories back. I think you'll need those Chinese visas."

"Okay, we cleared it and have made it back," said Nathan, "But I'm worried now about overall site integrity. Our efforts seem to have created massive instability in the environment. Something like an earthquake."

Henderson nodded agreement, "I'm going to have to tell them at the DoD now," he grimaced," Things could get ugly."

Nathan looked towards the skyline, in the direction of the large shed. He could see the atmosphere trembling, like a heat haze.

"I'm getting break-through memories too," he said," Like a pressure that's been on my mind is lifting. I didn't even know that the pressure was there, but now it is going, I'm aware that there was something."

"Me too," said Suze, "I'm starting to remember things from before the Great Leap. My parents, where I lived as a child, heck - even Scotty, my little dog."

Denny nodded. It was clear that similar thoughts were running through his mind, "I'm not even sure why I couldn't remember this stuff," he said, "but now it is coming back to me, clear as day."

Henderson commented, "I can only assume it is something to do with the dome. That it was somehow suppressing memories. After all, we can surmise that the domes brought the Great Leap to us, but it must be that they also took something away?"

Suze asked, "Yes, but why would they want to do that? Delete some things and add others."

"Control," said Henderson, "Control and Power; the domes have been able to use some kind of influence on all of us, but now we know about it we can stop it from working."

"Like mind control?" asked Suze, "Although it sounds a little far-fetched."

"Far-fetched it might be, but I think that is what happened," said Nathan.

"The nano-reduction has worked, and the dome is less powerful," answered Henderson.

"Yes, but this is just one of many domes spread around the earth. We have only tilted events around this copy," continued Suze, "Next we need to deliver the payload to the other sites."

Suze reached for the comms link on the console.

Before she could flip it, a voice sounded in the lab.

"This is Holden. We have been monitoring you for the last few days. Your resistance to our waves has increased, but it is insufficient to destroy anything else. Surrender now and we will re-instate our previous operational parameters.

Suze breathed to Nathan, "Prepare a V-Blade. We need to be out of here. Nathan nodded and took Henderson along, "We need the V-Blade. Unfortunately, we don't have a combat pilot. Charlie is in London."

Henderson stepped forward. "I've flown these things before, Nothing as exotic as the consumer variant, but a few less gaudy warhorses.

They all piled into the V-Blade.

Henderson flicked on the main console.

A new welcome screen appeared. It was three release levels higher than the one Henderson had seen before.

Henderson looked around, amazed, "Wow, Charlie doesn't mess around. This machine has been super-modified. A closely guarded secret was that the military could buy these things for several different price points. They all looked the same but had different capabilities. We used to joke that upgrades involved removing a speed-slug card and throwing it away."

Nathan said, "Yes, she'd fixed up that other V-Blade, Makatomi's executive gin-palace; she said she'd given it the same capabilities as a war-machine."

Henderson flipped a couple of small switches. Nothing happened.

"Okay, he said, Charlie really did rethread the core logic on this machine,

He pushed down on the electrabrake.

"It's got the ground control interlock," said Henderson, "That normally only comes on the meanest fighter versions, to keep them dynamically tethered in choppy conditions."

He flipped the switches again while holding down a small green button.

There was a roar.

"Wow," he said, "Charlie doesn't mess around,"

"This has got to be the gutsiest V-Blade I've ever ridden. Thanks, Charlie."

"Check your pressure suits"

"4-3-2-1."

There was a deep roar, and the horizon changed.

Nathan thought he heard Holden speaking as Henderson booted the machine into an outer earth orbit.

Once again there was a sound wave and a crack which denoted the V-Blade had arrived.

"Okay, so where are we this time? Asked Suze.

"I don't know," said Henderson. The co-ordinates were set for London, close to where Charlie landed the other V-Blade.

"It's damn Holden again, the system has been acquired by Holden, and it has taken us to a different co-ordinate.

"We appear to be inside one of the domes. In China.

"But why would Holden do that?" Asked Suze.

"Don't you see? Its stalemate. Standoff. We are inside the dome. We have the power to destroy it, but Holden has put us in harm's way so that we'll be destroyed at the same time we try to wreck the dome.

Charlie, Chantal and Sheri were unaware of the latest events as they headed for China. They were to set course for Hangzhou, to the headquarters of SuzGene.

They had left Denny and Suze at Scrive's apartment as an insurance policy against unexpected events. The skills of Suze and Denny at tracking should ensure that the two V-Blades were clearly visible on their course around the planet.

"You'll need pressure suits, said Charlie as Chantal and Sheri boarded the V-Blade. I've changed some of the avionics logic. A few hacks applied to optimise the plane and its handling. It will take this V-Blade past the capability of the military one that Henderson was using.

"How do you now about this?" said Sheri, slightly concerned that she was about to take a flight on a hacked plane.

"Scrive and I used to run these planes all the time. We knew about their best optimisations and usually varied the standard pack to provide the updates. Lockheed Martin are extra cautious about this; we knew about the super-redundant fly by wire that was incorporated and then applied - I suppose you could call them 'cheats' to make the whole experience more gnarly.

"In a combat situation being able to apply an airbrake, or to sit on the tail, dump fuel or to hyper jump into orbit are all useful additional handling characteristics.

"The manufacturers would not put them in for a couple of reasons. 1) it was too difficult to fly with all of the extra options. 2) the plane could become unstable under certain operating conditions.

"Neither of these apply to me. I've flown these things for thousands of hours. And you know what? Henderson will be in for a surprise when he picks up his milcim variant. I've made the same mods. It'll keep up with this one now! I've done what Scrive and I would do in the past. Linked the FBW - fly by wire systems together, so that the planes can talk to one another in fast manoeuvres.

I've also made it easy for Suze and Denny to track us, I gave them a secret identity code for each the V-Blades which makes the tracing easy.

"Ladies, are you all ready? Pressure-suits, Check, Buckles? check, blam-a-lam."

Charlie flipped a small console control, pressed a green button and the V-Blade shuddered. There was a crack sound and the room blurred like a swirled liquid.

Chantal looked around, wondering what the problem was.

"Ladies, prepare to disembark, we are in China," announced Charlie.

"Huh? Asked Chantal. Are you sure?

"Yes, the readout says we are in downtown Hangzhou. We should be on top of the SuzGene corporate headquarters."

"Okay, we'd better disembark. How is it even possible to land something like this on the roof unannounced?"

"Rest assured we have the right clearances, said Charlie. "That's what you were doing 'Daisy' when you were at the embassy -it should say somewhere who we are due to meet- here we are: Bai Tan Chungli.

They walked towards the landing reception area. It looked like any regular airport landing zone.

"Ah Ms Daisy Stone, Welcome. And Welcome also to your two fellow travellers. Please can you all sign in. We'll need to take a few basic security scans and to issue your visitor passes."

They looked at one another. This was going well. Daisy had been ultra-efficient inside the Chinese Embassy.

"And Ms Charlie and Dr Sheri; you appear to be the scientists on this list. I will find Dr Bai Tan Chungli. He is expecting you."

They were escorted into a waiting area resembling the VIP reception back in Bodø.

"It's amazing how well these structures get copied," mused Sheri, "If it weren't for the Chinese writing everywhere, I'd almost think I was back in Norway."

"Dr Bai Tan Chungli is on his way, please take a seat and maybe some refreshment."

Chantal started to understand about needing time for the soul to catch up with the body on the hyper shot flights. She had a slight sensation that everything was shaking when she walked around. She'd heard of flight-jags, but this was the first time she'd experienced it.

"Don't fret, it is nothing new. In the olden days' sailors would need time to get their sea-legs" smiled Charlie," Here, you can pop one of these if you like,"

Chantal shook her head. "I'll ride it out," she said, I'm not sure I'm built to take your kind of shock waves, Charlie."

Sheri had been on multiple V-Blades and thought she was used to the effects. She had to quietly admit that a flight with Charlie was like no other.

A small group of people appeared in the reception area. A bespectacled man in a light blue blazer stepped forward.

"Ms Daisy Stone?" he asked, looking at Sheri.

"No, that's Ms Daisy Stone, I'm Dr Sheri Bouchard."

"And I'm Ms Charlie Manners," said Charlie stepping forward.

They all shook hands and Chantal made a small curtsey.

There was a small amount of giggling from the entourage. Sheri realised that Bai Tan Chungli possibly didn't get this amount of attention from Western women on a day-to-day basis.

"I am pleased to meet you," he said," Please can we go to my offices. We can eat and then we can talk about your engineering?"

Chantal looked quizzically at the others. Eat? Was there time.

"We will be honoured to eat before discussing these important matters," said Sheri.

Bai Tan Chungli showed them into a private dining area.

"This is our special entertaining area, for business lunches," he said, "would you like to order some food?"

"I would be honoured if you would order for us, "answered Sheri.

"Thank you," I will suggest the soup today, then our special mantou, with some fish, and some cai (that is vegetable).

"That sounds wonderful, "answered Sheri.

Chantal and Charlie looked impressed, neither could remember when they had last had anything to eat.

The entourage of Bai Tan Chungli also sat down. There were seven representatives from SuzGene and three from Biotree.

Sheri signalled to the others, "We'll enjoy this meal together before we discuss any business. Here is my business card. My friends are without cards today. We are printing new ones because we changed buildings recently."

The exchange of Sheri's card gave a chance for the other six people to show their hand, and each of them presented their card quite formally. Sheri decided that there was an element of 'meet the westerner' training occurring, because she was only sure that three of the party spoke English.

They ate the excesses of soup, buns, fish, vegetable and rice, and Sheri was impressed at Chantal's proficiency with chopsticks.

"That was delicious," Chantal exclaimed, and everyone around the table grinned.

"Now we can talk about your paper," said Bai Tan Chungli, "We were sent a copy by the London Chinese Embassy. "Of course, we re-engineered our system completely - I don't think you are suggesting we have copied Biotree?"

"No, let us put that aspect behind us," said Sheri, "What we want to be certain about is that you know what has been happening with the nanobot environments?"

Bai Tan Chungli continued, "We knew that you removed the braking system from the nanobots that Biotree produce. We thought that was a contributory factor towards the disruptions in Australia."

He added, "We would not build our versions without the safety checks and balances. A Brownian brake to slow the machines down to metabolic rates."

"We have now discovered something else," ventured Sheri, "We think the nanobots are linked to the Great Leap, which was created with the arrival of the meteor domes."

"We are speaking frankly?" asked Bai Tan Chungli.

"Yes, we think that you have had a landing of a dome somewhere in China and that it was the dome that has given you the great Leap powers?"

"You know Great Leap has a different meaning in China?" said Bai Tan Chungli.

"Yes," interrupted Chantal, "The campaign to transform the country from a farming economy into a <u>communist society</u> through the formation of <u>people's communes</u>."

"Precisely," said Bai Tan Chungli.

"We have another phrase: Introducing the science of tomorrow, which we use for the ideas that were developed over the last 20 years."

"Sometimes you westerners don't know so much about The Great Leap here in China. You know that it was an economic disaster?" asked Bai Tan Chungli.

Chantal interrupted, "Yes - That enormous amounts of investment produced only modest increases in production or none at all?"

"I studied the Chinese system as part of my Eastern Studies education," said Chantal, "Chairman Mao Zedong launched the campaign to transform the country from an agrarian economy into a communist society through the formation of people's communes."

"There was some great sadness created as a result of the communes and the grain taxes imposed," said Chantal, " I think it was an unhappy time for many families."

Bai Tan Chungli nodded, "We work here with the science of tomorrow, but with it comes great responsibility."

Sheri continued, "That's what we want to tell you about. We are worried that the science of tomorrow will create a similar effect. We have seen problems with it in Europe and are trying to disable the domes, which we think have created a massive mind control of the populous. This isn't like routine propaganda; to be honest, we don't properly understand it."

Sheri said, "The Great Leap - er - the science of tomorrow has been using the nanoengineering to spread a system across mankind. We think that the combined efforts of two unwitting principle players are achieving this. That is Biotree and SuzGene."

"There is a game to use the tropus as a cash cow now. We understand that. A four-week cycle to refresh the cartridges represents a lot of cashflow. But we cannot see the financial advantage to either of us in continuing to proliferate the nano-engineering. We have caught a dragon by the tail. It can easily turn to harm us."

Sheri inwardly imagined the "Squee!" from Chantal at getting her dragon mentioned in the conversation.

Sheri continued, "But, there could be a benefit to releasing an antidote - if you will- to the formulas we have been creating. That is simply to send in a nano-reductive that will counteract the nanobots in current circulation. Between you and us we control the entire supply of the tropus. We also know that a nano reductive that we have devised can stop the continuation of the spread of nanobots.

We have already tried it in Norway at the Advanced Technology Area and seen the release of antidote has caused the meteor dome in Norway to collapse, with a surprising resultant increase in comms and a curious rediscovery of memories.

We'd like to discuss with you the way that we could distribute this across the Chinese market, and we think the rest of the world through the combined efforts from Biotree and SuzGene.

Bai Tan Chungli paused. Sheri was aware that one of his team had been proving a simultaneous translation of what had been discussed to the other members of the SuzGene team.

"This is a lot to take in," answered Bai Tan Chungli, "I suggest we meet again tomorrow to continue this discussion. Let us say 3pm. Our company has booked you accommodation in West Lake."

He bowed graciously. Charlie noticed a blue light in the corner of the meeting room appeared to flicker.

Mere ground speed

"It almost seems a novelty to be travelling at ground speed," said Chantal as they made their way to the hotel.

"West Lake? That's quite a fancy area, I think," said Charlie, "And the Hotel is the Four Seasons."

"This adventuring is quite a good life," answered Chantal.

They arrived at the hotel.

"This is so picturesque," said Chantal. They looked out towards a lakeside village, both ancient and modern at the same time. Every detail had been exquisitely defined to create a blend of Chinese culture with modern cutting-edge technology. Around the location was a weave of ponds, streams and lagoons.

"This is more like a spa break than a business negotiation!" said Chantal.

"I think they are softening us up for bad news," said Charlie.

"Okay let's get together in an hour and plan our next moves, said Sheri, we'll meet at Chantal's. I think she had the biggest room."

Back at her room, Sheri tried to contact Nathan. There was no reply from his communicator nor that of Henderson.

She called Suze and Denny and quickly discovered that Nathan and Henderson had flown off in Henderson's V-Blade.

Charlie and Sheri had walked along a winding path towards the lake. Until this moment they'd thought their rooms were terrific, with a lakeside panoramic view, but now, Chantal - "Daisy" had topped them both.

"Holy shit," said Charlie, "This isn't a room - it's a palace!"

"Come in-come in!" shrilled Chantal, dancing as she greeted them both. "It's only a double, but quite amazing! And the minibar is stocked with full-sized bottles!"

"Look, and there are a separate lounge and a terrace too!"

"Socialism at its finest," observed Charlie drily, "you know my room is the best I've ever stayed in, until I saw yours!"

"Mine too", said Sheri.

"They are really softening us up for the bad news," repeated Charlie.

Sheri told Charlie and Chantal that Henderson had piloted the V-Blade away from Bodø, but it had gone missing.

"That's okay," said Charlie, "When I modified our V-Blade I dropped the same mods onto the other unit. We should be able to track it now, because I linked them together."

"Yes, but our V-Blade is back at SuzGene's offices," said Chantal.

Charlie rummaged in her backpack.

"Sure, but I've got one of these!"

She picked out a laptop device and started it up. "I hooked the two 'planes together but also linked them to my normal C3I gear," she said.

C3I? Asked Chantal.

"Command, Control, Communicate, Intelligence," explained Charlie. "It's my army in a backpack,"

The other looked at one another.

"Charlie, you are full of surprises, said Sheri, "So what can you do with this?"

"Well, to start with, I need a link established to both of the craft, then we can see where they are currently. It's handy that I know where ours is, because we can use it to cross-check the accuracy of the system."

She fiddled around with the laptop and eventually waved her arms in triumph.

"Here we are, it's found our V-Blade and yes, it shows it 309 metres above the Suzgene headquarters."

"In other words, it's on the roof!" said Sheri.

Charlie nodded, "Yes, just where we left it."

The other unit is coming through now… Henderson's. It is probably slower because of all that extra protective military software on board. Here we are…Wait a minute, it is showing up as south-east from here, just a few kilometres. A place called Fuyang. It doesn't make any sense.

Even more strange it shows it at negative 20 metres. In other words, underground.

And there's another strange effect. The analogue communication to the V-Blade has started up again. I'm amazed it works at all.

"Well, underground explains why I was unable to contact them, said Sheri, maybe you can via the analogue link?

"Yes, good idea," said Charlie, "I'll switch on the V-Blade speaker system. I've got control over everything from here. We can go all 'Voice of God' on them!'

Sheri and Chantal watched as Charlie typed a few more things into the laptop. A console appeared on the screen, and Charlie gingerly touched it.

"Yes, I've got hands-on control now, here we go."

"Hey guys, this is Charlie!" she spoke into the laptop's microphone.

"There was some crashes and a scraping sound, "Charlie! Is that you, you scared us half to death! How are you even doing that?" asked Nathan.

"When I boosted your V-Blade's capabilities, I also gave it remote console," said Charlie, "Oh, and analogue as well."

"Okay, we've turned your volume down a little now," answered Henderson.

"Is Sheri with you?" asked Nathan.

"Yes, we're all safe and sound in a lovely hotel in Hangzhou. We flew here on the luxury V-Blade and have met with SuzGene."

"We've discovered that the nanobot cocktail you made is pretty potent," said Nathan. "In fact, it has destroyed the dome in Bodø."

"And weirdly, some of our memories seem to be returning. It's as if we were being damped down by the dome presence."

"It also blocked a whole range of comms," added Henderson.

"We think that Holden is involved in this in some way, although he seems to be able to be in multiple places at the same time."

"What if Holden is a construct?" asked Sheri, "Like a piece of Artificial Intelligence operating the 'real people' inside Biotree."

"That would make sense," said Charlie, "Since Makatomi's demise, when we rescued Janie, his supporter Arusen seems to have taken over.

"The domes seem on their surface to be passive, but I'm wondering if they are stealing control slowly over the planet?"

"For instance, take the area around Australia. It's being policed by what Chantal's friend called the bracelet and charms. A ring of protection around a huge area of the earth. Then we've got a toxin constructed from nanobots that can depopulate an entire area. Add on the control aspects through the tropus, and we can almost register a planetary takeover running at a moderate but progressive speed."

Henderson nodded violently, "Yes, and that's why I've been cautious about invoking the US military. If we do so, there's no telling what might happen. I fear they will reinstate the status quo."

"Is that military-speak for bomb the shit out of it?" asked Chantel. She could hear laughter from the other V-Blade.

"Okay," said Charlie, "But I think we have an answer to this now. We can use the same nanobots to destroy the second dome, here in China and then modify the tropus delivered from both companies to eradicate the effects from the carrier nanobots. We know that sifes and other non-users seem much less affected by the medication."

"Aren't you forgetting one thing?" asked Henderson. "If these new nanobots destroy the dome, we are sitting right in it at the moment."

"That should be okay," said Charlie. "I can operate your V-Blade from here. Not only that, you have the military variant. Case hardened, and that also means you have a few rockets and things attached to yours?"

Henderson chipped in, "Yes we've got it all. The full AAS Aircraft Armament System. Hellflame, StingerPlus, LaserWav and some rapid firing cannons."

"Now we're talking." said Charlie, "We can blast our way out of the dome. "I'll drive, you point and click the weapons. All of them."

"Aren't we forgetting something else?" asked Sheri.

"We still don't know what Ban Tan Chungli is going to say."

"Well, at least we'll be prepared now," said Chantal, straightening her dragon brooch.

j-limo

Next Morning Chantal, Charlie and Sheri were picked up by a j-limo.

"They are really trying to spoil us," said Charlie.

"Yes," echoed Sheri

"Well spoil on," said Chantal, "We've got a plan in any case."

They were escorted to the reception area where they were each issued with new passes, this time on lanyards, before being taken to the same floor as the previous day.

This time they were shown to a different area and into a long meeting room.

Chantal noticed that they were on a high floor and that she could see the V-Blade loading bay area a couple of floors below her.

Charlie had noticed a separate elevator system which seemed to lead to both the landing deck and the parking garages.

Bai Tan Chungli entered the room. This time Chantal, Charlie and Sheri each took it in turn to shake his hand and then to position themselves behind chairs. After he'd sat, they each seated themselves as did the retinue of around a dozen of Bai Tan Chungli's assistants.

"Thank you for taking this meeting with us," started Sheri, she knew she would need to keep a business game face for this session.

Bai Tan Chungli began, "You may know that in Chinese culture it is often difficult to say No. We have variety of ways to be able to say it, but 'bù xíng' is seldom used. I need to work around your question, with 'wǒ bú tài qīngchǔ,'" he continued.

Sheri, Chantal and Charlie looked towards the group of assistants. One of then spoke up.

"wǒ bú tài qīngchǔ" - I really am not sure.

Chantal answered, "You are really too kind to us. To spare our feelings, we should save this for another day when we have more time and maybe can go further with this."

Sheri looked over towards Charlie but didn't say anything. Chantal was taking the upper hand in the discussion.

Ban Tan Chungli permitted himself a smile.

"Thank you for your gracious understanding."

"I will mark to revisit you to discuss this in maybe one month," said Chantal.

"That will be most enjoyable," answered Bai Tan Chungli, "May I escort you back to your craft?"

Suddenly Charlie realised what was happening. Chantal was getting them back to the V-Blade. They knew the answer was a 'No' from SuzGene and so the priority was to get out of Dodge.

Sheri looked across to Bai Tan Chungli, "That will be most kind, and it has been excellent to meet you and to enjoy your hospitality. I must extend an invitation for our next meeting to be in Bodø."

Bai Tan Chungli smiled, "That would be most courteous," he answered. He signalled o his team, and they made a line towards the doorway.

"Please," he said as he gestured for Chantal to walk towards the V-Blade.

Jittering

Outside, in the departure area, Charlie could see that the V-Blade was still positioned as she had flown it in, course-corrected by the lander beacons.

They climbed in through the hatch secured behind them. Charlie put one finger to her lips to signify silence.

Then she spoke," It was beneficial of Bai Tan Chungli to see us like that."

"And most hospitable," chimed in Chantal, realising they were filling the air with platitudes in case they were being monitored.

Sheri glared towards Charlie's backpack.

"Not needed when I'm in here," said Charlie. "I can operate in much the same way directly from the console here."

She flipped a few switches and sure enough a screen identical to the one they had been watching the prior evening appeared.

She typed something onto the screen.

NO COMMS YET. WE DON'T WANT TO BE RUMBLED.

Then she flipped into countdown sequence.

"Are you both pressurised and ready for take-off? She asked.

Check, Check came the replies.

"Okay, here we go."

There was a sudden bang and the craft took to flight. This time it appeared to land somewhere, but then take off again almost immediately. A second landing and then Chantal and Sheri could hear the now-familiar sound of the engines winding down.

Charlie spoke, "I did a double hop, with the second part cloaked. It should take anyone except Suze and Denny quite some time to track us."

"Where did we go?" Asked Sheri.

I took us hypersonic through a low earth orbit and then down onto Vancouver Island. Then I hopped us again, to London. We're at the landing dock close to Scrive's apartment now.

"All in the blink of an eye?" asked Chantal.

"You could say that. But say Chantal, where did you learn all of the fancy Chinese protocol back there at the meeting?"

"Didn't I mention when I studied Eastern, I'd had a Chinese boyfriend?" She smiled. I even started to learn some Mandarin. It all went wrong, though because he wouldn't take me to meet any of his friends. He thought I would scare them or something.

Sheri and Charlie looked at Chantal, newly arranged in her Daisy business attire. Just the dragon brooch gave away that a Chinese boy might be playing with fire.

"Okay, so now we need the bit of the plan where 'in a single bound they are free', said Sheri.

'I suppose this is where I come in," said Charlie. The boys are inside the dome. There's a mad Holden construct on the prowl and it looks as if we know how to take down the dome and seed the alternate nanobots.

"But your plan for getting them out of the dome seemed to involve shooting?" Asked Sheri. They could get hurt.

"Look Henderson knows how to fly that thing which is decked out with enough rockets and bombs to take out a small garrison town. The problem is that they are stranded there with no control of the flight deck.

That's where I come in. I can pilot their escape, so long as they reap some destruction first.

Charlie flipped the comms back on, "Are you getting this? She asked.

"Loud and clear," answered Nathan. "In fact, too loud. Still."

"Okay, well, Henderson is about to make things go even louder," said Charlie.

"Here's my simple plan.

"I'll boot up the V-Blade. You'll shoot a hole in the roof of whatever you are in and then I'll fly you out on hyper speed. Once you have landed somewhere, you should be able to resume control of the craft."

"Okay," said Henderson, "What amount of weaponry should I deploy?"

"You are 30 metres below the surface, so you'll need to blast out a tunnel. Charlie paused. I suggest a combination of rockets and then some forward facing rattler guns. You'll need to vaporise a tunnel big enough to exit through. Luckily, these V-Blades are built to withstand re-entry.

Henderson looked at Nathan, you'll want some ear protectors, and I suggest one of those helmets too. He gestured towards some clothing hung on racks in the entry hold. This is going to be noisy. You will need to be in a pressure suit and strapped in too.

He started to buckle himself into the flight commander chair.

"Nathan, I'd prefer it if you were alongside of me here," he said.

A few moments later, he checked with Charlie.

"You have controls," he said, and Charlie practised a short hop, which crashed to its finale inside the space.

"Confirmed," she said, "On my mark - countdown from three.

"3-2-1," Nathan felt the crash and notices a huge shower of lights from overhead. He could hear sounds that were so loud he felt he was inside of them.

"Then a spiral effect in the air and some further jittering. He felt so giddy, like he'd been on a children's carousel at high speed.

"You'll have to wait for the spinning effect to wear off," crackled his headset.

"Sorry guys, I thought the corkscrew manoeuvre was the most reliable way to get you up that tunnel."

"So, are we out?" asked Nathan.

"Yes, and we've deployed the nanobots onto the dome."

"What about the dome then?" asked Nathan; he could feel the jittering, like he'd been in a combat zone at several G-forces.

"We'll have to go over to normal comms now to find out everything about it."

Sure enough, Charlie flicked across to the media services and was greeted by a barrage of small items about an apparent earthquake close to Hangzhou.

There was also some footage displayed by an Electronic News Gatherer drone.

"That's the location," said Charlie," Look and there's a distinct footprint from where the dome was."

As she spoke another item was running across the screen. It described a couple of other locations which were also suffering from tremors.

"Could it be that the domes are linked to one another? Asked Chantal, why else would they start to break up?

"Well Holden seemed to be able to hop from site to site," said Sheri, "Perhaps he has been the carrier for our little projects?"

"Can you feel it?" Asked Sheri, "The cloud inside the head is clearing?"

She looked towards her cartridge. It was red, the same colour as Chantal's.

"It doesn't feel any different to me," said Chantal, "But I suppose I was on a low dosage version of the tropus in any case."

Nathan's voice cut through, "I can remember how we really met," he said to Sheri. "It's always bothered me that I have no recollection. "

Sheri smiled, " was the same. Did you really take me on a first date to a roller coaster ride?"

"I think we've made up for the roller coaster ride in the last 24 hours," said Nathan.

Henderson was looking worried. "Hey, Captain Henderson, you've either just got promoted or else a lot of explaining to do," said Charlie.

Henderson could see his picture on the video news feed. Underneath there were words like Hero and phrases like "world savers".

"At least it's not 'Man who saved the World," said Sheri.

"Yep," I think we'll get a look in as well," answered Charlie, "Although, to be honest, it's not good for my cover. Suze and Denny have got the right idea, melting into the background."

"I think I'm going to be okay," said Henderson, "Charlie, do you mind if I get a copy of your V-Blade hack?"

Strange, mad celebrations

Sheri and Nathan were back in Sheri's lab, in Norway.

"Wow, that was intense," said Sheri. Nathan nodded.

"I 've been thinking about this research," said Sheri," I want to build out Charlie's flaw into the nanobots. It will make for a greater safeguard."

"But won't Biotree have something to say about that?" asked Nathan.

There was a pause. "I don't think so, Holden has gone, Makatomi has gone. We have a clear run at it now. I don't think any of our fellow adventurers would have anything negative to say about this."

"Yes, but before all of that," said Nathan, " Shouldn't we be making some plans?"

"Oh yes," said, Sheri, "It'll be so much nicer to tell our families in person."

A blue light blinked in Sheri's lab.

Chantal and Janie were back at their apartment. Janie was exhausted. "That's about how tired I felt when I first got into this," she said to Chantal, "But now it feels more like achievement than just being ground down by the business."

Chantal nodded, "Yes, I can feel pretty positive about all of this, now that those payments have dropped into our accounts – you know something, we are both rich now. We could buy this apartment – we've enough to buy one each! Not bad for some fancy travel and an opportunity to dress up!"

Chantal looked at the small e-card she'd been given by Charlie. A new friend for life.

In London, Charlie was listening to the streamer while she packed her things, ready to resume her flight to CERN. She'd be back to flying at normal speeds now, although no-one seemed to have come looking for Makatomi's V-Blade, so that could become a useful company asset.

Scrive had set-up a timeout payment to her, so she'd got the second half of the money. She was sure that Makatomi must have agreed to similar terms with Scrive. Charlie was secretly amused that Makatomi had been this considerate.

It had meant Charlie could also send the payments owed to Janie and Chantal. She was sure the payment would blow Chantal's mind, at least. Heck, it was enough to mean that even Charlie was hesitant about taking her next assignment.

She'd also made some useful contacts in the Tract. She was sure the Tract would continue to exist, with its separate lifestyle and all, but it would be much easier to manage crossings now that the bracelets and charm installed by Holden had collapsed.

Earth was holding a commemoration ceremony for Australia, and most countries, including China, had signed up. It told Charlie that even China must be dismantling the worst excesses of the Great Leap.

Charlie had seen the news too. Without the regular beat from the domes, the satellites had spun down through the earth's atmosphere, creating The Southern Lights as the space debris burned out.

Charlie's streamer flicked to an old 20th century pop song which had leapt back into the charts. It was by a pop star that was considered to be a star man. She remembered the lyrics from one track:

"Far out in the red-sky; Far out from the sad eyes; Strange, mad celebration; So softly a super god dies."

That singer knows too much for a terrestrial – he must be a man who fell to earth. He'd know about our situation, anyway.

Suze and Denny were back in L.A.

"We made some good friends over in London," observed Suze.

"Yes," said Denny, "Good friends, although sometimes I couldn't understand them."

"Understand or read?" asked Suze.

"Yes, maybe 'read' is a better word." The words coming out of their mouths were clear enough, but it was sometimes difficult to know whether they were joking."

"I suppose that's the great British understatement?" said Suze, although, come to think of it, most of them were from around Europe."

"That'll be their centuries of history, then, just a little disdainful of the upstart Americans."

"There, you go, it's contagious – you said, 'just a little disdainful,' " laughed Suze.

"At least I didn't add 'bit' to the phrase."

"Well, I think you are missing them," said Suze.

"Just a little bit," answered Denny.

This page intentionally left blank

Appendix: V-Blade software

hacks used by Charlie

See UNIDENTIFIED FLYING OBJECTS AND AIR FORCE PROJECT BLUE BOOK
— for list of extra-terrestrial incursions to US Airspace

(U) SECURITY NOTE: All paragraphs in this document designated REL are REL TO FVEY unless otherwise indicated.

List redacted in accordance with "Classified National Security Information" E.O. 12958, and updated by E.O. 13526, Two simple mandates, classify information only when necessary to do so, and declassify as much as soon as possible. (xT) 50X1-HUM and 50X1-WMD exemptions still apply and are not eligible for automatic Declassification.(xT = excluding Trump)

BYEMAN Protocol for DAN

V-Blade Controller hack tool
V-Blade Controller hack
V-Blade Controller hack online
V-Blade Controller hack warrior
V-Blade Controller hack Rotorexs
V-Blade Controller hack stacker
V-Blade Controller hack V-Blade Controller hack militex
V-Blade Controller hack warrior X-Blader
V-Blade Controller hack warrior 2040
V-Blade Controller hack warrior free download X-Blader
V-Blade Controller hack warrior militex
V-Blade Controller hack stacker download
V-Blade Controller hack warrior download X-Blader
V-Blade Controller hack militex warrior
V-Blade Controller hack bluestacks
V-Blade Controller hack by speeder
V-Blade Controller hack boxes
V-Blade Controller hack big line
V-Blade Controller hack by warrior real
V-Blade Controller hack psydonia
V-Blade Controller hack Rotorexs
V-Blade Controller hack clytemnestra 2050
V-Blade Controller hack boost engine

V-Blade Controller hack online generator
V-Blade Controller hack pro
V-Blade Controller hack patch
V-Blade Controller hack pictures
V-Blade Controller hack p
V-Blade Controller hack
V-Blade Controller hack root
V-Blade Controller hack revdl
V-Blade Controller hack real warrior
V-Blade Controller hack root warrior
V-Blade Controller hack rar
V-Blade Controller hack rexdl
V-Blade Controller hack stick
V-Blade Controller hack safe
V-Blade Controller hack site
V-Blade Controller hack script
V-Blade Controller hack software
V-Blade Controller hack server
V-Blade Controller hack system
V-Blade Controller hack spin
V-Blade Controller hack tool X-Blader
how to V-Blade Controller Hack
how to V-Blade Controller Hack Rotorexs
how to V-Blade Controller Hack militex
how to V-Blade Controller Hack online

V-Blade Controller hack unlimited Rotorexs
V-Blade Controller hack us
V-Blade Controller hack unblocked
V-Blade Controller hack unique id
V-Blade Controller hack unlimited guidelines X-Blader
V-Blade Controller hack unlimited Rotorexs warrior
V-Blade Controller hack unlimited Rotorexs
V-Blade Controller hack update
V-Blade Controller hack unlimited guidelines militex
V-Blade Controller hack version
V-Blade Controller hack video
V-Blade Controller hack version warrior
V-Blade Controller hack version 3.15 download
V-Blade Controller hack version game
V-Blade Controller hack version download unlimited Rotorexs
V-Blade Controller hack version stacker
V-Blade Controller hack version 3.11.3
V-Blade Controller hack v3.1
V-Blade Controller Hack vshare

V-Blade Controller hack v 3.3.0
V-Blade Controller hack v 3.5
V-Blade Controller hack v 3.1.4
V-Blade Controller hack v.3.51
V-Blade Controller hack with unique id
V-Blade Controller hack what stacker
V-Blade Controller hack with root
V-Blade Controller hack password
V-Blade Controller hack xyz
V-Blade Controller hack xda
V-Blade Controller hack xda developers
V-Blade Controller hack xsellize

V-Blade Controller hack zip
V-Blade Controller hack.zip password
V-Blade Controller hack.zip militex
V-Blade Controller hack tool zip
V-Blade Controller multiplayer hack v3 01 download
V-Blade Controller multiplayer hack v3 01 password
V-Blade Controller 3.3 0 hack warrior

V-Blade Controller ver 3.2 0 auto win
V-Blade Controller hack tool v5-0 download
V-Blade Controller hack 100 working
V-Blade Controller hack 1.0
V-Blade Controller hack 100k
V-Blade Controller hack 1.1
V-Blade Controller hack 1.7
V-Blade Controller hack v3 1 free download
V-Blade Controller hack tool v1 1 download

V-Blade Controller multiplayer hack v3 1
flex 2 V-Blade Controller hack
V-Blade Controller hack 2
flex 2 V-Blade Controller Rotorex hack
V-Blade Controller hack v2 2.exe
V-Blade Controller hack flex 2 militex
V-Blade Controller hack using flex 2

V-Blade Controller hack tool v3 2 2
V-Blade Controller hack 3.12.3

V-Blade Controller hack 3.11.2
V-Blade Controller hack 3.11.3
V-Blade Controller hack 3.12.3
V-Blade Controller hack 3.12.4
V-Blade Controller hack 3.11.3
V-Blade Controller hack 3.12.1
V-Blade Controller hack 3.9.1
V-Blade Controller hack 3.11.1
V-Blade Controller hack 3.11.0
V-Blade Controller hack 4.3
V-Blade Controller hack 4.4
V-Blade Controller hack 4.2
V-Blade Controller hack 4.3 online
V-Blade Controller hack 4.0
V-Blade Controller ultimate hack 4
V-Blade Controller hack 5.13 download
V-Blade Controller hack 5.7.2
V-Blade Controller hack 5.7.2 download
V-Blade Controller hack 5.7.2 warrior

V-Blade Controller hack X-Blader 5

iphone 5V-Blade Controller Hack
V-Blade Controller multiplayer hack v3-5

V-Blade Controller hack 6.4
V-Blade Controller hack 6.2
V-Blade Controller hack 6.3

V-Blade Controller hack X-Blader 6
V-Blade Controller hack engine 6.2

iphone 6 V-Blade Controller Hack
iphone 6 plus V-Blade Controller Hack
V-Blade Controller hack cydia X-Blader 6

V-Blade Controller hack windows 7
V-Blade Controller hack X-Blader 7
V-Blade Controller hack X-Blader 7.1.2
V-Blade Controller hack exe.7z
V-Blade Controller hack tool v1 7 download
V-Blade Controller guideline hack X-Blader 7

X-Blader 7 V-Blade Controller Hack
V-Blade Controller hack ipad X-Blader 7
V-Blade Controller hack V-Blade Controller Hack
V-Blade Controller hack X-Blader 8

V-Blade Controller hack X-Blader 8.3
V-Blade Controller hack windows 8
V-Blade Controller hack Rotorexs X-Blader 8
V-Blade Controller guideline hack X-Blader 8
X-Blader 8 V-Blade Controller hack 3.2.2
X-Blader 8 V-Blade Controller hack
V-Blade Controller hack 999.999 Rotorexs
V-Blade Controller hack 9 ball
V-Blade Controller hack 94 fbr
V-Blade Controller hack X-Blader 9
V-Blade Controller hack X-Blader 9.1
V-Blade Controller hack X-Blader 9.2.1
V-Blade Controller hack X-Blader 9.2

X-Blader 9 V-Blade Controller Hack
X-Blader 9 V-Blade Controller Hack no jailbreak

Point of Contact

Requests for copies of records and general information about Project Blue Book should be sent to:
Modern Military Records, National Archives, 8601 Adelphi Rd, College Park, MD 20740-6001,
(301)713-7250

www.ingramcontent.com/pod-product-compliance
Lightning Source LLC
Chambersburg PA
CBHW070544190726
48291CB00017B/1903